Juleps, Jockeys, & Justice

Mary Seifert

Books by Mary Seifert

Maverick, Movies, & Murder
Rescue, Rogues, & Renegade
Tinsel, Trials, & Traitors
Santa, Snowflakes, & Strychinine
Fishing, Festivities, & Fatalities
Diamonds, Diesel, & Doom
Creeps, Cache, & Corpses
Pranks, Payback & Poison
Juleps, Jockeys & Justice

Visit Mary's website and get a free recipe collection!
Scan the QR code

Juleps, Jockeys, & Justice

Katie & Maverick Cozy Mysteries, Book 9

Mary Seifert

Secret Staircase Books

Juleps, Jockeys & Justice
Published by Secret Staircase Books, an imprint of
Columbine Publishing Group, LLC
PO Box 416, Angel Fire, NM 87710

Book layout and design by Secret Staircase Books
Cover images © BooksRme, Dianneslotten, Naddiya, Cynthia
Hanevy, Jmpaget
First trade paperback edition: March, 2025
First e-book edition: March, 2025

* * *

Publisher's Cataloging-in-Publication Data

Seifert, Mary
Juleps, Jockeys & Justice / by Mary Seifert.
p. cm.
ISBN 978-1649142115 (paperback)
ISBN 978-1649142122 (e-book)

1. Katie Wilk (Fictitious character). 2. Minnesota—Fiction. 3.
Amateur sleuths—Fiction. 4. Women sleuths—Fiction. 5. Dogs in
fiction. I. Title

Katie & Maverick Cozy Mystery Series : Book 9.
Siefert, Mary, Katie & Maverick cozy mysteries.

BISAC : FICTION / Mystery & Detective.

813/.54

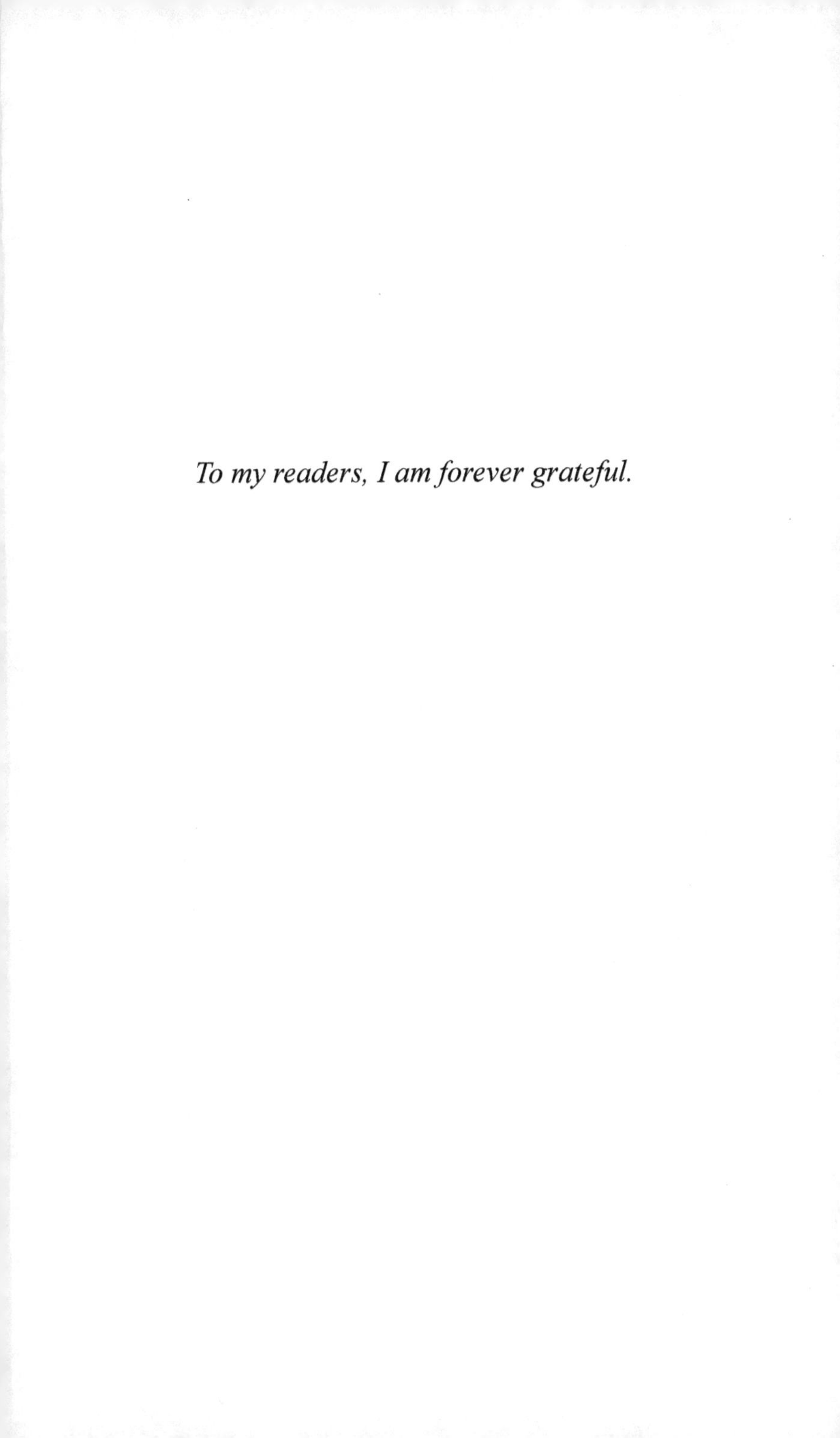

To my readers, I am forever grateful.

ONE

After almost completing my first edifying year teaching high school mathematics, you'd think I'd be ready for anything, but that Monday morning took me completely by surprise.

As the kids congregated for first hour, I had seven precious minutes before the starting bell rang, and I was hurrying to post the day's assignments on the whiteboard when one of my students swept into my room.

"In the absence of gambling, horse racing would cease to exist." Lorelei Calder flipped her long sandy hair over her shoulder, uncovering the Cougar emblem, Columbia High School's mascot, on her gray polo shirt. She never failed to drag us off topic with her intensity, and her friends watched the impending interaction with amusement. "Ms. Wilk, do you think it's true?"

I curled my forefinger over my lips and brushed it down

my chin, turning her words over in my mind. It seemed my second exposure to horses was going to be just as complicated as my first. "Where did that come from?"

"The Kentucky Derby runs Saturday." Her eyebrows rose, and she tipped her head as if I'd asked a rhetorical question. "It's all over the news."

A smile tugged at the corners of my mouth. "Can you give me a bit more to go on? Why do you think gambling is so fundamental?"

"I didn't know anything about horse racing, so I began to explore the topic." Lorelei slid her glasses from her nose to the top of her head. "It's been going on since ancient times and predates many other types of physical contests. Did you know the original Olympics included chariot races?" She stopped.

"Wait for it. She's not finished," one of her classmates tittered. "She's just taking a breath. Her rants always have more."

"And you have no idea how many different forms of racing exist." Lorelei raised her chin in answer to the challenge. "Modern gambling began in the 1600s with King James I."

"Seems a little contradictory. Isn't he the same guy who proposed a new translation of the Bible?" asked another classmate.

Lorelei ignored the slight dig. "Last weekend, I read two Dick Francis novels." She ticked off the list on her fingers. "I watched an old Charlie Chan film, a *Murder 101* rerun, *Secretariat*, *Seabiscuit*, two other obscure racing films, skimmed the Britannica version describing the Triple Crown, and listened to a gruff podcaster barely scratch the surface explaining how betting works. I still don't get it."

My mouth dropped as I tried to wrap my head around Lorelei's exhaustive research habits. A year younger, she held her own among her senior classmates, and her academic talent and intelligent focus warranted advanced studies in math and science. More and more of the glass ceilings have been shattered by women in science, technology, engineering, and mathematics, the STEM tracks, but she'd met resistance among a few of her classmates and a teacher her savvy parents told her to ignore. Going the math route, I'd encountered many of the same obstacles and hoped to provide a haven for her and room to spread her wings. I was fortunate to be stuck with her.

"In some circles," she continued, "it's considered America's first major sport, and the game of chance has been one of its important tenets. I think we should organize a Derby celebration."

All eyes turned to me. I hid my grin and worked hard to temper her enthusiasm. "You're not of legal age to wager on horses."

Three blue-eyed blondes cast laughing glances back and forth, and from the back of the room said in unison, "But we are."

I shook my head and Lorelei continued.

"We can study various aspects of mathematics in horse racing like measurements of the horses, gait, length of stride, speed, acceleration, distance, heart rate, respiration, and expenses in addition to the fundamental economics surrounding the sport, but deciding on a winner through the odds is by far the most common numerical occurrence and an integral part of the race proceedings. And there is an unending list of attempts to beat those odds, legally and not so much."

I disguised my amusement by covering a cough. Little did she know how delving into a student-led math topic delighted me. "I'm sure we can apply numbers and formulas and make it relevant."

"My mom and I already talked about what a small gathering would require," she said offhandedly. "A mere shadow of the elaborate parties thrown every year, and it would only last a few hours. Just through the race."

Her heavy backpack slid from her shoulders and thudded onto her desk. She retrieved an anniversary edition of *Run for the Roses* and cracked it open to reveal a photojournalist's spread of beauty, power, and dignity. "In fact, she and Mrs. Clemashevski have already spoken about our science club hosting a derby party."

I froze for a moment. If my landlady, Ida Clemashevski, was in on the discussion, it was already a reality. She was a force of nature.

"She said she'd be honored to provide the fancy food and divine hats so we can experience the race hullabaloo ourselves. My parents would take care of the tent and the invites. The guys could rig up the screening. That is, if it's okay with you. Please?" she implored with a tiny whine.

As the school year neared completion, and with so many activities taking up students' time, our science club had decided to hold a meeting if, and only if, requested. And now Lorelei waited for my definitive response.

I ran my finger along the perimeter of one page of Lorelei's book, drawing a border around a tall dark brown horse draped in a blanket of red blossoms. "I suppose, if Mrs. Clemashevski is going to cook and provide *les chapeaux*, who am I to refuse?" I drew my hand back from the book and laced my fingers together. When the best cook in Columbia, Minnesota, wanted to host a Derby party, how could I deny her?

"Derby dalliance at Ms. Wilk's," a deep voice said from the doorway. Two juniors from my science club, Galen Tonlenson and Carlee Parks-Bluestone, caught my answer, raised their fists in victory, high-fived each other, and silently pounded the air as they shimmied into their adjacent classroom.

"That remains to be seen," I said to their retreating backs, loud enough to be heard over their guffaws. "We'll need a short meeting after school." I lowered my voice, saying more to myself, "I'll add a reminder to the morning announcements. It should be easy to incorporate the subject of odds in a lesson plan involving chance, ratios, probability, and statistics." My fingers flew over the computer keys to share our meeting information. Before I typed my name, Katie Wilk, on the bottom line, I glanced up to gauge the students' appreciation and watch their reactions. "You understand, no money will change hands." Setting the restrictions up front made the process easier to manage and would save time arguing later.

Lorelei and her friends nodded. I hit send and crossed my fingers as the remainder of my first hour students filtered in for class.

In the fleeting moments I had throughout the day, I hit up our school librarian for articles mentioning the Kentucky Derby (of which there were too many), scanned book blurbs for titles relating to horses, sorted through the archives about horse racing, reviewed the scant information I could find on odds and betting, perused the online material about Churchill Downs, and compiled a succinct glossary of terms specific to the equestrian.

The original handful of science club members joined in the fall merely to have a co-curricular affiliation look good on their resume. Over the course of the year, our roster had grown to ten, and they'd become serious participants, offering experiments, concocting hypotheses, building confidence, making new friends, and having fun.

As the first of the membership assembled after school, I

dimmed the lights and played snippets of significant historical horse races for an introductory backdrop. Pulsating hooves pulverized the tracks and resounded in the enclosed space. When one race ended, I'd spliced an additional clip to another heart-stopping finish. The majestic animals momentarily mesmerized the kids, and some of them found it difficult to navigate the rows of desks, bumping into one after another while staring at the screen at the same time.

When the video ended, I flicked on the lights. "We can talk numbers, but I don't have too much for you." I handed out the results of my investigation. "A live specimen would contribute so much more to understanding the statistics, so I can honestly guarantee today's gathering will be short since I don't have a horse."

Lorelei stood at the whiteboard to take notes as the group's secretary. Her face crinkled. "I read that many horse racetracks have the word 'Downs' in their name because downland is an area of open chalk countryside in southern England and are often referred to as downs, derived from the Celtic word for hills."

I shrugged. *Of course she did.*

The club president, Ashley Johannes, called the meeting to order and immediately abdicated, giving me the floor.

I furnished the sheet of terms, and we discussed horses in general, but before we could look at the other math involved, Lorelei said, "Please tell us how to figure odds."

I had to smile. That girl was like Maverick with a tennis ball.

"Horse racing uses an involved method called pari-mutuel betting. This is a simplified version of the way I understand it.

"Bets placed until the start of an event make up a pool of money for that entire race and no more bets are accepted. If there are ten entrants, there are ten possible victorious outcomes. Let's say the total amount collected on wagers to win is two thousand dollars. In addition to concessions, ticket sales, and merchandise, the track makes money on a user tax, and the house may assess up to twenty percent of the two thousand for their take. How much would that be?"

"The pot could be decreased by four hundred dollars to sixteen hundred," said Lorelei.

"If a total of fifty dollars has been bet on Horse A to win, and Horse A is victorious, the pool of sixteen hundred dollars is divided into fifty shares. The payout is thirty-two dollars for each share or dollar wagered. That makes the odds on having Horse A win thirty-one to one. If I bet ten dollars on Horse A, I would have won ten shares of the pot or three hundred twenty dollars."

"That's three hundred twenty dollars per race? I can see how this could look like a good gig," said Brock Isaacson, waggling his eyebrows. He and Lorelei met in science club and had been an item since the beginning of the year, and she tried, in vain, to overlook his relentless teasing.

"If the house knew what it was doing, it predicted similar odds. Long shots pay out more, but betting is never a sure thing."

I took a deep breath. The arithmetic didn't thrill everybody. Disinterested, glassy eyes stared at me, but I'd planned ahead. I came prepared with individual packets of chocolate candies. Before I could explain how we would use the confections, Galen grabbed one, tore open the cellophane, and popped a handful of the sweets into his mouth.

I put up my hand. "Wait, wait. I brought the candy to use as our currency. You'll need three unopened packets."

My suddenly enthusiastic students leaned forward and grabbed the packages with feigned interest in the discussion.

"I have video of three races which took place two years

ago. We're each going to choose a horse and check the odds as they were posted before each race. Let's see how well we do. Lorelei, click on Race One Descriptions."

The file contained a photo, name, physical description, age, number, and colors worn by each horse. "What else would you like to know in order to place an educated bet?"

Galen said, "It would help if we knew if the horse ever won before and how long ago."

"And we'd want to know if the length of the race won and the race going to be run are the same." Ashley twirled a blond ringlet around her finger. "Track conditions and weather might play a role."

"And maybe knowing a little about the stable and if the trainer helped other horses in the sport of kings," added Brock. He winked at Lorelei. "I know things."

Lorelei buried her head in her hands and rubbed briskly. I thought I heard her mumble, "Boys." She dragged her fingers down the edge of her face and raised her head, ignoring Brock. "The odds indicate the expected winner," said Lorelei. "And it might be helpful if we knew a bit about the jockey."

Carlee said, "There are statistics sometimes available to tell us how each horse does under specific weather conditions."

"The next screen lists some of that additional information on each horse." I nodded to Lorelei.

Lorelei clicked on the arrow as she spouted a factoid. "The Kentucky Derby has been won by the favorite over thirty percent of the time, but the payout is much better for an underdog."

Ashley chewed on the end of her pencil. "I like hot pink. I'd bet three bags on Number Seven."

"And I'd take that bet," said a chipper voice from the doorway.

TWO

"M s. Mackey!" My excited students and I joined in one voice.

Jane Mackey taught history. We began the school year together, and she'd seen me through months of ups and downs. She was the best friend anyone could have.

"I never, ever place a bet based on the silks—the colors the jockey wears. Why would you do such a thing? Successful racing animals have specific conformation and musculature which can impact a horse's athletic ability and lead to faster horses. A horse can move best with a shorter back and a longer neck. And you can tell a lot by their bone structure." She gave every indication she understood aspects of horses we'd never considered as she tucked long golden tendrils behind her ears. "Everyone knows you choose winners by the sound of their names."

I blinked back to reality and laughed along with our students.

She planted her fists on her hips, and though she usually had to look up at each of us, she acted much taller than her petite frame allowed. Her dark eyes narrowed. "I'm serious. What better way to select a winner? Many of the animals don't get their names until they've been tested and observed on a track."

I stifled the end of my chuckle. "How do you know so much about horses?"

Jane's stiff shoulders sagged, and she admitted. "I spent summers on my grandparents' farm. My grandmother called herself Lady Lone Ranger and her horse Golden. I think it was a play on the names of her favorite vintage television characters."

My eyes met hers, and she looked away. With brutal honesty called for, I asked my question directly. "How many horses do you own?"

"None." She relaxed and threw her shoulders back, but her face turned a deeper shade of pink.

"Ms. Mackey?" I raised one eyebrow.

Jane had a difficult time fudging the truth. I watched the wheels turn behind her sparkling brown eyes. She vacillated but capitulated under our silent, spellbound gazes. "Dad has a stable with eight Thoroughbreds."

Her dad owned Sapphire Skyway, a premiere private airline in the Southeast, best known for catering to the jet set. She came from money—oodles and oodles of money.

"Did someone say Thoroughbreds?" Kindra Halloran breezed through the doorway and her bright tone alleviated some of the tension. Her sister, Patricia, followed, words and fingers flying. Although Patricia lost her hearing a few years ago, she continued to communicate well with the rest of the world, though Kindra worked diligently to improve her American Sign Language, enabling her to fill in blanks if Patricia missed something.

Kindra repeated the comment. I didn't understand her rapid finger spelling, but I smiled, and Patricia giggled as we both recognized the sign for horse.

Lorelei said, "Can you teach us some equine ASL to use at our Kentucky Derby party?"

Kindra began to repeat Lorelei's question, but Patricia waved a hand and cut her off. "I know what Lorelei said." Patricia turned to Jane and me as she spoke and signed, "I wish everyone faced me and enunciated as clearly as Lorelei. I could read their lips." She plopped on top of a desk. "Who's hosting the Kentucky Derby party? It sounds like a riot."

Brock tapped Patricia's shoulder. She turned to face him. He articulated with deliberation and more volume than necessary, "Mrs. Clemashevski is hosting, and we are learning about betting odds."

"The Kentucky Derby is the most exciting two minutes in the sports world." Patricia didn't wait for us to respond. "We watch the race every year and often catch the Preakness and the Belmont as well. They make up the Triple Crown." She sighed. "Someday I'll have my own horse." She made an L-shape with her thumb, middle and index fingers, tucking her pinkie and ring finger against her palm. Her thumb touched her temple, and she bent the two fingers down twice. "Horse," she repeated with a huge grin.

"We're viewing old races and using candy as currency to test the odds." I offered bags to each girl. "Do you want to play?"

Kindra and Patricia joined their teammates and took

seats. The students stared at the video and tried to glean which information might prove beneficial in wagering successfully. They jotted notes and discussed characteristics of a possible winning entry.

Jane folded a piece of paper into an origami hat and wore a somber expression. "We'll keep it simple today. In our first attempt to study the game of chance, if your horse wins, we'll simply divide the reward for choosing the right horse with the other winners. Next time, you can throw your offer into a collection, and we will repay winners according to the predicted odds."

Jane had practical knowledge, and I couldn't help myself. I blew out a sigh of relief as the film began.

The first movie clip flickered on the eager faces as the challengers chased the first-place winner across the finish line. The students hooted and whistled an I-told-you-so for successful picks and hissed at the results of poor choices, exchanging chocolate candies with our temporary bookie, Jane.

After the three races, Patricia gloated behind the largest pile of candies.

"You're awfully lucky. Care to share your system for choosing the victors?" Galen scratched his head as he popped his last two chocolates into his mouth.

Patricia acted as though she hadn't noticed him speaking, nibbling on her pile of winnings, but she couldn't ignore him tapping her arm for attention.

"I love horses." She lowered her head. She reduced her mound of treats by half and confessed, "I may have seen these races before and knew the outcome. But it's even better when you know the competitors. You should come out to our farm and meet TnL."

"TnL? Is that a fast cow?" Brock mooed and laughed.

Debora Halloran, the girls' mother, operated a high-tech dairy farm, but I had a hard time visualizing a cow race firing up the same enthusiasm as did horses.

"Our dairy operation is set up on an adjacent farm site, so we have extra room. We board four horses. TnL and Demon Dancer are Thoroughbreds," Kindra said around a mouthful of sweets she'd confiscated from Patricia's haul.

Brock laughed. "Ya gotta shovel out the …" Jane cleared her throat, and he caught her subtle hint. His smile faded. "Manure, right?"

"Muck out the stalls, yup." Kindra acted put out, but she beamed.

Patricia gazed at the ceiling. "We feed and water them and curry their coats. We exercise them as often as we can. His owner calls him TnL, short for Thunderbolt and Lightning. Horses are so much better in real life. Do you think we can take a field trip?"

"A live specimen would be better," Lorelei parroted.

Jane's hopeful eyes met mine. I loved my job.

Jane padded to the filing cabinet and extracted our red folder containing the necessary authorization forms for any excursion. "Fill out these permission slips and return them with a parent signature for a field trip tomorrow—and two successive trips, in case we need to go back. Ms. Wilk will reserve a van." Her brow furrowed. "What should they enter under purpose and expectations?"

"I think we'll use Lorelei's initial inquiry about mathematics in the equine industry and the timely coincidence of the Kentucky Derby." I wrinkled my nose, putting the week together in my head. "I'll talk to Mrs. Clemashevski tonight, and we'll hand out another form if the party comes together."

"What makes TnL a Thoroughbred?" Carlee asked as she loaded her backpack and slung it over her shoulder.

Kindra shrugged and looked to Jane.

"Thoroughbred horses trace their origins back to three sires, or fathers: Darley Arabian, Godolphin Arabian, and Byerly Turk," Jane said. "Their owners transported the horses to England from the Middle East around 1700, and they've been bred for stamina, strength, and speed ever since."

"I don't know about that, but Mrs. Brown has the handsomest horses in the county. Patricia and I have permission to ride them for their workout once in a while, but not often enough in my book. I think TnL is especially beautiful, but my personal favorite is Demon Dancer."

"Why does Mrs. Brown keep her Thoroughbreds on your *dairy* farm?" Brock narrowed his eyes and scowled.

"Mrs. Brown moved here last year, supposedly to escape the constraints of corporate life, but couldn't find the right hobby farm. She met Mom at a techie geek thing and griped about the 'paucity of property' available." Kindra gestured with finger quotes and rolled her eyes. "Mom offered space and helped Mrs. Brown build her stable on our farm site. She's kind of distant with the animals, but she sure likes to call herself a horse owner." She caught herself and said, "Just calling it as I see it. But Patricia and I are lucky. We take care of the horses and mom splits the fees with us."

"That reminds me." Jane pursed her lips as she was known to do when the story had, shall we say, a few colorful elements. "The last time my dad and I visited Churchill Downs—"

An immediate response bubbled among us. Brock said, "Go on, Ms. Mackey."

"Do you still have your hats?" said Kindra.

"How's the food?" Galen, wrestler and consummate foodie, rubbed his belly.

I ignored the banter. "The last time? How many times have you attended the Kentucky Derby?"

"We've visited Churchill Downs too many times to count, but we've only attended the Derby three times." All kidding and chatter ceased. She'd hooked them. "Some years, the track is riddled with controversy. The last time I attended, quite a while ago, one of the horses tested positive for betamethasone and the trainer was suspended. And the time before that, race officials caught one of the jockeys betting on another horse, which didn't look good. Someone always tries to beat the system."

"Did you ever bet? Did you pick any victors?" Patricia asked.

"Won some. Lost way more." Jane shrugged. "That's not to say my method of choosing a horse is invalid."

The students packed up, and on our way past the admin office, I reluctantly requested a vehicle large enough to accommodate our science club.

Jane held me back as the kids left the building. "You don't seem thrilled to be taking the students to see a Thoroughbred during Kentucky Derby week. What's up?"

"The first and only time I rode a horse was when—" I choked up and puddles filled my eyes. "We saved Maverick's mom from the iron teeth of a trap, and I discovered Charles had a secret life."

THREE

We stood in the entryway, and Jane's eyes grew big and round. "Whaaat?"

I inhaled and exhaled slowly. "We'd nearly finished our program in cryptanalysis, and the instructor assigned Charles and me the task of tracing some harassing text messages. The man behind the posts had dyslexia and intended the amorous words for his fiancée instead of the annoyed recipient, Lady Victoria Colton. In gratitude, she invited us to celebrate at a picnic-on-the-grounds of her breathtaking seventeenth century estate." My thoughts drifted back in time, remembering my handsome Charles lifting his head and tossing back a lock of wavy blond hair as his twinkling blue eyes spotted me across the crowded yard.

Jane touched my forearm, and her concerned voice brought me back. "If it hurts to remember, you don't have to tell me."

I grinned. "These are wonderful memories. Really." I shook myself and straightened my shoulders before continuing. "After the delightful lunch, Lady Victoria led us to her stable and gave us permission to ride. She had fabulous horses, but I'd never been in a saddle before, so I approached the entire experience with trepidation. Charles, on the other hand, seemed quite at ease. He helped fit me with proper attire and headgear to ride." I chortled. "You'll never believe this, Jane, but my first mount ever was named Abacus."

She clasped her hands together and tried to stifle her laugh. "Math is your fate."

"Charles hoisted me on my horse's back, and we'd begun to follow the well-worn trail when an anxious young boy, a groom, told us Lady Victoria's purebred British Labrador dam, Bonnie, had nosed open the gate again and was on the loose. We joined in the search. I had little control over Abacus, and he followed an invisible trail straight up to her. She'd been caught in a trap." My heart beat against my ribs, bringing back the overwhelming fear for Bonnie's wellbeing and my conscious effort to remain calm as I raised my voice to summon help from Charles. I blinked away the recall.

"Charles rushed her to the onsite veterinarian." My nose turned up. "He was a stuffy little man I've had to meet twice too many times in my life."

I focused on my hands. "That's when the vet addressed Charles as 'your lordship.' Until that moment, I thought what we had between us was the real thing. I'd wanted to marry him, spend the rest of my life with him, but I felt betrayed when he turned out to be the biggest puzzle in my life, with so much I didn't know." Jane cleared her throat, and I looked up. "I almost gave him up that day."

"But you didn't."

"He didn't give up on me. But…" I tamped down my

unease. "Among other feelings is a guilt I can't seem to shake. Horses still remind me of my unreasonable reaction to Charles's revelation."

She threaded her arm through mine, and we approached the double doors. "What about Maverick?"

My eyes welled up. "Charles arranged to surprise me with one of Bonnie's puppies from her unplanned assignation that night. After Charles was killed, I almost didn't accept Maverick, and now I don't know what I'd do without him. He's one of the best gifts ever." I swiped at my eyes and turned my head toward her. "And whatever would I do without you, Jane?" I squeezed her hand. "Thanks to you, I'll have the opportunity—" I teared up.

"You're welcome." She waved as she climbed into her big green SUV.

Hot tears pricked the corners of my eyes. Dizzying scenes from the bike trail made my head swim. Dad had yelled a warning but was hit first—a shot to his head—and was downed feet from me. Charles had charged me, crashing us both to the ground. The bullet struck him and forced air from his lungs. His lifeblood poured out. I held his head in my lap and agreed to everything he'd asked as long as he vowed to stay with me, but seventeen days after we'd married, he was gone.

I wiped my eyes and shook my head. I would lead a good life as Charles had requested.

Equine thoughts filled my head as I slid into my trustworthy Focus and made my way to North Maple Street. Meandering down our driveway, I glanced through the kitchen window and caught sight of a black blur leaping away from the sill. I squelched the admonition on my lips and chalked it up to Maverick's deep, abiding love for me and excitement at my return. With my arms loaded, I bumped the car door closed, lumbered down the walkway, shuffled into my kitchen, and prepared for an enthusiastic dog greeting.

Instead, a singsong "Kay-teeee," came from my landlady as she waddled her full-figured form through the adjoining door of our apartments. She attacked my cheeks with both hands, pinching and pulling back and forth. "How was your day?"

"Great," I burbled as my lips flapped. "And yours?"

She sported a satiny purple skirt and flowing floral tunic belted in yellow patent leather with aplomb. The skirt swirled around her feet as she glided across the kitchen to the refrigerator and nabbed a pitcher of some beverage with floating limes and mint leaves. Try as I might, I couldn't pull off her bright mismatched colors and incongruous fabrics. At least one of the hues accentuated her baby blue eye shadow and set off her freshly colored red hair.

"Wonderful." Her emerald eyes glimmered. "Marietta Calder and I have come up with the best idea for your science club."

"Lorelei told me."

"Thoughts for this weekend's bash are coming at me from all sides, but do not fear. Themed parties are very much my vibe." She must have seen my curious glance. "What? I listen to the kids, and I'm always ready to update my lingo. I haven't been out of teaching that long. Now, let's get to work. We've got a party to plan."

My jaw dropped, wondering when it devolved from *she* to *we*, and what she expected me to do. Her eyes twinkled merrily, and she bobbled her head to show off her silver hoop earrings. She selected a pen and notebook from my desktop and picked up the pitcher. The beautiful big old Queen Anne home provided ample space for both apartments, and she marched through the doorway to her living quarters at the front.

Ida stopped and sighed. Her shoulders slumped. Less than a month had passed since she'd survived an unsuccessful scheme of vengeance. We thought she'd shown signs of early dementia, but instead she'd been drugged. I gently laid my hand on her back. "You don't have to host the Derby party, you know. We could do something else."

Ida raised her nose, snubbing the pessimism. "It's time for positive energy. This isn't the first Derby party I've ever hosted, and knock on wood ..." She rapped on her own noggin. "It won't be the last, but it will be the best so far." Her head swung to watch my face, and she eyed me with uncertainty. "The kids are coming, aren't they?"

"They're definitely planning on it. How did you think I found out?"

She threw her shoulders back. "Let me show you what I've collected."

I followed her the rest of the way into her house. "Have you seen Dad today?"

"Yes. He's out on assignment—gathering fresh mint leaves for the juleps."

I cocked my head and eyed her warily, watching for signs of a relapse of her dementia symptoms. "You know the kids can't have mint juleps, right?"

She'd been a high school art teacher. She knew the rules and nodded absently. "Of course not, dear. Not with the bourbon. But they can certainly have my Kiddie Mint Mocktail which is the beverage we'll serve with the kids onsite."

Her mental faculties were as sharp as ever. I relaxed and smiled as she plopped into a chair at the head of the dining room table, pointing to an adjacent seat, the only empty place for me to sit. Dumbstruck, I stopped in my tracks. My mouth gaped, and my eyes popped.

I noted elegant, fancy, tulle tufted hats in cardinal red,

Columbia Jaguar blue, shamrock green, daffodil yellow, and Viking purple on display—straw hats, felt fedoras, velvet cloches, satin and lace fascinators with intricate detailing—hanging from the backs of the remaining seats around the table she'd extended to its longest length with three extra leaves.

Bolts of fabric, jars of buttons, feathers, ribbons, and sundry crafting supplies surrounded piles of papers, recipe cards, magazine articles, books, and pamphlets, covered half the area. She pointed to the artsy end of the table and announced, "For those who'd like to design their own hats."

I nudged the polished, filigreed silver platter containing three different types of finger sandwiches back from its precarious position at the table's edge and accidentally brushed up against the glistening glass serving bowl jam-packed with dill pickles, wrapped in prosciutto and oozing cream cheese. The vinegary filling I licked from my fingers puckered my lips and I nodded in approval. Ida lightly slapped my hand when I reached for a flaky fruit tartlet from among a plateful nearly obscuring a ceramic dish designed in the shape of a leaping steed. "Marietta is coming for a taste test." She waggled her forefinger and pointed down the table.

Hand painted glassware, fancy flatware, stacks of small red-rose rimmed plates, and multi-colored napkins in a shiny fabric embroidered with large numbers filled a sizable portion of the credenza under the window, lined up next to another tray of open-faced turkey sandwiches dripping with cheese sauce covered with sliced tomatoes and crisp bacon.

"Those look delicious. May I taste one of them?"

She nodded. "My take on the Kentucky Derby Hot Browns."

I could barely contain my groan of delight. Maverick sat near my feet at the ready and lucked out when a bit of bacon squirted from my second bite. I swallowed with relish and so did he. "How many guests are you expecting?"

She shrugged and opened her planner to the page marked invitations. She ran her finger down the long page as her lips moved, whispering the names. "Not quite enough, and as it's so last minute, the kids are in charge of sending backup evites."

I swiped at my lips with the back of my hand. "And you put this all together today?"

Ida rolled her eyes and dragged a stack of fill-in-the-blank invitations across the table.

"Of course you did." I needed fuel to deal with my landlady's over-the-top ideas and snatched a confection from a two-tiered stainless-steel platter, popping it in my mouth. "That chocolate truffle was calling …" I muttered around the sweet as a burst of a very spicy liquid cherry exploded in my mouth and my eyes flew wide. "… my name," I garbled and forced a swallow.

Ida poured a measure of liquid from the pitcher. Condensation dripped through the magnolia pattern painted on the side of the ice-cold glass. She placed it in my hand and firmly wrapped my fingers around it securing the bottom so it wouldn't slip. With a smug smile, she clucked her tongue.

Leery of surprise ingredients in the beverage after the most recent taste of the filling inside the chocolate, I asked, "What's in it?" She crossed her arms and mimed zipping her lip and tossing the key. I hesitated but only a moment before sliding the leafy sprig to one side and glugging the drink to tamp down the fire on my tongue. A bright fresh minty zing hit my palate. My eyes closed, and a guttural sound hummed in my throat.

She tried to wait for my opinion, but her question erupted

in earnest concern. "Don't you like the beverage either?"

After another long slurp, I said, "Yes. This is wonderful."

"Careful." One eyebrow rose to her hairline, and she sniggered. "It's light on the alcohol, but that's a real Mint Julep." She unrolled a swath of blue velvet and artfully wrapped it around a hat form, cutting the excess, zipping five long basting stitches, and pinning the gathered fabric with a gold brooch. She turned me to face her and fitted the creation over my light brown hair, swiping wisps away from my face.

I turned my head right and left, examining my reflection in the mirror. "I bow to your extraordinary decorating talent."

"Derby hats are to die for."

We couldn't know how prophetic her words would be.

FOUR

After school, we loaded the students into the van, and Jane pelted each rider with questions as she manned the sliding door. "These spring days in the month of May are flying by. How did yours go?" She genuinely cared for our kids as much as I did and prodded each with individual attention. "What's the school day countdown? Are we ready for the state mock trial meet?" Though she sometimes pried into their personal lives as well with "Who are you taking to prom?" and "I saw you with that basketball player. What's up with that?"

The students took her good-natured interrogation in stride but didn't feel compelled to answer all her questions and often teased her back, asking about her fiancé, the dashing Agent Andrew Kidd. Drew started the school year as a condescending high school communications teacher, but he actually worked undercover as an agent for the

Bureau of Criminal Apprehension until the drug pipeline he'd investigated had been disrupted. After too many sub-par substitutes, the school finally replaced Drew with an overqualified retired journalist who might be persuaded to take the job for at least another year.

For the umpteenth time, I glanced at my naked wrist as Kindra and Patricia crammed into the seat behind us next to Lorelei. They silently but furiously argued over directions for the best and fastest route home. Jane kept an eye on Patricia, awkwardly mimicking the signs she gleaned from their exchange.

I'd visited the dairy operation and knew the general location of the farm, but step-by-step instructions removed the unknowns from the equation.

"Our farm site has been annexed and is within city limits now, but because of the pond, to access it we have to come in from the county road." I followed Kindra's confident instructions penetrating the chattering voices of her classmates.

Lorelei spoke a bit haughtily. "I talked to Mrs. Clemashevski right after school, and she gave me a rundown of the menu and entertainment she's organized. She's hosting the best Derby party this side of the Mississippi. After her trauma last month, I was worried at first it might be too much, but she said she's looking forward to it." Lorelei radiated happiness.

Kindra tapped the back of my headrest. "Take the next turn on the left, after the line of trees, toward the water." I checked with Patricia in the rearview mirror who nodded. From this distance, the pond appeared small, but I had a feeling there was much more around the corner.

We pulled up to the gate. Kindra jumped out and unlocked it. She hopped back in, and we followed the crushed stone driveway around the bend. A pristine house came into view. Debora ran a tight ship, and her business venture had finally come into its own and afforded them the luxury of updating the antiquated white two-story. The fresh siding and contrasting black roof and shutters made it an oasis amid the numerous dated deep-red outbuildings and the two gleaming white metal barns with the Halloran Dairy insignia on the sides.

"Oh," Patricia pointed at a metallic green-colored SUV and complained. "Why'd she choose today, of all days, to be here at this time?"

Jane signed as she spoke. "Who's here?"

Patricia crinkled her eyes and pursed her lips. "The horses' owner, Mrs. Brown. I was hoping we'd have my majestic friends to ourselves."

Kindra put a hand on Patricia's wildly bouncing knee. "I don't think she'll mind sharing. She's always inviting us to ride, and she knows her animals gets their best treatment from my little sister."

Carlee gravitated to the window, jabbing a finger toward a vehicle parked across the driveway. "Look at that boxy contraption. I've never seen anything like it."

"And you probably never will anywhere else," said Brock, wide-eyed. "It's a Mercedes-G63 four-by-four-squared."

Carlee wrinkled her nose and shrugged. "It's not my thing, I guess."

Brock sighed. "Won't ever be mine either. That machine costs more than some houses."

Galen glanced up from his phone and studied Jane. "You told us about the fathers of Thoroughbreds, so who are Magic, Herod, and Eclipse?"

Without missing a beat, Jane said, "They are the offspring of the initial fathers, and the foundation sires. It's what relates them all. The Jockey Club has maintained proof of the entire

Thoroughbred line in the American Stud Book for over a hundred years."

We piled out of the van, and Jane stopped to gaze over the gently rolling, green hills surrounding the farm. "This is lovely."

Kindra nodded. "We think so." Patricia led us behind the house to a new red shed with a black roof. Sparks of a palpable exhilaration followed in her wake.

"How many of you have ever ridden a horse?" I asked.

All hands rose but two. "But I would try in a heartbeat," said Brock sheepishly.

Patricia took a deep breath and exhaled before she thrust the big door to one side with a rumble. Sheets of sunlight streamed in behind me, and it took a moment for my eyes to adjust to the shadowy interior. I blinked. In the dim light from a bare bulb, I made out the silhouette of a short, robust figure stationed in front of a stall, reaching up to pet the nose of a dark horse.

The woman turned toward the light, shading her eyes with her hand. "Patricia, dear. And ..." She stammered. "... Kindra. So nice to see you both. It's been a while."

"Hey, Mrs. Brown," said Kindra as upbeat as she could be. "We're planning to celebrate the Kentucky Derby with a party and brought friends to visit your—"

As if Kindra had not been speaking, Mrs. Brown said, "TnL has been asking for you, Patricia." An answering whinny came from deep within the recesses of the barn, and a mottled gray face bounced up and down over a stall door. "There he is now. And I see you brought reinforcements." Mrs. Brown stepped toward me. "I'm Mia Brown. And you are?"

"Ah," I spluttered, a bit apprehensive yet mesmerized by the large dark-brown horse eyes winking at me from between the wispy feathers and shiny baubles adorning a red hat sitting jauntily on Mia's head. "I'm Katie Wilk. I'm the advisor of our high school science club. We came out to study some of the numbers surrounding horses. Yours, in particular."

"What can I tell you?" she said in a dulcet voice.

"He's quite a specimen," said Jane, her tone odd.

"He is, isn't he? I'm so fortunate." Mia turned her head to the right and to the left, and stretched out an elegant hand, dripping in shiny stones. "Do you like it?"

"Like it?" I accepted the hand she offered. She locked our grip, clasping with both of her hands and shook.

"My Derby hat. I noticed you admiring it. Whether I go to the Kentucky Derby or not, I order one every year from Hood London."

I'd been staring at her horse, but she didn't need to know. "It's remarkable. Are you attending this year?"

She shook her head, still squeezing my fingers. "Sadly, no. I'll miss the action and passion of the event this year. Too much to do." She raised her tawny eyes to the sky as if longing to find an answer written there.

"My friends and I are helping host a Derby party Saturday," said Patricia tripping over her words, reiterating her sister's explanation for our visit. "It's our science club's mission to learn about numbers among the horses."

"What a unique reason to throw a party." She pumped my hand again.

"Are you amenable to a few questions now?" I asked. The strength of her grasp surprised me. I reclaimed my hand and surreptitiously rubbed the feeling back into my appendage while directing her attention to the gaggle of students and the unending list of questions they'd devised on the short trip from school.

"Patricia," Mrs. Brown said, "you and ..." she stuttered,

again at a loss, seeming to forget Kindra's name, "… your sister, please prep the horses while I entertain your guests. You may take your friends out to the paddock to ride. I didn't get to exercise the horses today. You could take Demon Dancer out with TnL and the quarter horses. I know that's not usually part of your daily routine, but all the horses are antsy and could use a good romp."

When Kindra finished signing the communication, Patricia saluted. I don't think anyone but me saw the withering look Kindra shot Mrs. Brown before she turned and trailed after her little sister.

Mrs. Brown gauged her crowd and bowed. A lock of black hair fell over her face, and as she raised her head, I could almost hear her neigh as she shook her own mane and righted her hat. "I love an audience. What can I tell you?" Her shoulders rose to her ears, and she rubbed her palms together in glee.

"What's a hand?" Galen's first question was met with a befuddled look.

Brock nudged his friend, "And how tall is TnL, Mrs. Brown?"

"Oh, that." It seemed a light came on, and she said, "Please call me Mia. And to answer your question, TnL is sixteen hands." Mia Brown held her palm out to us. She followed an invisible trajectory up and furrowed her brow, then turned her palm ninety degrees and grinned. "This is the hand I use to measure from the ground to his shoulders."

"You mean withers." Jane raised an eyebrow and stared intently.

"Yes, of course, the withers."

"Where are the withers?" asked Ashley.

Mia mimed brushing her hand down a mane and stopping in the middle of what *I* would've considered shoulders, but what did I know? I wasn't a horseperson, at least not yet.

"How old is TnL?"

"We celebrated his tenth birthday in January."

"I always wanted a horse." Carlee smiled longingly.

"Join the crowd. There are relatively few horse owners but millions of enthusiasts."

Reacting to what I considered a rude comment, I felt my lower lip protrude in a sulk.

"Has he ever won a race?" came a question so quickly, I couldn't identify the source.

"Several. In fact, I believe he still holds the record for the most wins in the shortest amount of time on his home turf."

At the same time Jane asked, "Where is his home turf?" Brock asked, "How much did he win?"

Mia chose to answer the latter. "There are a number of variables, and the amount can only be determined by calculating the odds and tallying the bets placed for him to win, place, and show." She caught Brock's confused, screwed up face. "Oh, sorry," she sniggered. "You didn't mean how much wagerers won by betting on him. You want to know the total of the purses he took in." She smiled crookedly. "According to his previous owner, TnL won a lot."

With that ambiguous opening, Lorelei and Brock led the barrage of questions and comments, facts and fiction regarding horseracing. Mia parried well, her facial expression inviting an open dialogue.

She concluded with her assessment of the economic footprint of the racing industry. "The business of horses has over a hundred-billion-dollar impact on the United States economy. Racing alone is linked to over a million full-time jobs, from trainers, groomers, and jockeys to equine therapists, nutritionists, and bloodstock agents. Minnesota ranks eighteenth in the list of state horse populations, providing fifteen thousand jobs."

When the inquisition slowed, Carlee asked, "Has TnL fathered any kids?"

"None that I know of." Mia Brown's eyes sparkled and her artfully shaped eyebrows danced with innuendo. Given the furtive looks among them, I'm certain my students understood her intention.

Mrs. Brown scanned the discomfited faces, enjoying her center-of-attention status.

After a slight lull, Brock said, "Mrs. Brown, you should come to our Kentucky Derby Party on Saturday." Oblivious to the quizzical faces encircling him, he added, "The hostess with the mostess is holding a dynamite party around race time."

"I'd love to attend. Give me the time and place, and if it works, I'll be there. I love horse talk, and I'll have a place to wear my hat."

Her hands came together in front of her cheery face. Before she could continue, the awkward conversation changed gears with a clip-clop from the side of the barn, and the kids swarmed Patricia and Kindra, each leading two saddled and bridled horses and carrying two helmets.

The sun bounced off the smooth, shining, reddish brown coat of the taller animal next to Patricia in sharp contrast to the midnight-colored second horse. Kindra cradled a dusty-gray nose between her head and her shoulder, while muttering sweet, calming words to both of her charges, answered by nickering and affirmative head bobs.

The gray horse raised its tail, and my students chuckled as the horse relieved itself. Kindra dusted its rump and turned toward the barn, but Mia said, "Don't bother with that now. You can take care of it later." She clapped her hands. "Who wants to go first?"

The kids eyed one another nervously until Galen said, "I will," and reached for a helmet.

"Have you been on a horse before?" Galen nodded, and Mia continued, "Just like on TV, stand on the left side, grab that protrusion, and put your left foot in the stir—"

"If it isn't Mystical Mia, the horse Houdini." We turned to the abrasive voice roaring behind us. "And you, kid, stay off my horse."

FIVE

Trying to disentangle himself from the mount, Galen bounced on one foot while freeing the other from the stirrup and nearly toppled when he released his grip on the saddle. Carlee caught him.

The black-haired fireball stomped across the yard, pointed at Mia, and barked, "I've finally found you." She skidded across the wet vegetation and came to an abrupt halt. A groan emanated from deep inside as the fresh mound of manure threatened to suck the Wellington off her foot.

Kindra drew in a quick breath and stepped forward, ready to lend a hand, but retreated as the newcomer's eyes blazed, and the woman exploded. "Mia, this is all your fault." She attempted to shake the horse chips from her cherry-red rubber boot and tottered but waved off assistance as she adjusted her balance.

Mia hid her chuckle behind the fingers she brought to her

lips. "Hey all, meet my sister, Penny Gyles."

Heads swiveled from one to the other and sure enough, although Penny Gyles was the antithesis of Mia in temperament, I could see the similarity. Penny's hair was cut in the same blunt style, but her roots needed a touchup. Mia's soft smile and lightly made-up pale eyes distinguished her from Penny's blood-red grimace and heavily lined squinty eyes. Mia wore lightweight colorful fabric. Penny wore black. Aside from their contrasting personality traits, they clearly shared DNA, and under the right circumstance, they'd look like twins.

"Sister, shmister," the woman snapped. "It's Penelope." She stepped, lurched, and shook her boot, repeating as needed in an angry march across the narrow strip of yard. She snatched the reins from Patricia. As she stretched to stroke his nose, TnL raised his head out of her reach. Penelope yanked on the reins, bringing him close enough to touch, but her hand stopped inches from the horse's face. "Where's his stripe?" She examined the visage from all angles, then bent down and ran her hand down his leg. "What did you do to my horse? Hey Liam, get your lazy bones over here," she called over her shoulder.

An ultra lean, wiry, compact man with short-cropped curly red hair emerged from the rusty, old baby-blue cab. When he slammed the truck door, it crunched, and I thought it might fall off. He scurried next to Penelope, who pointed to the horse.

Mia inhaled. Penelope crossed her arms over her chest and gave a smug grin. She said, not caring who heard, "Beggars can't be choosers. Got to watch him though. He likes to gamble." Mia's eyes widened. "Loves horses but couldn't sell his soul to get a job."

Liam pulled a fistful of sugar cubes from his grubby

jeans pocket and held them out on a flat palm. Gobbling contentedly, TnL allowed Liam to peer into his eyes, stroke his nose, rustle his ears, and swipe a hand down the thick, black mane, halting on, perhaps, the withers, and dropping to the hooves. Liam got to his feet and caressed the horse's nose, whispering soothing words, then turned up the horse's lip and peered at some markings. He removed a small notebook from his khaki shirt pocket and flipped it open. After scanning the page, he hesitantly met Penelope's fretful gaze. His jade eyes flashed, and he shook his head.

Penelope Gyles spoke through gritted teeth. "I should've microchipped my horse. Then we wouldn't have this problem."

In answer to my unspoken question, Jane leaned over and whispered, "She'd be able to electronically scan and determine ownership of this horse."

"Where's my Foggy Bottom?" Penelope wailed.

"I don't know what you're prattling about." Mia glided to Patricia's side. "This is not your horse. This is Thunderbolt and Lightning."

Penelope squinted, counting on her fingers as she mumbled to herself. "You know better. That name's too long."

"I am perfectly aware we are only allowed to use up to eighteen characters, so his official name is TnL."

"You can't change the name of a winning horse willy-nilly. It's not le …" Her words tapered off as she scrutinized the animal and frowned.

Mia held out her hand, accepting the reins Penelope was all too happy to get rid of. Mia passed them along into Patricia's trembling fingers.

"If he's not Foggy Bottom, what did you do with my horse?"

"I have no idea where you lost your horse." The bickering began in earnest, and Kindra and Patricia withdrew to the barn, towing the powerful creatures.

"You owe me," said Penelope.

"I don't know what you're going on about," answered Mia, laughing lightly as if the complaint was by far the craziest thing said.

The kids gawked in rapt attention. I took small steps toward our van and herded them in front of me. They continued to rubberneck, watching the disagreement, oblivious to our destination. The finger pointing lessened, and the hollering softened, but by the time Patricia and Kindra emerged, we'd taken our seats in the van, and I'd inserted the key, intent on quickly extricating my crew from the troubling tableau of the terrible twosome.

Kindra hopped in and sat on the bench seat next to Lorelei. Patricia had one foot on the running board when Mia's voice sounded behind us. "Patricia, bring your friends back day after tomorrow. Penelope and I will have this sorted out by then."

Patricia waved. She plopped onto the seat and slid the door closed. "Can we come back?"

I observed her eager reflection in the rearview mirror. "I'll try to reserve the van again. How many of you can come Thursday?"

There were more hands raised than kids in the van.

"Then we'll try to make it happen."

"Mrs. Brown depends on us to attend to most of her stock. We'll have to be there anyway," said Kindra. "I'm not sure she could do it without us."

Lorelei requested data—numbers for horse stats, jobs, economic impact—and recorded them on her notepad to justify our trip. I caught snippets of excited conversations about stealing horses, sisters fighting, disappearances, odd cars, racing, and money, but Jane focused on the road in front of us. My best friend's rare quiet demeanor raised the hairs on the back of my neck.

By the time we returned to school, we'd been on our field trip long enough for the office to be locked up for the day and only ten percent of the cars remained in the parking lot. After promising the students I'd make the return trip happen, I accompanied Jane into the building.

"Why so serious?" I asked.

Rather than answer my question, she asked her own. "What did you think of Mia and Penelope?

"I don't know. Patricia and Kindra really love the horses. Mia Brown's a little different—"

"A bit ditzy, I'd say. All I wanted to do was brush the coats. They were a lustrous black, gorgeous red, and a silver-gray begging to shine. I can't figure out Mia Brown. And don't even get me started on the sister." She huffed wisps of hair away from her face.

One corner of my mouth smiled in agreement. "Too bad we only have that fragment of today's crabbiness with which to judge them."

Jane snorted, and we walked to the math office. "By the way, I'm sure Mia doesn't do much of the day-to-day care of her horses. She must leave it all up to Patricia and Kindra. She seemed distracted until she spouted a bunch of statistics anyone can get off the internet. She sounds like a front-office mouthpiece for some horse business. I think she cares, but I just didn't see the passion. It's Kindra and Patricia who have to get their hands dirty."

"Did you see how Carlee's eyes glowed just mentioning the possibility of owning a horse? Mia tried to dampen her enthusiasm, but I've got to bring it up with her parents.

Maybe she'll become a vet like her dad."

CJ and Danica Bluestone had reconnected after discovering their beautiful, hardheaded, intelligent teenage daughter, Carlee, had survived being kidnapped as a newborn. Parenting was new to them. They lived across the street from Dad, Ida, and me, and were on the prowl for parenting hints. This one could be life-altering.

"I'd like to ask CJ if he'd talk to our kids about more of the mathematics of horses." I chewed on my lip before continuing. "I'm sure I can work the veterinary school angle into the conversation somehow." I watched Jane's brow furrow. "What else is bothering you?"

"Liam." She stopped walking and so did I. "He looked so familiar, but I can't place him. I wonder if he's a jockey. He's the right size. Of the three of them, he seemed as if he truly liked and understood the horses."

"How would you know a jockey in Minnesota? Have you been going to the races without me?" I asked.

She sniggered and shook her head. "I frequented the stables with my granddad back home."

"Do riders from Atlanta race up here often?"

"I don't think so." She shrugged. We started walking again, and she said so quietly I strained to hear her. "I wanted to be a jockey."

"Really?" I continued to discover how different we were. Jane's interests and intelligence continued to amaze me, and I wondered how she put up with me.

She nodded. An embarrassed giggle popped out, and she covered her mouth, and we parted ways at the stairs.

At my desk, I opened my computer, my fingers hovering over the keys. Not yet quite at ease with the possibility of revisiting the horses, my nervousness increased when I encountered not one single problem requesting the van again.

"My work here is done," I said to empty air.

I dashed home to feed Maverick so he wouldn't gnaw on the edges of his new interactive puzzle. Built for mental stimulation, he had to solve various problems to overcome the impediments blocking his way to the tasty treats I stuffed inside. Sometimes that meant chewing the plastic out of the way.

The minute Maverick finished gobbling supper, my phone rattled on the counter. I read the display, and my excited heart skipped a beat. I put the phone on speaker.

"Hello, handsome," I said in a way I thought might be considered a tiny bit seductive.

Dr. Pete Erickson said, "Did I get the right number?" He chuckled. "Just wondering if my girlfriend would like me to accompany her on a dog walk and then stop at Schmitz Tavern patio for a burger. They allow pets."

"Absolutely, but you'd better make it quick. Said dog heard the 'W' word and he's wagging himself into a tizzy." And hearing the 'G' word did the same thing to me.

"No problem," he said. I turned to a knock on the door and my heart pitter-pattered. "I'm right outside."

SIX

A sappy smile split my face remembering my prior evening with the hottest doc in Columbia, and probably reflected my students' fatuous grins. Pete made everything seem alright, even a note from the principal: *You have a new student in your last hour class. Justine Wright moved from Chicago, and she's finding small town life challenging. The applied math class is the only one she requested.*

I was requested. Wow. Well, my class was requested at any rate. I intended to honor the request and make it worth her while.

Even though I didn't have a window to the outside world, I could always tell when the sun shone in a cornflower blue sky. My scholars would beam and pretend to pay attention, but when I called on them, many shook themselves and politely asked, "Would you please repeat the question?"

The students told me they'd enjoyed my puzzles and

riddles, but were distracted by the lovely weather, the promise of summer, the need to complete homework as quickly as possible, or the myriad activities filling the days. Not many chose to look at the brainteaser for the day. However, my last hour applied math class knew how to milk my offering and get out of an assignment.

"Can you show us how it's done?" Patricia asked.

"Absolutely." I answered all the questions throughout the demonstration, no matter how seemingly insignificant because you never knew what might flip a pro-math switch for my students who didn't believe they needed to learn numbers.

"Do you have another like it?" Kindra asked.

"Of course."

"Please show us," said Justine.

After a very short pause, because I had math magic at the ready, I said, "I will predict an answer given any three-digit number in which the first and third digits differ by more than one." I scribbled a number on a corner of notebook paper and handed it to Patricia—she always sat in the front row— and covered it with her short stack of textbooks.

"Seven hundred," shouted a student from the back of the class.

"Reverse the digits." I waited.

"Double-o seven," said Kindra, chuckling.

"Subtract the smaller from the larger."

"Six hundred ninety-three," called another voice.

"Reverse the digits again."

"Three hundred ninety-six," sneered Patricia. Most of these students could perform math operations with ease but lacked confidence in their ability to take additional math classes. Not Patricia. She'd had a difficult start at her last school and was allowed to come home because she purposely did poorly, but she was forging her way.

"Add the two numbers."

A few different voices answered simultaneously. "One thousand eighty-nine."

Patricia peeled away her protective book pile. She held up the page from the notebook and smirked. "One thousand eighty-nine."

I bowed and said, "You will always get the same answer, and if you want you can finagle a secret message. Add zeros and subtract a string of numbers you've already designed. Replace each digit in the solution with an assigned letter and—"

"But your message can only use ten different letters to match with the ten individual digits," Justine clamped her lips in a smirk, sat back, and crossed her arms.

"True, but even just coming up with the numeric answer, one thousand eighty-nine, will amaze your friends and family."

Astonishingly, the bell rang, and the snickering students stampeded through the door.

"Well played," I conceded. No assignment again. I raised my voice a tad and said to the retreating backs, "You'll get twice the homework tomorrow."

Kindra and Patricia piled their things together on one desk and set to work, helping me get the room ready.

Methodically stowing her belongings, Justine watched, eyes wide. "What's going on here?" she said, looking at Patricia.

"We have a mock trial rehearsal," answered Kindra, sliding desks across the floor.

Having feigned fascination, Justine smirked. She tucked a stripe of red hair behind her ear, and against the black it looked like a headband. "What's with her?" She pointed to Patricia.

Kindra swallowed her facial contortions as she worked out what to say. "My *sister* is deaf."

Justine shrugged. She lugged the backpack strap over her shoulder, turned to exit, and bumped into Galen.

"Hey," he said, not unkindly, but her navy-blue eyes flashed something I couldn't identify, and she kept walking.

His wary eyes followed her out of the room. "Where did she come from?"

"Hinsdale, a suburb of Chicago. What a shock we must be." Patricia never looked up but kept right on talking. "She's staying with her dad. She said he wants her to play hockey and figured she'd get to do that here."

The rest of my mock trial team filled the empty seats. No longer merely learning the ropes, we decided to meet as often as necessary to polish their delivery. By all indicators, they were seasoned student-attorneys and finely tuned witnesses, ready to take on the best the state had to throw at us. As our attorney coach had directed, they'd learned the art of observing behavior, reading body language, watching for clues, and listening for contradictions. We had five rehearsals remaining until the state meet, and each time, my mouth hung open in awe. If I were in legal trouble in ten years, I wouldn't hesitate to hire one of them to get me out of a jam.

Some of my students participated in both of my extracurricular activities. I'd like to think I drew them in with my sparkling personality and rapier wit, but, in reality, the kids got along well and generally enjoyed each other's company performing in a courtroom or practicing experiments. The students had become friends. So, after a quick run through, those in the science club shared an invitation to the Derby party with their mock trial teammates and the guest list grew.

"Respecting Mrs. Clemashevski's wishes, we'd like your definitive RSVP by Friday, at the conclusion of practice."

Lorelei reloaded her backpack. "That way we'll have enough food."

My thoughts drifted to Ida's dining table. She always had enough food.

"And she has plenty of materials for us to make hats, which is a horse racing tradition."

"Is it okay if we wear our own hats?" Jane asked, winking a priceless, mischievous, twinkling eye.

"I think that would be great," said Lorelei. "I'll RSVP for you, Ms. Mackey, and indicate you'll be wearing your own hat. That way, Mrs. Clemashevski will have an idea whether she has enough supplies. Will it be for one guest or two?"

Jane raised two fingers and winked coyly.

Ashley wrapped her long hair in a roll at the back of her head and secured it with a pin. "Will anyone dress up with me? This is the perfect opportunity to go all out." Brenna and Allie warily raised their hands but questioned just how fancy they were expected to be.

Brenna tipped her head. "I'm not buying a second prom dress."

"No, no," said Ashley, leading the group. "Just fun and fancy. Maybe skip the blue jeans?"

"Do you think Mrs. Brown will really attend our Derby party? She sounded very interested," Lorelei asked, glancing from Kindra to Patricia. "And do you think we should invite the sister? I'd hate to widen the rift between them."

"We can extend the invitation if we see one of them, but I don't have Mrs. Gyles' contact information." Kindra screwed up her face. "Don't expect them to RSVP. They'll just show up anyway. It's sort of their style."

The students disappeared before I remembered to ask who still planned to ride along to the Halloran Farm. I clung to the small hope no one would want to go. I could maintain a clear conscience and not face my peculiar aversion to the memories horses evoked.

SEVEN

The first email of the day originated in the principal's office. The admin, Mrs. McEntee, told us there was a chance for severe weather and asked us to keep an eye out. Minnesota weather could turn disastrous as quickly as Maverick could snag an unattended wedge of Dad's favorite Jarlsberg cheese.

So far, May had been dry, and after the much appreciated but dreary day-long shower, students and teachers failed to notice the lack of sun. Undaunted by the pattering, we ignored the persistent rain drumming the math commons windows until the first few minutes of the last hour of the day. Booming reverberations drowned out the eloquent opening lines of my lecture. I peeked out my doorway, intending to silence the annoying disruption with a wicked glower.

Wild gusts splattered the torrent of droplets at a thirty-degree angle and rattled the glass panes. The deluge blurred the view to the outside. As the tempest gained momentum, distant thunder rumbled. Within moments, tumultuous gunmetal gray clouds plunged the school yard into a greenish-brown hue. Lightning bolts coincided with the roar like a train, and winds buffeted the exterior. Computer screens blinked out, and an inky black blanket fell over my interior room. Although school had a no-phone rule, I couldn't fault Justine pulling out her device, but when turned on, the multiple alerts added to the cacophony of sounds. The rest of the phone flashlights flicked on amid a restless muttering but no outright panicking.

Over the wailing severe-weather siren, a monotone voice on the loudspeaker repeatedly directed students and staff into the hallways away from possible shards of shattering windows and flying debris. We made our way toward the hazy, dull greenish-yellow light in the commons. The storm raged and my charges calmly filed toward the door, voices muted by the weight of the ultra humid air. My urging for a speedier exit went unheeded.

We marched steadily from the room—the farthest from the exit—in single file close to the inside wall. Kindra made it to the corridor entrance when tree limbs smashed against a section of the huge plate glass behind her. She staggered and clutched her books to her chest. Patricia smirked at the response, oblivious to the angry sounds of the turbulent storm in the world around her but nudged her sister ahead to the supposedly safe haven in the wide passageway.

Before taking the final steps to shelter, clattering golf ball sized hailstones drew the attention of the remaining few students who stopped to gape at the ice chunks bombarding the east side of the school. Patricia froze, noting the horrified looks on her classmates' faces. She frowned and turned to see what had caught them unprepared. Her jaw dropped, witnessing the ferocious gale wreaking havoc on the swaying trees arching toward the earth, ripping loose tender young leaves from the monstrous oaks, towering elms, and full maples, and hurling them willy nilly. She stood transfixed. I prodded but she jerked her arm away, stuck in place.

Kindra nabbed Patricia's sleeve and hauled her through the doorway, and as the few remaining students headed out, I felt the need to search for stragglers. I scurried through the eight rooms, checking to make certain no one had been left behind. By the time I entered the last room in the math department, the howling squall had abruptly ceased. As quickly as it began, the tempest stopped.

Unfortunately, in ZaZa's room, I discovered two girls gazing through tiny prism-like raindrops at the destruction left in the wake of what might have been a tornado. Safety first, but ZaZa would hear about her lax supervision.

One of the girls jumped to attention and stammered when I asked in a calm but serious voice, "What are you still doing here?"

The other announced, "I want to be a storm chaser, and Cecilia stayed behind with me. Ms. Lavigne never missed us."

"How on earth did that happen?"

The weathergirl-wannabe snorted, but her cohort confessed. "We'd just come from the restroom and snuck past her in the hallway."

"Next time, you must leave with your class. You could've been seriously hurt."

Cecilia lowered her head. "Yes, ma'am."

Her friend blustered, "Whatever," never exactly acquiescing, and turned back to the scene outside.

I shook my head and sighed at their fortuity before following their gazes. Brilliant sunlight peeked through the dissipating clouds, painting an awe-inspiring double arch stretching one hundred eighty degrees across the sky.

The droning voice announced the all-clear over the intercom. Lights flickered and computer screens popped on as the rooms hummed back to life. Students reentered, unsure, parked halfway in and out of the math department commons, blocking the doorway.

"Come look," I beckoned.

Patricia slid into the space next to me. Staring, she signed a graceful arc and circled her face with finesse. "Gorgeous rainbow," she said. Dazzled as we were by the vibrant colors, we almost didn't notice the speed at which the clouds scattered in front of the sun.

Students plodded through the entry, lining up at the window with the best seat in the house from which to view Mother Nature's paint strokes. Kindra tugged Patricia close and dropped her head on her sister's shoulder, admiring the panorama.

Over the intercom, the admin, Mrs. McEntee, announced cancellations and the rescheduling of after-school activities. I tapped Patricia's arm and nodded toward our room. She and Kindra dragged themselves away from the amazing vista, and I expected them to follow me, but they, along with half my students, disappeared. I ignored the grumbles of those rule-followers returning to my classroom. With such little remaining time, the braver souls had elected to call it a day, and before I thought to assign homework or take roll, the bell rang, and I was alone.

Jane bounded in and excitement replaced my short-lived disappointment. "Do you think it was a tornado? I didn't see any funnel clouds, but I only have the one window."

"And I have none. I could see out the glass in the commons, and the wind gusted ferociously."

"You'd never know now—"

"Except for everything blown all over." I retrieved the key for the van to take our students to the Halloran Farm and tossed it from palm to palm. "Can we still go?"

The door banged, and in walked a sheepish looking Brock. "Oops."

Lorelei followed, glaring at him. Galen and Carlee brought up the rear.

"Lorelei got permission from Mr. Ganka to go to the farm today, but you only have to take the four of us. Kindra and Patricia are going to meet us there," Galen said.

"That answers that," said Jane.

Before Jane made it out the door, Carlee added, "And Patricia invited Maverick and Renegade. The dogs have been cooped up all day in this mess, and Patricia misses them."

Galen cleared his throat. "Fess up."

"And I want to make sure they're doing all right too."

My lips formed a crooked smile remembering a moment in time when Patricia needed my trusty canine, and he'd gone to her rescue. The sweet bond between them matured with every visit. Jane sidled next to me, threading her arm through mine. "What ya thinkin'?"

"How this year has flown by."

We opened the door to the parking lot, and the smile dropped off my face.

"This year flew by as well as everything within five hundred yards of the school, it seems," said Jane soberly.

The wet pavement glistened beneath scraps of soggy paper, shredded leaves, rain-soaked black twigs, and flower petals of all colors. Rivulets of water left trails of dirt washed out from the edge of the yard. We passed my Focus, and I inhaled the clean air tinged with a hint of lightning and earth—petrichor in its finest glory. I released my breath slowly, grateful my car sustained no damage.

The van was unharmed as well, and the six of us drove Columbia's main streets at a snail's pace, following a long line of gawkers. Peering out the van windows, we waved at community members collecting rubbish and constructing small refuse piles, localized along an invisible line. Cruising Maple Street, however, we would never have detected a storm had coursed through.

My passengers' prattling stopped as they noticed party preparations begun in earnest. Four young men from the rental company stood under the awning of a huge white tent in Ida's front yard. Two swung sledgehammers at long stakes in the ground and it appeared the shelter had prevailed against the storm.

Carlee crossed the street and retrieved her yellow Lab, Renegade. I opened my kitchen door to a super-energized pup. The dogs met for a brief sniff, and we easily coaxed them between the seats to take up residence on the rear bench between Galen and Brock, happily panting, and we continued our trek.

The sights changed again near Columbia's outskirts. At the rail yard, a long line of empty boxcars rested on their sides surrounded by men and women with shovels and trash bags. The railroad crossing sign bent in the middle and bowed to the ground. A stream of gravel had been washed out from a story-high heap next to the track. Leafy canopies ripped away left gaping, jagged trunks. Strange indeterminate projectiles had been launched at the industrial buildings and splatted against the siding like bugs on a windshield.

Outside of the city limits, we could more easily see the pockets of extensive damage, almost as if a giant crushing pogo stick had stamped down at odd intervals, flattening one area and hopping to the next. We dodged shingles, branches, timber, and twisted shapes we didn't recognize. The gentle rolling hills surrounding Columbia took on greater significance as water pooled in the shallow valleys, mercurial mirrors inching across the road.

We drove through the unlatched gate behind Kindra and Patricia. Kindra parked their car, and they trudged up the walkway. The house and visible outbuildings stood untouched, but the wind had ripped the yard apart. Patricia crawled over a huge, uprooted elm sprawled across the gravel road. Maverick barked and frightened a rabbit he eyed gnawing on a pink and white petunia. It hopped between the two large planters smashed against the pavement and vanished. Giant branches littered the lawn. Shining puddles dotted the lush green grass.

Kindra turned to the sound of our vehicle and discreetly wiped her eyes.

"Careful," I said, shifting into park. "Watch where you step."

Jane rolled out first. She caught Kindra in her open arms and wrapped her in a huge, rocking clinch. Ahead of her, Patricia gingerly picked her way over the debris, heading toward the horse shelter.

I followed Patricia around the house and stopped in my tracks.

EIGHT

The wind had ripped off the roof and half the front face of the building. Small unidentifiable scraps, impaled in the siding, left pockmarks, dimpling what remained, and the twisted red metal screeched and moaned against the unfairness.

Maverick and Renegade easily overtook Patricia, bounding from one small clear patch of earth to another, avoiding overturned tufts of grass and clods of dirt, racing to the stable. They halted six feet in front of the mangled door, and barked with every ounce of energy they could produce.

All eyes, but those of the single-minded quadrupeds, rotated at the growl revving around the trees. Two white trucks, emblazoned with Halloran Dairy on the doors, careened down the drive and lurched to a halt. Debora leaped from the first, sprinting to Kindra and engulfing Jane in her hug as well.

The driver's door to the second truck squawked. Ransam, Debora's fiancé and business partner, climbed down, put his hands on his hips, and slowly swiveled his head, releasing a pent-up breath. I think he might have been expecting worse.

When she released them, Debora took her daughter by the shoulders, holding her steady so she could study her face. "Are you okay?" Kindra nodded. "Where's your sister?"

Kindra glanced toward the stable where the dogs barked and wove figure eights in and out of Patricia's legs. Patricia shoved them away, and in an irritated voice repeated, "No, no." Renegade grabbed her by the shirttail and amid, "Drop, Renegade, drop," she struggled to gain footing as the pup tugged her away from where the door might have once been. She couldn't win, swimming against the dog-powered rip current.

Renegade released her into Debora's grip. Realizing who and what had grabbed her, Patricia melted into her mother's embrace, sobbing, "The horses." As Debora ascertained her daughters were well, Maverick ceased barking and disappeared into the wreckage.

I raced after him, my heart in my throat, slipping and sliding over the obstacles in my path, listening for the familiar yip, and hearing nothing but the voices behind me. With barely enough room for my dog, I ducked and shimmied through the narrow opening at the bottom of the bent door, calling "Maverick," and caught the back of my shirt on something sharp.

I wrested free and wobbled as I stood, coming face-to-face with one of the quarter horses. Frozen in place and wedged between what remained of the wall and a large piece of metal fallen from the roof, as if peeled back with a can opener, he had no room to move and blocked my path. His nostrils flared.

I rotated in the vertical tunnel and kicked at the opening with all I had in me, loosening it enough to shove a piece out of the way, and edge him toward the escape. I directed the chestnut horse forward to the whistle and clucking Patricia made summoning him. He tossed his head, trying to back away, but I slapped his rump to give him a little more incentive. Startled, he bolted through the opening.

"Katie," Jane said in a voice an octave higher than usual. "What do you think you're doing?"

"Getting Maverick," I mumbled, swiveling in place where I ran into a second obstacle. Demon Dancer had poured his more than half ton mass into the space vacated by the quarter horse. I pointed him toward the opening, but he stubbornly planted his hooves on the floor. He snorted at my feeble attempt to shove him forward, throwing his head in the air. The gap looked small, though it had been safe enough for one horse. I crammed myself into the confined space and braced my back against the frame, standing and pushing to enlarge the slit. My grunting was met with, "Katie, get out of there."

Metal shrieked, and the pieces separated. Heaving again, a big chunk broke away. Maverick's warning woof from somewhere deep inside frightened Demon Dancer. On his dash to freedom, he knocked into me, and I lost my balance. I pitched forward, wrenching my knee, and landed on my outstretched arm. I expected a jolt, but my hand sank into the cavity between the door and the partial wall tightly packed with lots of green and white rectangular bricks wrapped in clear waxy wrappers. I brought one closer to my face. If they were authentic bills, I'd fallen onto a humongous pile of cash.

A throbbing pain shot down my leg. In my clumsy scrambling to extricate myself and get assistance, and unable to find purchase, my hand slipped deeper into the mix and landed on a cold, heavy, metal cylinder. I patted around and found the cylinder attached to a grip with a hammer and a trigger. Rapidly retracting my fingers as if they'd been burned, I landed on my backside.

Money and a gun, but I still hadn't found Maverick.

With limbo-like movement beneath a stall door, I crab walked deeper into the ruins, calling my dog with more insistence. His muffled response sent chills up my spine. Where was he? Was he hurt? Did he find something? He was exceptional at locating both the expected and the unexpected.

CJ Bluestone, Carlee's dad, rigorously trained Maverick and Renegade to improve their discovery skills. Maverick had rightfully earned his credentials as a probationary search and rescue canine, and Renegade was well on her way. They had the heart, head, and nose to do the work. Sometimes, however, I had to take a deep, calming breath, realizing my dog easily clambered in where pit bulls feared to tread. Had he forged ahead into a new, dangerous situation?

I snaked through the detritus, lifted planks, skidded siding out of the way, and wormed onto my belly, jarring a support beam, and hurriedly steadied it until Maverick's incessant yipping drew me to the threshold of darkness. As I became more accustomed to the gloom, I used my elbows to army crawl to the edge of a gaping hole in the floor. Maverick gazed up at me with his soft brown eyes from a five-foot drop. He barked once and sat. He tilted his head and his tongue hung out.

"What did you find, my friend?" As I peered into the dim breach, a piece of roofing rained down, and I covered my face in case anything else should fall from above. When the space quieted, I peeked past my elbow and followed the shifting dust motes in a newly exposed shaft of light, to my dog. I gazed, disbelieving. The cone of the dingy spotlight caught Maverick and, next to him, reflected off the short dark hair and glassy eyes staring beyond at some undefined corner of the structure above me. "Oh, Maverick."

Maverick sat next to a crumpled body. It could have been Penelope.

As I peeled my phone from my pocket, it pirouetted on my fingertips and tumbled into the chasm. Maverick barely acknowledged the phone landing nor the chunk of two-by-four crashing into the hole immediately after. He glanced down at the timber and back at me. Unwilling to crawl into the abyss next to him and unable to call for assistance, I scoured the subfloor hollow to devise a way for him to safely get out of there as soon as possible. We needed help.

On the far side of the rift, a narrow metal sheet about six feet long and a foot wide stood against the one intact wall. I slithered close enough to knock one edge over the lip and maintain a grip on the other. Maverick looked at me and cocked his head. He examined the makeshift incline and found me again. His baleful eyes produced a pang of guilt. "Come on, boy. We've got to get out of here." He jumped onto the proffered, jerry-rigged exit ramp and bounded next to me, slathering me with tickling kisses. I wrapped my arm around him. A crack sounded from the dark recesses of the barn, and I held him tight.

"Hello? Anyone there?"

A large piece of plywood broke away and descended with the precision of a guillotine. It struck the floor inches from my foot and sent up a puff of dirt. I glanced longingly at my phone as I wrapped my fingers around Maverick's collar so he could read the seriousness in my tone and pointed. "Let's go, my furry friend." Maverick bounded toward the narrow opening I'd made for the horses, glanced back at me tediously dodging the obstructions, and fled. I inhaled deeply and caught the pungent smell of dung mixed with the sweet scent of hay and something floral.

Scrambling behind him, I tripped and crashed into a support beam. Another piece of roof toppled from above, and I sheltered my head with my forearm, trying to fend off an avalanche from the rafters but sustained a hard conk. The ground turned ninety degrees and came up to meet me.

* * *

The next thing I remembered was a warm, wet tongue washing my face clean of dust and grime and sweat and makeup and any hint of lunch. I felt a tugging sensation at my sore shoulder followed by being dragged across the rubble on the floor. Blinking, I breathed a sigh of relief when a beam of warm sunlight from the makeshift doorway hit my face.

"I'm good," I mumbled, squirming and tugging myself free from the jaws of life. Wriggling to crouch, I emerged from the wreckage and carefully navigated the residual refuse. Looking up with a sharp pain crowding out the muddled thoughts in my head, I shielded my eyes and caught a welcome figure. "Jane?"

She stood stock still with her hands planted on her hips, wearing a scowl. "You took your sweet time. What were you doing in there?" she hissed. "I thought something happened to you."

I rubbed the knob on my head and peered at my watch. It wouldn't tell time ever again. "I went after Maverick." I surveyed the yard. "Where is everyone?"

Her anger dissipated, but she ignored my question. "That place is a death trap."

Unbidden words crept into my head and silently answered

her. *Little does she know.*

"It's falling down."

I sorted my fuzzy thoughts and looked back at the barn, a flashback knocking on my brain. Maverick planted himself on his rear end and followed my line of sight. My heart thudded in my chest. He nudged me, and I turned to my friend. "Jane?" my voice squeaked. Tiny bits of the recent sight took shape in my head spinning together like pieces of a puzzle.

Jane's keen sense detected my anxiety. Her brown eyes widened. "Debora and Ransam invited the kids inside to make ice cream sandwiches. What's wrong?"

"I've got to get back in there." I tried to sort the images bombarding my mind.

A loud crack followed by a boom had clouds of dust extruding like sausages from the cracks in the building. Jane ducked, and I shielded my head.

"Oh no you don't."

I recalled the glassy eyes and familiar face and prepared to bolt inside, but she grabbed my elbow and held on tight.

"Call 911. There's someone in there."

"Who?" She examined my face and said in disbelief. "Not again."

NINE

"I think so." I screwed up my face. It wouldn't be the first body I'd discovered since moving to Columbia. Or the second.

"We can't go in there."

I marched toward the house. Ransam and Debora would know what to do.

Jane hustled to keep up. "Dead or alive?" She tried to read my face.

I shook my head the tiniest bit and kept my voice low. "I don't think she's alive." What I remembered was tragic.

"Who is it?"

"I couldn't get very close, and the light in the barn is dim, but the body has short dark hair and wearing black like Mia's sister, and I—"

Penelope's battered blue truck roared down the drive, crunching gravel and honking its horn, spewing exhaust, and skidding to a stop next to the farmhouse followed by a second vehicle. Debora and Ransam trudged onto the porch. Multiple doors thunked closed, and though I thought it impossible, I recognized the grating voice. "Where's my sister? Where's Mia?"

I suppressed a shudder, leaned into Jane, and whispered, "I'm not sure who's in the barn. The woman talking to Debora right now looks and sounds like Penelope and is looking for her sister, Mia, so she can't be the one to have fallen through the floor."

I needed to know if I'd dreamed the body. I cradled my forehead in my hand, trying to convince myself I was wrong and fend off the ache.

Her eyes grew round. "Is it bad?"

"Shh!" I didn't want to point out another catastrophic loss, identify the wrong person, upset the kids, or call attention to an imagined vision. I shook my head, and amid the hammering, the kaleidoscope of parts shifted into place. "I'm sure there was a body. At least I think there was a body, but the building isn't very stable, and I don't want anyone else to get hurt or ruin the chance of getting inside. I'll try to take Debora or Ransam aside. Maybe we can shore up the supports, but we need law enforcement help to determine the manner of death." I mentally shrugged away the sight of the unnatural position of the woman's body at the bottom of a gaping hole.

And I remembered the blocks of money. And the gun. *What money? Whose gun?*

Jane groaned and scrubbed her face. She drew her phone from her bag and tapped the keypad, turning away and pressing her finger to her ear to drown out the sounds around us.

At first, I thought the slight man standing near Debora

and Penelope was Liam, but today he was a head taller than Debora. He'd exited the tan sedan, and, although he wore jeans and a similar khaki shirt, if he stood sideways and stuck out his tongue he'd look like a zipper.

"On their way." Jane materialized at my elbow, pocketing her phone and scrutinizing the twosome walking with Debora. "You thought the body might've belonged to Penelope, but she's right there." She pointed with her chin and gave me a questioning look. "And who's the guy with her?"

As I blinked away the sunshine, Penelope strutted toward her truck. "Byrne, get out here. Halloran says it could have been so much worse, and she's celebrating their good fortune."

I cringed and rubbed my forehead, fending off the ache narrowing my field of vision. *How could it have been worse?*

Penelope lowered her voice. I strained to hear her as she said, derisively, "If this is luck, I wouldn't want to experience their misfortune."

Liam startled me, his bantamweight popping up from inside the cargo bed of the pickup—the absolute worst place to ride—and dexterously vaulting over the side.

"That should be illegal," I said, and my breath hitched. "Jane, what if I'm remembering wrong? The details are a little hazy."

"We'll know soon. I got some pushback, but the dispatcher said he'd send someone out as soon as possible. An F3 tornado touched down on this side of Columbia, and they're assessing what's been left in its wake. So far, they have everything under control, but their plates are full."

Patricia closed the distance between us. "I knew it was a tornado. There's an awful lot of damage on our end of town." She'd read Jane's lips and understood most of the words. "Was anyone hurt?"

Jane worked an unsure smile onto her face. "I don't *know*

if anyone was hurt in the tornado."

Patricia inspected her wind-torn yard and turned to Jane. "You said, 'he'd send someone out.'" She cocked her head. "Who's on their way out where?"

"Officer Christianson is coming out to your farm," Jane said.

I flinched. Why did it have to be Ronnie Christianson? I never knew where I stood with him, but we needed assistance. Maverick sensed my additional unease and prodded my fingers for attention.

"Why?" Patricia blinked. "What's happened?"

Jane and I exchanged a silent communication. We wouldn't disclose anything—yet. If there was a body, revelation of a death would be traumatic, and the kids would need all the support they could get. I hoped I was wrong. "He's checking damage done by the storm." I pointed toward the farmhouse. "Your mom is having the team in for a snack. Let's join them."

"No can do. The other two horses are in the paddock behind the barn. They have to be frightened. I've got to round them up and see if they'll go for a short ride. And all four need to be situated in a temporary shelter. It's my job to take care of them."

"Jane, you join the rest of the kids and see if Debora needs any help. Patricia and I will see to the horses." I inwardly trembled.

"Ms. Wilk, thanks for the offer but," Patricia almost laughed, "be honest. What do you really know about horses? I believe Ms. Mackey is better equipped to help." She winked a cornflower blue eye.

"She's got you there, Ms. Wilk." Jane smirked as they headed to the paddock. "Besides, it's been too long, and I could use the ride," Jane called over her shoulder.

I trudged to the house, intent on breaking the news

to Debora when a Corvette, the color of a fine red wine, rocketed around the corner and slammed on its brakes mere feet in front of me. A police vehicle followed closely behind, blaring an earsplitting whoop. A man jumped from the sports car and stomped toward the house, seemingly oblivious to the wailing siren.

The vacuum created when the police officer deactivated the noise sucked me forward, and I lost my footing. The door of the blue SUV opened and divided the white letters of the word "police" in two. The occupant dropped one cowboy-booted foot at a time, and I heard the eerie whistled theme from *The Good, the Bad, and the Ugly* in my mind. Ronnie emerged, breathed deeply, and hitched his belt.

"Ronnie?"

"In a minute, Katie." He ran his hand along his front fender as he approached the speeder. "Sir," Ronnie said. Ignored, Ronnie's face darkened, and his irritated voice boomed. "Stop, sir."

The middle-aged man turned at Ronnie's incensed tone and yanked wireless devices from his ears. "What do you want? Can't you see I'm in a hurry?" When he recognized the uniform, a smarminess flooded his patrician features, and he nonchalantly pocketed the earbuds as he delivered his next words with a fawning that made my skin crawl. "Detective, what can I do for you?"

"It's Officer Christianson." Ronnie narrowed his dark eyes and set his fingers lightly on the butt of his holster, stopping in front of the Corvette. "And you can hand over your license and registration."

"I know I was traveling slightly over the speed limit, Officer Christianson. I am truly sorry." He raked his fingers through his mahogany-colored hair and gave the officer a curious once over. "But I'm looking for my wife and with the storm and everything—"

"License and registration."

"Yes, sir." He saluted and plastered on an unctuous smile. "Anything for an officer of the law." He straightened the front of his gray suit jacket and retraced his steps to the car, sliding across the grass, cleaning his muddy soles. "This place is a mess," he grumbled, opening the passenger door and retrieving the papers from the glove box.

The corners of my mouth turned down and my nose wrinkled in disgust. What on earth had he expected after the storm? And who was he?

Ronnie took the identification cards and retreated to his vehicle. I wanted him to throw the book at the slick sweet-talker, but Ronnie's quick turnaround time didn't give me much hope, until he held out a tablet and said, "Sign here, Mr. Enzo Gyles."

Mr. Gyles snatched the writing utensil and read the page. Instead of signing, he tossed his head and banged the tablet against his leg. "Two hundred fifty dollars? That's highway robbery. I couldn't have been going much over the speed limit on these God-forsaken winding roads. What kind of rinky-dink cop are you anyway?"

A genuine smirk inched its way onto my lips. He was messing with the wrong policeman. I might not be Ronnie's favorite, but he was no-nonsense and knew the regs. He'd take the driver down a peg, and the man would never see it coming.

"This rinky-dink cop will arrest you for breaking the law if you refuse to sign. Your choice."

Mr. Gyles released a puff of air, then scribbled on the tablet and shoved it back at Ronnie. "For your information," Gyles sputtered, "I know all the right people."

"I don't know what the law is in ..." Ronnie leaned back

to get a better view of the license plate, "Kentucky, but for your information, it's illegal to drive in Minnesota wearing earbuds." Ronnie pointed to the pocket containing the errant devices. "You're lucky I didn't add that fine to your ticket. Would you like me to write another citation?"

Mr. Gyles paled. He seemed to be biting down awfully hard, and his jawline turned white.

"You might need to cool down, Mr. Gyles." Ronnie said calmly. "Why don't you take a hike?"

Gyles spun on his heels, and breathing heavily, stomped down the drive, and out through the open gate.

Ronnie's smirk morphed into a frown when he saw me. "Jane called and said I was urgently needed at the Halloran Farm. Don't tell me it was for that hog's ear. Was he causing the problem?"

"It wasn't for him, I assure you."

He scrutinized my face. "What happened to your head?"

I swiped my hand through my hair and my fingers came away sticky with blood, bringing back a rush of memories from almost two years ago. I had thoughts of zooming the verdant bike path near home with my husband, Charles, and Dad. I'd lifted my feet from the pedals, letting gravity draw me down the incline when Dad's hoarse voice yelled, "Gun." Even his streaking by us didn't register alarm until Charles crashed into me, knocking me off the trail, and throwing us both to the asphalt. Charles took the bullets I still thought were meant for me. "Promise me you'll be happy. Lead a good life," he said. I turned my hands over, expecting them to be covered in blood.

"Katie?"

I shook away the painful memories and focused on Ronnie.

"Do you need medical attention?"

"No," I said harshly. Someone else might really need help. "I'm perfectly fine." I closed the gap, lowered my voice, and gave it all the weight I could. "I found a body in the barn."

"This some sort of joke?" He snorted.

"No joke."

"You're a magnet for trouble, Katie." Ronnie squinted as if using his X-ray vision on me, and I tried not to wince. "The storm damage was patchy, and in some places, worse than we expected, but I thought we dodged a bullet this time. No one had reported injuries anywhere else. A horrible accident here?" He searched my face. "Are you sure? What happened? Where's the victim?"

I processed his words and wondered about what I'd seen.

"Why are you at Halloran's?" Ronnie pulled out a notebook and pen and began to write.

"The Kentucky Derby is running Saturday, and Ida and Marietta Calder are planning a party for the kids. We came out to see the horses." Ronnie stopped moving for a moment at the mention of students and searched the grounds. His eyes alighted on our obvious mode of transportation, the van sporting the district number on its side. "The members of our science club are with Debora in the farmhouse."

"You realize no one should've disturbed the scene."

"Jane and I haven't told anyone what I've found. No one has been in there."

"Speaking of Jane, where is she?"

"She's with Patricia—"

He held up his hand. "Who?"

"Patricia Halloran, Debora's daughter. They're rounding up the horses in the paddock and moving the Thoroughbreds."

"Debora has Thoroughbreds?"

"No, but she and Mrs. Mia Brown built a barn, and Debora's daughters, Kindra and Patricia, take care of the horses Mrs. Brown boards here." I pursed my lips, wondering what I could share and not sound like an old gossip. "There was a little tiff between Mia Brown and her sister, Penelope Gyles, when we were here on Tuesday." Ronnie looked over his shoulder in the direction Enzo Gyles had marched, and his left eyebrow rose. I shrugged. "Maybe they're related. Anyway, Penelope accused Mia of having a horse by the name of Foggy Bottom, but the young man with Penelope examined the horses and indicated they weren't the same."

Ronnie shook his head. "Just the facts, Katie. Where's the body you and Jane found?"

"Sorry. Just me. I found the body. It's in the barn right next to where I lost my phone, so Jane called it in. Follow me." Maverick bolted toward the horse barn. "Or rather, follow Maverick." I lifted my leg to crawl over the fallen elm, and Ronnie grabbed my shoulder.

"Did you notice all the destruction here? It's too dangerous. I'm not taking a civilian into these ruins, especially you, until I see it firsthand. Just tell me what you've found."

"I know my way in and out. It'll be easier if I show you where she is."

"No. Describe what I should be looking for, and I'll call for reinforcements."

I gave him as much detail as my muddled mind could remember. After he called out the cavalry, he crawled beneath the demolished siding and maneuvered his bulk through the narrow, improvised entrance.

Fifteen minutes later, he emerged, red faced and visibly annoyed. He strode toward the driveway, shaking his head, as a second patrol car arrived with the county coroner wagon in tow. My heart skipped a beat, and my cheeks ached behind my gigantic grin when Pete Erickson unfolded his long, lean legs from the front seat. As county coroner, it was his job to ascertain cause and mode of death and collect evidence to support his determinations. I shielded my eyes against the bright sunlight as I neared them.

Ronnie's scathing voice stopped me midstride. "Wilk, it's a crime to make a false police report."

A chill ran up my spine. "What are you talking about?"

"I searched the entire barn." He glowered. "There's no body."

TEN

Did you look through the hole in the floor? Maybe part of the ceiling fell on top of the body?" I rubbed my head and dismissed thoughts of everything but the body. I scrambled over the fallen tree and marched toward the shattered horse barn. "Maybe you were in the wrong place. I'll show you where the body is."

The more my mind cleared the more vivid the vision. I was sure I'd seen a corpse, maybe victim of the storm or something more egregious, but now Ronnie said there was none.

"Wilk." Ronnie's harsh tone brought me up short.

"What?" I said sharply and turned to glare at him. He tantalizingly dangled my phone from his fingers, and I stammered, "I don't understand. My phone fell next to the body." New questions clicked into place, and I focused on the shelter again. "We have to keep looking. Maybe she's dazed and hurt and wandering around."

"There was no sign of anyone in the pit. Squandering precious police time in your flight of fancy is a waste of valuable resources, especially today."

My mind swirled. "But she was there. I saw her. Ask …" Ronnie cocked his head. But he couldn't ask Jane. She hadn't seen the body. No one had. Except for my dog, I'd been alone.

I gathered my thoughts and sought comfort and confirmation from Maverick. With a spurt of energy, words tumbled from my lips. "What about the money?"

Ronnie crossed his arms and set them on his paunch. "What money? You never said anything about money."

"There were packages of money—many packages of money—deep in the crevice between the doorway and the wall." He'd believe me when he saw the money. And the gun. "Can I show you? It's right inside the entrance to the barn."

Ronnie jerked his chin up, affirming my attempt.

I picked my way across the yard and pointed through what remained of the doorway. *Please be there. Please.*

Ronnie stuck his head in, and I heard rummaging around, sure footed steps, and a shuffling of heavy things. My hope was dashed when he came back into view and squinted dark, beady eyes at me. "In my book, you're as bad as Gyles." He smashed my phone in my hand. "Lucky your head took a hard knock, or I'd cite you for obstruction of something. Good day to you."

In a tizzy, I teetered. Was it real? What was wrong with me? Had the knock to my head given me a daydream, a false memory? The vision had seemed genuine, but I doubted it now and I stutter-stepped. A strong hand cupped my elbow.

"I've got you." I closed my eyes and inhaled Pete's scent, leather and fresh cut pine. He led me to the porch, righted an overturned Adirondack chair, and lowered me into it.

Kneeling, his eyes were in line with mine, and I melted into the gorgeous milk chocolate orbs. He tenderly took my hand and tilted his head, examining my injury. "What do you think happened, Katie?"

"What do I *think* happened?" My shoulders sagged. He didn't believe me.

"You hit your head." He examined my scalp with a gentle touch, but bright flashes of pain shuttered my eyes. He slid my hair over my shoulder and tipped me forward. "And your shirt is torn. You have a long gash." Although he tugged softly, a quick burning seared my back, but even my bizarre contortions didn't allow me to see the injury.

I caught Officer Christianson leaning against his vehicle, watching the spectacle, gloating. And I groaned. Was he right? I know I didn't intentionally make her up, but did I hallucinate everything?

"The bleeding has stopped. From your recent medical history, I know your tetanus is up to date, but you should go to the ER, and have the wounds cleaned and dressed. Susie's there now and I'm on call tonight."

"I can't go yet. I will." My need to know what happened overrode even the most wonderful, concerned, brown eyes. "I promise." I nodded and meant it but recoiled at the throbbing I felt. I'd been so focused on first Maverick and then the body, I hadn't felt any pain. It hadn't hurt much, but now I couldn't think of anything else. I'd make a visit to the ER—after.

"There *was* a woman. You believe me, don't you?"

"I believe you saw something." Pete searched my face. "You're not going to let this go, are you?" He smiled indulgently. "Ronnie," he called out. Ronnie's hand rested on the car's door handle. "Do you think it's stable enough for me to take Katie to check out the barn. I think she needs to see what you saw. I promise we'll be careful."

"There's not much left to fall from the ceiling." Ronnie refused to look at me and opened his car door. "But don't say I didn't warn you. Watch yourselves."

He recalled the second policeman, and both patrol cars spit pebbles as they hurried back toward the town's tornado troubles.

Pete held back the outside metal strip. My dog dashed inside. "Maverick," I called. He disappeared. I lowered my head and slithered through, hunched against the twisted flexible panel of siding used as a brace for the gap. When we slipped inside and Pete let go, the waves in the metal released a sound like faraway thunder.

Together, we tracked the powerful beam from Pete's lamp and climbed over and around the barriers felled by the mighty wind. Pete studied the existing supports, jostling a few, testing the lingering rigging, observing the soundness of our surroundings. Maverick dashed ten steps ahead, turned, and waited for the beam to light up his eyes before bounding to the next clear section of floor until padding down my homemade ramp and stationing himself in the beam of sunlight next to a pile of blankets and a pair of leather work gloves where I was absolutely certain I'd seen the body.

Pete took a deep breath before taking hold of the battered, splintered edge of the floor and lowering himself into the space next to Maverick.

He swished his pointed finger and said, "Out." Maverick responded by climbing next to me and observing Pete as he squatted and carefully scrutinized the ground. He pulled on nitrile gloves before sweeping aside the blankets and assorted riding gear. He jimmied free a board display of twelve braided black mane patterns and looked up at me.

Dark fabric. Fingers. Black hair. I rubbed the sore spot

on the back of my pulsing head. *How could I have been so wrong?*

Pete retrieved a spray bottle from his bag and removed the cap. Giving me a reassuring wink, he spread the contents over the ground to allay my fears. He reached for his Maglite and turned it off.

The ground glowed light blue.

Seconds later, the blinding light clicked on. Maverick's ears flopped as he tilted his head back and forth, inspecting Pete's work, eyeing my reaction, and waiting for a conclusive answer.

Pete frowned. His head dropped forward, and I wanted to brush back the dark curl falling onto his forehead. He shook his head from side to side, and I could almost hear his words echo Jane's, "Not again."

"Katie." The way he said my name made all my questions disappear. "Are you okay?"

"Great," I squeaked but immediately changed my answer to, "Good," when I remembered why we stood on this spot.

Indicating the trace left by blood, he said, "The blood sign could have been here a while, but I'll talk to Amanda and see if we can't get out a search party, just in case. With the pandemonium surrounding the storm, it might take her a while. Don't worry. Your mysterious woman must've been okay enough to get out of here."

"If I saw someone." I had to be mistaken. The woman I saw didn't look like she'd been well enough to breathe. Maybe I'd jumped to an erroneous conclusion, and it was a terrible accident, and she would be found.

"You and Maverick, wait out in the yard, please."

His head bent to the task in front of him. As Maverick and I picked our way over the detritus, I heard him say, "Amanda, I think we might have a situation."

I wondered what had happened to the woman in the pit. I knew what Pete didn't want me to think about. Even if she'd removed herself from the chasm, she could still be badly injured.

Or dead.

ELEVEN

Chief Amanda West had been assessing the destruction left in the wake of the storm on this side of Columbia and arrived minutes later. "Join your students, Katie," she said. "As soon as we survey the site, we'll be in to talk to Debora and your kids. One of them might have seen something. We can determine the next course of action. Then you'll be free to leave." She and Pete beelined to the barn.

I might have been right, but I didn't feel good about it.

I took a calming breath through the thick, warm humid air. Ice cream sandwiches sounded like a welcome diversion. Rustling Maverick's ears, I whispered, "Ice cream." His tail swished every which way but loose.

I stepped onto the porch and raised my knuckles. My fist hovered next to the door as a woman's bossy voice hissed, "What do you want?"

I leaned closer and turned an ear toward the door.

"Now Mrs. Gyles, don't get so worked up. It can't be good for your heart." The man's low drawl was so smooth, and he spoke so slowly, I strained to catch all the words through the heavy wood. "That in turn wouldn't be good for my pocketbook."

"And don't you forget it."

Footfalls crunched on the drive, and I turned to see Enzo Gyles strutting toward the house. I wiped beads of sweat from my forehead and retreated a few inches before I knocked.

Gyles stepped onto the porch at the same time Kindra pulled the door wide to admit me, but when she caught sight of Gyles, she let the door partially swing closed to block out the newcomer. "Who are you?"

"I'm looking for my wife, Penelope Gyles. Is she here?"

Kindra's eyes flew from me and back to Gyles. She looked uncertain, gauging how to answer the stranger or if to answer at all.

"Chief West and Dr. Erickson are checking your property ..." The mention of their appearance should make her feel more at ease, but what should I add? What would I be able to say without giving away the wrong information? "For storm damage."

She relaxed and motioned for us to follow her. The kids had mounded multiple pairs of footwear on a black plastic mat under a wall of coat hooks. I slid my sneakers from my feet and stacked them on top of the pile. Before I could stop him, a self-absorbed Gyles marched into the noisy kitchen, leaving behind oozing, oily black shoe prints on the light-colored linoleum. I cringed. He stopped in his muddy tracks and scanned the festive group.

My boisterous students sat around a long rectangular wooden table with small bowls of do-it-yourself fixings in front of them, a rainbow of sprinkles, silver dragées, sparkling glitter, chopped nuts, chocolate and butterscotch chips. Large round chocolate chip cookies shared an aluminum baking sheet with an equal number of dark chocolate chunk cookies. Lorelei plopped a mound of soft vanilla ice cream between one of each and rolled the edge in shiny green sprinkles before passing the scoop to Brock. She took a big bite and giggled as the ice cream spurted out and dribbled down her chin.

"What's going on here?" Gyles glowered, and Lorelei stopped mid-swallow.

"Want one?" Carlee mumbled around a mouthful, holding out the tray of cookies.

Gyles' eyes went wide when he caught sight of Mrs. Gyles in the corner, glowering. "Penelope, I've been looking all over for you."

She narrowed her eyes in mock scrutiny and with a big fake smile said. "How did you find me, Enzo? You got a tail on me?"

Everyone in the room stopped talking to hear the response, everyone except Brock.

"Do you have the FindMyPhone service turned on?" asked Brock, seemingly unconcerned as he eyed the sparkly, sugary red edge of his treat. "It's a cinch to keep track of someone." He glanced up in the uncomfortable silence. Without moving his head, he slurped the melting goo, and his eyes raked the curious faces staring at him. The ice cream dripped, and although he seriously considered it, he caught himself before licking his fingers, and dabbed the towel on the table before saying, "What'd I say?"

Penelope glared at her husband, and the look on her face could have frozen a river of lava.

Amanda didn't bother to knock, and her hasty entrance sliced through the tension in the room.

Debora raised a brow and said, "Hello, Chief. To what do we owe this pleasure? Care for a homemade ice cream sandwich?"

"No thanks, but you go ahead."

Enzo Gyles plastered a wide smile on his face. With nauseating sweet flattery, he said, "Chief? What a progressive community you have out here in the boondocks. Bypassed Officer Christianson, did you?" His sycophantic tone reminded me of Eddie Haskel from the reruns of *Leave it to Beaver* my dad watched.

"And you are?" Amanda cocked her head, and her long black braid fell over her shoulder. She'd faced many detractors on her path to chief of police and wouldn't be taken in by his ingratiating attitude.

"Enzo Gyles at your service, madam." I wondered if he would approach her in a quest to have his ticket thrown out.

Chatter picked up slowly. Amanda curled her finger, drawing Debora and me closer. "Actually, Debora, could you join Katie and me on your porch?"

Hearing porch, Enzo said, "Allow me." He propped open the door and bowed at the waist.

"What's going on?" Penelope demanded.

Amanda spun around and carefully regarded the stranger. "May I have your name?"

"Why do you want my name?" Penelope threw back her head in a show of haughty indifference. I knew from personal experience Amanda could wait a very long time, and Penelope caved. "I'm Penelope Gyles." She raised her chin so she could look down her nose at Amanda. "And that is my ..." she grumbled as if smothering the word, "husband, Enzo Gyles."

Amanda acknowledged my students with a nod—they'd met before, and she led us out the front door. Debora had been put through the ringer this year, arrested for a murder she hadn't committed, and she asked cautiously, "What's this all about, Chief?"

"Do you know if anyone has been hurt on your farm recently? Any mishaps?" Debora shook her head. "I'm sorry to be the bearer of bad news, but Dr. Erickson wants to check out blood spatter he found in your horse barn."

The color in Debora's face faded and she closed her eyes. She looked more confident when she opened them. "Absolutely."

Penelope had followed us to the doorway and overheard one word. "Blood?" she repeated to the world in a loud, horrified voice.

Chairs scraped across the floor and footfalls pounded over the tile as the entire room readied to ascertain what was going on or help—whichever made the most sense. As they poured onto the porch, Amanda put up her hand. "Everyone, please remain here until we have a better understanding of what we're dealing with."

With a single nod from his boss, Officer Daniel Rodgers assuredly stepped onto the porch. "We'll need to take statements and record contact information. Let's head back inside."

My lower lip puffed out. What does it say for our year's experiences when my students were not put off at the first hint of trouble. Rather, they were visibly disappointed they wouldn't be allowed to witness the action.

However, before they could take a single step in the direction of the kitchen, Galen pointed toward the paddock and said, "Hey, look at Ms. Mackey. She sure looks upset."

We turned as a single unit. Jane stomped ten feet closer. She clenched her jaw, pointed her thumb behind her, and jerked her fist—the international get-over-here gesture. Debora took three uncertain steps, gasped, climbed over the fallen tree, and broke into a run, matched stride-for-stride by Amanda.

What happened to Patricia? My throat closed up.

Galen and Brock bolted after Jane, magnetically drawing us behind, a jumbled, worried army of friends. We rounded the corner of the horse shelter and stalled behind the boys' outstretched arms, halting us at the edge of the fence. Thirty feet into the paddock, Patricia held the reins of a royal horse, whinnying, snorting, and vertically shaking its head. Pete knelt over a mound crumpled at her feet. His sad eyes met mine.

Penelope and Enzo blustered their way through my students. "What's going on?" she said.

Enzo Gyles scaled the fence. Holding onto the post with one hand, he hung over the rails. From the look on his face, his vantage point allowed him to see the answer. He gave a strangely sad look. "Looks like that horse killed someone."

TWELVE

Pete estimated the time of death less than three hours prior and wouldn't allow anyone to get close and contaminate the scene. Kindra accompanied Patricia and they led TnL to the temporary shelter—an ancient barn on the outer edge of the farm site. Amanda herded everyone else back to the kitchen.

My resilient students had seen more than trigonometric functions and derivatives this year. Together, we'd weathered drugs infiltrating the school, a kidnapping, the defense of a parent, a threat of physical harm, and the reunion of a family. They mattered to me. I wanted to shield them. I had them check in with a parent before Amanda calmly asked for their insight and intelligent comments about the horrible accident and fielded those questions they could truthfully answer. Jane, my science club scholars, and I had battled the loss of electricity at school during many of the crucial hours. After arriving, none of them had seen anything resembling normal on the storm-torn farm grounds, but they couldn't add useful information nor had any of them been alone.

Renegade growled and snapped at some unseen pest, maybe a fly, so Carlee leashed her. She and Galen took a short jaunt down the drive to exercise the energetic pup. Upon their return, Renegade briefly caught sight of a thick brown strip of fur taunting her and circled, chasing her tail, bringing a brief moment of levity while we waited for Lorelei's mom who would help Jane transport the kids back to Columbia High School.

The choice of Marietta Calder for chaperone was calculated. She knew her daughter's friends. As a clinical psychologist, she'd be able to observe my kids, advise us on proper watchfulness, and alert us to possible difficulties. She'd hitched a ride with Ronnie Christianson, and he reparked his vehicle on the turf now resembling a parking lot. She hugged Lorelei and corralled her friends, funneling them to the van with expansive gestures.

"We can't leave Ms. Wilk." They fussed for only a second before Jane gave them *the look.*

She inhaled deeply and said, "We can, and we will. She'll return with Dr. Erickson."

I half expected a snide whoop, but the kids quietly stepped to the vehicle, and Jane gave me the "call me" sign.

The newly constructed, organic dairy barns stood on an unattached parcel of property, miles down the county road. Ransam, Debora, and two of their farmhands had braved the wind and rain to protect the herd and salvage as much as they could if the need arose. The cows were safe. Ransam and Debora hadn't seen anything or anyone, hadn't been to the home site until they joined us, and had witnesses to back them up.

Amanda questioned Penelope, Enzo, Liam, and the other skinny guy separately. I wished I could be a fly on the wall and hear what they came up with for alibis. One by one, they peeled off into their vehicles and played a life-sized game of Tetris to juggle an escape path to the road.

Amanda saved my confidential interview for last, and I worried through the wait time.

What had I seen? Should I have done more? If the victim had been dead for two hours, she couldn't have moved to the paddock by herself. Had I imagined it? Was it some kind of premonition? Mental aberration? How hard had I hit my noggin?

The puzzling memories didn't quite fit together in my pounding head. I sat at the table, watching the colored trails made by stirring colored sprinkles into the melted ice cream, reminding myself to follow Pete's instructions to go to the ER until Amanda cleared her throat.

"Are you ready, Katie?"

"As ready as I'll ever be."

"Dr. Erickson found the blood spatter following up on the statement you'd seen a body. Who knew about your discovery?"

"I told Jane, and she called 911." I chewed on the inside of my cheek. I couldn't very well accuse Ronnie of blowing me off, although that's exactly what it felt like. "Officer Christianson didn't find anything and attributed my vision to the bump on my head."

"Why were you in the barn? What happened?"

"Maverick took off and slipped inside. He wouldn't come out, so I went after him. He'd alerted at the body." I *had* seen the body and so had he. "I must have tripped on something in the barn on my way out and fallen. I can't quite pull that up from my memory. In fact, a lot of my thoughts are jumbled. Pete convinced Officer Christianson to let us search inside.

He sprayed luminol to assure me nothing had happened, and he found the blood."

"Is the victim the same person you saw before calling Ronnie?"

"I didn't get a close look at either body. It could be. However, the only light in the barn came from my phone, and that was fleeting. I hadn't seen much before I dropped it next to the body." My trembling fingers touched the cut on my head.

"No one can confirm your—ahh—sighting."

"No one but my dog. I could've sworn it was Penelope. The dark clothes had me fooled."

"Penelope is beside herself."

"Obviously, I was wrong." I shook the surprise from my head.

"Mia had been absent for almost a year. Penelope never expected to find her, and she admitted to being overcome. They argued but reconciled almost immediately, and now she lost her for good."

"Did the sisters decide to do a lookalike thing?"

"It's hard to get a complete sentence from her, but in answer to your question, yes. Although they had quite separate identities, in the past, they'd been able to fool people who didn't know them well by dressing alike. They patched up their differences on Tuesday and decided to have some fun and go for it again." Amanda slumped into the seat next to me. "There's no indication how the body had been moved, Katie. No obvious drag marks, no blood trail. So far, I can't explain the blood in the barn."

I was certain I'd seen the body in the barn. I hadn't dreamt it, but how bad was the knock to my head?

As if she could read my mind, Amanda said, "Mia could have been knocked out by a horse or the barn caving in, regained consciousness enough to walk to the paddock, and died there."

But the timing is off, I thought.

She put her hand on my shoulder and her compassion-filled eyes met mine. "Do you remember where everyone was from the time you entered the horse shelter until Officer Christianson pulled in?"

"Lists I *can* do." I laced my fingers together on the table and stared at them, lifting one at a time as I described the location of each group. "Patricia and Kindra were with Debora and Ransam near the trucks." Thumb. "My four students stood in a close circle by the van." Forefinger. "Jane hollered at me, standing next to the fallen elm tree." Middle finger. A giggle burst, and Amanda frowned. "She was livid, but when Maverick dove into the barn, I had to go after him." Ring finger. I bit my lip and for a moment wondered if Maverick had been chasing Mia's scent. He has a good search and rescue sense. I closed my eyes, allowing the events to scroll by like an old movie, and clasped my hands tightly together. "I hit my head and lost a little time, I think. I can't tell." I held up my wrist. "My watch stopped."

"You don't know where Mr. and Mrs. Gyles or their two workmen were?"

"Mrs. Gyles, Penelope, drove in about the same time Jane called 911 for assistance. She had Liam riding in the bed of her truck. Idiots." I shook my head. "And the other dude ... Who is he anyway?"

"His name is Tony Relando. He says he buys and sells horses, but I need to check his credentials."

"The Relando guy drove in behind them. And Ronnie has the scoop on Enzo. I would imagine all the info you need is on the ticket he wrote."

Amanda's eyes widened.

"What did I say?"

She shook her head.

"Thanks for your help." Amanda's lips cracked a momentary smile. "You should go to the ER. Get your head examined."

Pete knocked on the door jam. "We're all finished. The body's being transported to the hospital morgue. I'll get you my report as soon as possible."

"Amanda, I've been wondering." I dragged myself to standing and lumbered to the door. "How did Penelope find Mia in the first place?"

"Go home and get some rest. And Katie?" Her tone of voice hardened. "We'll take it from here."

"Yes, ma'am."

My salute halted midair as a nasty cackle sounded from out in the yard and another voice yelled, "What do you think you're doing, you old coot?"

THIRTEEN

Amanda pushed past me. Maverick flexed his muscles and dragged me after her onto the porch. Amanda's gaze lasered in on the miscreant at the far end of the fence. "What's going on, Ransam? Who is that?"

Ransam's neck cracked when he stretched and rotated his shoulders. Towering above Amanda, he took a few deep breaths to settle his annoyance. "Ole. Again. He appears and on occasion, he insists we've stolen his treasure."

The scrawny man with long, white snarly hair and a ragged beard hopped from one foot to the other. One strap of his shabby denim overalls flapped against his bare chest. After he hurled another goosebump-inducing hoot, he gave a gap-toothed grin, applauded, and dashed around the corner, out of sight.

Amanda pounded down the steps, and Ransam called after her, "You won't catch him. We've tried."

Amanda hurdled the fallen debris, but her shoulders dropped when she reached the side of the building. She stopped and rotated, determination etched in the set of her jaw as she tromped back. "He's a possible witness." Amanda's brow furrowed and her eyes darkened. "What's he doing here?"

"His daddy, Sven—"

Amanda covered a cough.

Ransam shook his head. "Yeah. I know. Anyway, Sven was the third generation to own this property, but Ole decided he wasn't cut out to be a farmer. He was too good for it and fled to Florida."

"What did he do there?"

"He held odd jobs like tending bar, washing windows, or playing the role of pool boy."

My eyes almost crossed. Ole Severson in a Speedo did not fit any pool boy mold I could fabricate in my mind.

"He even tried his hand at professional chess for a while. His mother, Astrid, coddled her baby boy." The last two words came out dripping in sarcasm.

Bartender? Custodian? Pool boy? Chess master?

"You wouldn't know it by looking at him now, but he played defensive lineman on the state-qualifying football team back in the day, and he was ripped. I'm pretty sure he's doing—" Ransam side-eyed Amanda, suddenly aware his words could have legal implications.

"Drugs? Maybe meth. You don't have to say it. It looks that way to me too. What happened?" Amanda glanced across the yard.

"Sven proposed a partnership with his son, but Ole refused. He didn't want to have anything to do with the farm." Ransam picked up a few of the smaller tree branches and launched them onto a growing stack lining the gravel drive. "Debora's husband skipped out about the same time. She needed additional income, and with her help, Sven kept the farm in the black. She's an amazing woman."

"You couldn't be more correct." Pete smiled appreciatively. "Debora has taken the farm into the twenty-first century."

A small laugh hiccupped from Ransam. "Sven invested in Debora's business to help her qualify to purchase this farm from his estate."

"Was that good or bad?"

"The return on his investment took care of his outstanding bills and provided a little nest egg. He stayed on the farm in his home, and Debora took over the day-to-day operations. Sven sat back and watched the New Age enterprise come into its own. Kindra and Patricia loved him and called him Gramps. They were extended family. And with Sven as a resource, Debora was able to handle every contingency. When he succumbed to his cancer, Debora was devastated, but he'd prepared her. Her successful organic dairy continues to pay off the note and support her and her daughters."

"What's Ole's problem with Debora?"

"It wasn't like he didn't benefit from Sven's life insurance policy when he came back for the reading of the will, but he was surprised his assets no longer included the farm. Debora owned it. He sued her, but, of course, it came to nothing. He's hung around in the area and shows up now and then to annoy Debora, but he wouldn't hurt a fly. He's harmless. Debora knows she's earned the farm, but still feels his loss and indulges him. Debora doesn't care if he visits as long as he stays away from her girls."

"Even so, I'd like to talk to him. He might have seen something. Where does he go when he's not harassing you?"

"I'm not sure. Nor have I seen where he accesses the acreage."

"If he's using drugs, he might become volatile and unpredictable, even if he's been the epitome of congeniality up to this point. I don't think he should be trespassing on private property. Call us next time, and we'll try to put an end to his intrusive behavior."

Candidly chastised, Ransam nodded and said straight-faced, "But first you have to catch him."

"I'll put your farm on one of our patrol officers' routes. We'll keep him on our radar."

Ransam bent to the task of painstakingly cleaning up the yard, and I slid into the County Coroner van next to Maverick. Pete had a few words with Amanda before taking the driver's seat. He copied her perfect three-point exit in exactly seven turns, but I didn't say a word. It had been a long, convoluted day.

My hazy memory threatened my confidence. The idea of a mental aberration or hallucination made me shudder. I trusted in my recall ability.

Although the music emanating from the radio was a rousing Bach fugue, the mood in the van was subdued. I peeked at Pete and noticed him squinting and gritting his teeth. He clenched his chiseled jaw. I didn't know what I could do to ease the tension, so I tapped my finger on the dash in time to the music.

The fugue ended, and Pete switched the radio off.

"We're going to get the scrape on your back taken care of first." His jaw line turned white as if he'd clamped down even harder. He cleared his throat. "Ms. Brown died from a blow to her head, and it could have been one of the animals. A horse would have been capable of dragging her across the paddock. We'll have to see."

My heart threatened to jump out of my chest and the palpitations compounded my anxiety remembering Dad's recuperation. He spent months recovering from his traumatic brain injury. On occasion, I caught a glimpse of indecision on his part, a hesitancy he didn't have prior to his injury. A blow to the head would have been debilitating and could have easily been fatal.

"Katie?" The concern in Pete's voice broke through my barrier of thoughts. Had he been talking?

"Sorry. What?"

"I won't know until I finish running all the tests, but I think you might be right. The body had been moved. But I know you, Katie." He raked his fingers through his dark curls. "You have to let this go. Promise me."

"I'll try." I believed I meant what I said but often found it easier said than done.

FOURTEEN

Before my first hour class, the morning began with a profound debate among a smattering of my science club students whether or not we should continue our plan for the Kentucky Derby party.

"Will it be in poor taste if we didn't know the victim all that well?" Ashley shrugged.

"She was a nice lady," said Carlee. "But the race'll still go on. I've watched it before, just to see the gorgeous animals. Talking about the physics and math involved has made the topic much more engaging." She smiled shyly. "And I think I've picked a winner."

The arguments, pro and con, waned until Lorelei bounced in and hurled a cardboard box onto my desk. "Sorry," she said a little breathless, straightening her hot pink skirt and the cuffs of her crisp white blouse. "It was getting heavy." She raised the flaps and removed a stack of linen envelopes with a fancy script across the front. "Mrs. Clemashevski copied her painting of a Thoroughbred onto the invitations. Everyone gets a frame-worthy print for themselves, one for their parents, and two more for whomever."

When no one grabbed an envelope she said, "What's going on?"

"We're debating whether we should still have the party, what with the death and all," Carlee said.

"I'll admit, Mrs. Brown's death tempered my enthusiasm, but our parents have been communicating. They want to observe, firsthand, the benefits of being part of an academic club, and this particular opportunity only comes once a year. Mom and Ms. Halloran had a long conversation late last night with Mrs. Clemashevski and concluded the lesson is still on. If someone doesn't want to attend, no problem, but no griping from the sidelines afterward." Lorelei doled out four cards to each student and reached in for a handful of blue pages. "Here are stats sheets for the horses running tomorrow, answering many of the questions we raised in order to make an informed choice." Her eyes shifted among the girls, and she jammed her fists onto her hips. "And why is no one wearing pink? Didn't you get the text?"

"I did." Brock swaggered through the door and heads turned. He sported khaki shorts and a hot pink polo shirt. "Anything for you, Lorelei." He winked, then tugged his collar up, snagged the sales tag, and snapped it free. Lorelei groaned, albeit with affection.

Galen reached into the box and peeled off two blue pages and a handful of invitations. "Why pink? It's not really a color I have in my wardrobe."

"The Kentucky Oaks race takes place today. Pink honors the official Oaks flower, the stargazer lily, and celebrates Churchill Down's advocacy and fundraising efforts for women's health issues."

"I wish you would have explained all that in your text." Carlee wriggled uncomfortably. "I thought you were just being bossy."

Galen dug deeper in the box and extracted a stack of pink T-shirts. "I don't suppose there's one for me?"

"I have twelve extra-large. Do with them what you will."

Galen donned a skin-tight version and handed around the spares. I pulled one over my head. It hung to mid-thigh and framed the beautiful graphic—a field of four horses ridden by pink-togged jockeys with a garland of pink flowers encircling the caption 'Lilies for the Fillies.'

Carlee drowned in her T-shirt, but she nabbed another off the pile and said, "I gotta see this on Ms. Mackey. See you later." Galen shrugged and hurried after her.

As Ashley and Allie tried out various knotting and tying techniques to cinch the shirt and make it more stylish, I calculated nine science club students, two parents and two guests apiece, five responses for each of the mock trial students, Mrs. Clemashevski, Jane, Drew, Dad, Pete (if I was lucky), and me for a grand total of—

Kindra spun around the corner as if she held onto a Maypole, her pale pink skirt swirling with the agitation of a cyclone. "Ms. Wilk, Mrs. Gyles must have heard about our Derby party and told her husband. They're coming for sure to honor the memory of Mrs. Brown. That's okay, isn't it?"

I felt the corners of my mouth turn down. "I'm sure it is. I'll give Mrs. Clemashevski a heads up. Do you need an invitation for them?"

"No, I've given them the information." she said, slyly. "We need to include Mr. and Mrs. Gyles in our count. And maybe that Relando guy, Liam, and Mrs. Brown's secretary."

I stared at Kindra. "Secretary?"

"I didn't see her often. She stopped out once a week to pay Mrs. Brown's bill, but usually when Patricia and I were in school. She came around last night, terribly distraught. My mom had a horrible time trying to get her to calm down. She couldn't believe her boss was dead. She stayed and wailed for hours about what she'd need to do while my mom loaded her with iced tea. I felt so bad for her." Kindra bit the inside of her cheek before going on. "After she left, Mrs. Gyles showed up. She'd forgotten her jacket and came back to get it. She caught Patricia and me trying on some old hats from a trunk we found in the attic. I felt we had to explain. She was so emotional, and she said the party would be a perfect tribute to her horse-loving sister."

There was that.

Not that I didn't believe Lorelei, but at the end of first period, I texted Ida to make sure she had no reservations regarding the party and to up the number on her invitee list. Her answering emojis, imbued with winking and big grins, left no doubt she'd accept additional guests. Periodically, throughout the day, she sent a growing inventory: updates to the menu, arts and crafts, games planned, and the up-to-the-minute odds on her favorite horses.

Before our mock trial practice, I organized the desks in semblance of a courtroom. With the judge's bench remaining, I held the gavel over the block but dropped it, startled when ZaZa poked her head in my room.

"Aren't you the least bit nervous," she growled, glowering, her lustrous brown hair pinned up atop her head.

ZaZa and I had studied cryptanalysis together at the Royal Holloway in London, and while there, she'd secretly harbored thoughts of a future with Charles, but he fell in love with me. She'd never forgiven us, and I never understood why she left her security job in Paris to teach mathematics in Columbia.

Careful not to offend, I blinked several times, and said politely, "What are you talking about?"

"Have you even sought permission to hold a party … for students?" She narrowed her exotic amber eyes. "With gambling? You think you can do anything you want."

My inability to come up with a suitable answer gave her plenty of time to spin on her Manolos and sashay through the math commons. I knew we were doing everything we could to make it a healthy experience for the kids, and I never thought anyone would think otherwise. I should have known ZaZa wouldn't be happy, but I'd never seen a first-year instruction manual on how to teach. I called the principal's office, and his admin answered after the first ring.

"Office."

"Mrs. McEntee, this is Katie Wilk. Would Mr. Ganka have a minute available for a quick chat?"

"You may come right down."

She never asked why. "I'll be there in three minutes."

I taped a quickly scribbled note to the door frame, informing whoever showed up for mock trial I'd be right back, grabbed my lesson plan file, and raced to the office.

Mrs. McEntee kept her eyes on her keyboard. She waved a finger in the direction of the principal's office and resumed her diligent typing.

I knocked tentatively on the door.

"Come," Mr. Ganka replied in his customarily terse way.

The door didn't make a sound as it swung open. I peeked around the edge of the door. Mr. Ganka sat at his desk, his fingers tented in front of his pursed lips. One eyebrow crept to his crewcut hair line over discerning, vivid blue eyes.

"Ms. Wilk, what can I do for you?"

"My science club students want to study odds. Is it okay to have a Kentucky Derby party? I don't want to break any school rules."

"And just how do you think you could be breaking the rules?"

I took a deep breath. "We're studying the varied aspects and impact of economics in the horse racing industry." I peeled four sheets off the top, copies of my lesson plan. "Here are our objectives and the procedures we'll be using and how they align with the math education standards."

His eyes traveled over the pages, and he gave an approving nod. "It's a departure from the norm, but it'll also be an efficient means to teaching a bit of physics, accounting, probability, and statistics." He ran his finger down the page and looked up. "What's the problem?"

"Maybe nothing," I said. "But we'd like to try using the probability theory proposed in the sixteen hundreds by Pierre de Fermat and Blaise Pascal to place…" I winced, watching his eyebrow raised even higher as I laid it on a little thick. "A wager. With candy," I added hurriedly.

He selected an invitation and gazed at the beautiful painting of a midnight black horse gracing the front. "The game of chance. No alcohol. No money. But fine food, hats, a horse race, games, and prizes. The invitation indicates parents are invited, and Mrs. Clemashevski is cooking." His eyes met mine. His chair squeaked as he heaved his powerful Marine body forward. "I've missed Ida. Her retirement came too early as far as I'm concerned. You don't suppose …"

I hoped I read his body language correctly. "Oh, I do. I most certainly do. Would you like to join us?"

He accompanied me across the room, raving about Ida's extraordinary and unusual teacher appreciation teas. As he opened the door, we came face to face with ZaZa, preparing to knock. "Ms. Lavigne," Mr. Ganka said. "Are you joining us for the Derby shindig on Saturday?"

Even her blood red lipstick paled as she stammered a negative response.

I breathed more easily on my return to the math department, but my relief was short lived. I opened the door to loud voices and scurried into my classroom.

Jane's arm hung over Kindra's shoulders. Carlee sat on my desktop, listening intently to someone on her phone. And Patricia pounded across the floor, her fingers flying, communicating with an imaginary listener. The rest of my students had backed up against the walls, watching the drama unfold from a distance.

Kindra saw me and began to quake.

FIFTEEN

That secretary wants to put TnL to sleep."

Jane patted Kindra's shoulders. "Hogwash. There's nothing wrong with Thunderbolt and Lightning. Why would anyone want to hurt him?"

"She's blaming him for Mrs. Brown's accident."

"Do they even know the cause of death?"

Carlee pocketed her phone. "Dad said the secretary doesn't care. But it's wrong. It's just wrong." Tears glinted in her silvery eyes. "He's been asked to shelter the horse until they sort out who owns TnL, and the final decision is made."

Jane said, with more assurance than I'd ever heard in her voice, "Dr. Bluestone will know what to do. Trust me. But right now, we have a rehearsal to undertake. I want you to make it to nationals."

When the final mock trial participant entered the room, the students unenthusiastically took their assigned places and, obviously caught in the throes of other thoughts, went through the correct motions and proceeded to regurgitate a less-than-mediocre performance. I didn't have the heart to have them repeat anything. We still had one week to go.

"If you aren't aware, the science club is throwing a Kentucky Derby party on Saturday. Are any of you planning to attend the shindig at Mrs. Clemashevski's?" Jane took another stab at making the students relax. She shimmied in her extra-large pink shirt, belted at the waist. On her, with gray leggings and leather sneakers, it was a style statement. She'd make a plastic garbage bag look good. "If you need any info, we'll give you the low down."

Two hands raised. The other mock trials students filed out of the room, apologetic about other plans made for race day and a Saturday to boot. Lorelei handed out invitations. If everyone who responded attended, counting Mr. Ganka, the grand total neared sixty. Ida's idea to erect a tent got better and better.

"Don't forget. Try to up your wardrobe game." Ashley struck a swanky pose.

She was quickly ignored and pouted when Lorelei's excited voice overrode Ashley's expected complimentary comebacks and waved us around her phone. "They're lining up for the Kentucky Oaks. Post time is in ten minutes. We should each choose a horse." She dashed the names onto the board and handed out rectangles torn from a sheet of notebook paper. Each student accepted the challenge and scribbled something down.

Lorelei rubbed a knuckle against her chin. Her eyes lit up concentrating on her phone. "Look at all the pink."

Rather than crowd around a hand-held screen, I brought the race up on my computer mirrored on the Smart Board. The kids spilled into the desks and leaned forward, eager to see the horses run. The camera panned the sea of undulating color from magenta and orchid to fuchsia and puce, male and female supporters and race attendees wearing pink hats, dresses, shirts, pants, jackets, pocket squares, purses, boutonnieres, and even stilettos. The picture circled back to the gate, and an announcer introduced the horses and jockeys. The views parried between the track and the box seats housing owners with proud faces, zooming in on the applauding and nail-biting fans.

"It'll take the three-year-old fillies less than two minutes to run a one and one-eighth-mile track." Lorelei glared at the screen with fire in her eyes. "The race is an eighth of a mile shorter than the Kentucky Derby because the powers that be didn't want to push the female of the species." Watching the firm set of her jaw, I felt those powers were fortunate to safely live nine hundred miles to the southeast.

We watched with rapt attention. When the horses lined up at the starting gate and settled, a loud bell clanged, the doors opened, and the long legs gobbled up the dry track, sending small puffs of dirt into the air around their hooves.

For two minutes, we watched and waited. No one said a word until Patricia and Carlee cheered, "Yes!"

"Winner, winner, buy me dinner," said Galen, prancing and waving his victorious prediction in the air.

"Amazing," signed Patricia. "Someday I'll go to Churchill Downs, but meanwhile, we'll make the best of our local Kentucky Derby bonanza, right, Ms. Wilk?"

"Of course. I'm thinking, if anyone has a little time on their hands before Mrs. Clemashevski's soiree tomorrow, perhaps I could get a volunteer or two to stop by and help get everything ready. She's expecting quite a horde of race enthusiasts."

Every one of my students raised a hand.

I choked up. "Thanks. Let's congregate around three." Then Ida wouldn't have the time or opportunity to ream me out for overstepping my bounds. She could, however, take advantage of the extra hands.

The kids disappeared in a frenzy, but Jane hung back, helping me put my room in order. "How are you doing?"

"I'm still trying to wrap my head around what I saw, knowing Pete thought the body might have been moved. It's like I listened to the beginning of a movie from another room and walked in right after the climax. How could someone have moved her? Why? And who? How about you?"

"I'm upset I didn't protect Patricia from seeing the body. You haven't heard how the victim died, have you?"

"No, and I doubt I'm on the list of those with the need to know." I stacked the pages and courtroom paraphernalia precariously in my arms and headed toward the commons.

"What are you up to tonight? Anything fun on the agenda?" Jane flipped the light switch.

"Pete's working tonight so he can come to Ida's party tomorrow. I'm going to walk my dog and chillax." Jane gave me a suspicious glance. "You know, chill out and relax."

"I know that. I'm just surprised you do." Jane chuckled and shook her head, snatching the pages fluttering off the top of my pile, and setting them on my desk. "Have a good night, Katie." She scurried away, her eyes aglow with thoughts of love.

"You two, too," I said to the closing door. I tossed the loose pages onto my desk and pulled out the mock trial drawer in my filing cabinet. I organized the scripts, notes, list of objections, notebooks, reference books, pens, gavel, and block. Beneath the seemingly unending pile of *Titanic* trial material, I found a strange white legal-sized envelope with what looked like 'Wilk' scrawled across the front in thick pencil. I picked it up by the edges and turned it over, looking for some identification of the sender. Jane? One of the kids? One of my teacher friends? The school admin? Finding none, I wriggled my desk drawer free, searched for an opener, and decided on the scissors to do the honors.

I slid the sharp edge under the flap and sliced an opening. A single white, folded sheet floated to the floor. I grabbed it and flattened it on my desk. A single diagonal line covered each square of an eight-by-eight grid. I rotated the page, searching for a signature, clues, or a legend to decode the pattern. Everyone knew I enjoyed a good puzzle. I chewed on my lower lip, wondering which of my cohorts or students left the enigma for me.

The office was so quiet I could swear I heard the digital clock ticking away the minutes I could be spending with Maverick, so I gathered my belongings, including the errant grid, and set off for home.

I never caught my big boy atop the kitchen table. However, the water dripping from the vase of yellow tulips in the center still gurgled from a recent spill, and I rescued a brown paper bag, bearing my name, from utter ruination, so he must have done something untoward. I wondered how to reprimand Maverick, telling him he shouldn't anxiously await his mistress from a platform three feet off the ground when I'd only belatedly witnessed him languidly stretched out on his cushioned doggie bed.

"Dad?" No one responded. When nothing but my rumbling stomach answered my knock at Ida's adjoining door as well, I said, "Guess we're on our own tonight, Mav."

My strengths did not include cooking. In fact, the kitchen cringed, and I frowned as I searched the refrigerator for easy fixings, settling on a peanut butter and jelly sandwich for me and kibble for my companion. Seated at the table, I peeled open the soggy paper bag and found my old Mickey Mouse watch.

"Thanks, Dad," I said to the air. "At least now I can tell time." I laid the leather band over my wrist and buckled it tight.

I extracted the curious envelope from my briefcase and while I munched on my supper of salty-sweet squares, I squinted, trying to imagine a purpose to the tangle of line segments. I turned it face down, and on the back in the corner I read tiny digits. Recognizing the north and west indicators of latitude and longitude, I entered the numbers in a convertor, and a map with a red rectangle popped up. I enlarged the map and recognized the road names and route numbers.

I stuffed the last bite into my mouth and chewed quickly. Maverick's leash usually hung by the back door, but he'd already dragged it from the hook and waited patiently with the lead dangling from his mouth.

I pocketed the puzzle and said, "Let's take a short road trip, and we can go for a walk."

I'd taken the road twice this week. Third time could be the charm.

<h1 style="text-align:center">SIXTEEN</h1>

I opened the car windows and created a gentle wind tunnel as we crawled through the familiar streets. I glanced in the rearview mirror and bit back a smile watching Maverick's ears and lips flap softly against the breeze as he stretched his nose to catch the passing scents.

We slowed even more when confronted with evidence of the twister's passing. Columbia had been famous for its stand of sky-high, century-old Norway pines lining the northern avenues and populating the wildlife refuge in Hamilton Park. The storm cleanup left heaps of wood chips where too many of the beloved state trees of Minnesota had been taken out, opening circular tunnels to blue skies never before visible. Buzzing saws severed dangerously dangling limbs and thrummed like a swarm of nasty bees. I waved two fingers at the garbage collectors inching down the pavement, working hours of overtime. Much had been tidied in the individual pockets of damage, but it would take a while for the tornado footprint to be completely erased.

We eased out of the town proper. The turns dictated by my phone's GPS directed me past flat fields sprouting parallel lines of short green leaves, crops breaking through the rich black soil. I stopped and viewed the blinking box indicated on the screen—one half mile to the destination. I teased the paper from my pocket and glanced out the passenger window. Across the expanse of water sat the Halloran farm, but the grid page still meant nothing. I sighed and took a warm, wet swipe across my cheek from Maverick before slipping the paper into my pocket and clipping on the leash. We hopped out of the car. I didn't know what I was looking for, but the coordinates piqued my curiosity.

The road curved around the small body of sparkling water, edging toward the far end of the Halloran farm, and we trotted down the dirt path until we'd eaten up fifteen minutes by Mickey's hands. I pivoted to make the return trip, but Maverick stopped and sat. No amount of cajoling could get him moving.

"What do you see, big guy?" I surveyed the unremarkable acreage.

Here and there trees dotted the countryside, sprinkled sparingly for wind block or to hold the earth in place. Maverick stared at the huge solitary oak tree nearest us. It stood atop a knoll, a sentry guarding a snarl of weeds and dead branches. Maverick wouldn't move forward so I stepped back and noted that the tree also stood watch over a ramshackle shed, almost completely shrouded by ivy climbing the walls and choking off the sunlight glinting from the windows.

I gingerly opened the paper with the grid again and tapped my forehead. Where had I seen the configuration before? Maverick pulled the leash.

"Do you want to go there? Shall we visit?"

Maverick rose to all fours and took off at a dog-gallop. Tall reeds created a challenging course, and I slalomed behind him through the damp grasses. My reprimand came out in fits and spurts. "I. Was. Kidding." He halted and I skidded in front of a wall of planks fitted into grooves across an entry of sorts. Maverick rotated his head, ping ponging between the access and me. He stood and woofed, ordering my participation.

"Shh. Let me think. Something is scratching at my memory, and your barking is chasing it away."

Maverick shifted from one paw to the other, took two small steps forward and one to the side, then sat.

"Jane's not here, and I don't dance, but you do a fine waltz. Keep up the good work. She's proud of you and so am I." I blinked several times. It couldn't be that simple, could it? "Do it again, can you?"

He looked at me quizzically. I fished around in my brain for a familiar tune and hummed "The Skaters Waltz."

Maverick stood, stepped forward twice, once to the side, and sat.

I inhaled noisily and, standing in a cloud of pollen, sneezed. I sniffed, "I think you've got it." I yanked free the grid paper again and examined the matrix, flicking the fingers of my right hand against the flimsy page. "A Knight's Tour." Maverick's warm brown eyes watched me with curiosity. "Let me explain. The knight's tour is a chess problem, and the goal is to visit all squares of an empty chessboard only once, moving as the knight's piece, advancing on an L-shape course, two steps one way and one on a perpendicular route." My forefinger followed the path indicated on the grid. "Each of these segments intersects only one square. Surely, I've mentioned it before." He tilted his head. "The puzzle has been around since the Middle Ages. If I remember correctly, this is one of over thirty-three trillion possible solutions for an eight-by-eight grid."

Maverick blinked, unimpressed.

"I learned about it when studying Ann Zeilinger Caracristi, a code breaker with the Army Signal Intelligence Service. She employed computers larger than this shed to aid in collecting and deciphering covert communications. She was the first woman named as NSA Deputy Director and her honors included the Defense Department's Distinguished Civilian Service Award and the National Security Medal." Maverick woofed. "Yes, back to the task at hand. But where do I begin? If only Ms. Caracristi were here now." I scanned the nondescript area around us. "What's the scale?"

I stumbled on a possible connection to the page but couldn't determine a solution with so many unknowns. Hoping for a revelation or someone to assist, I knocked on one of the wooden boards and it fell to the ground. We jumped back as the rest of the beams followed in rapid succession. When the dust settled, I peered through the entry into a dark and dismal cavity.

"Hello. Anyone home?" I contemplated entering the small space as my phone rang. I read the display.

Rats. Caught.

"Hi, Pete," I said as brightly as possible.

"We're having a slow night so I thought I'd see if you have anything I can help with for tomorrow's affair."

Maverick barked, yanked, and the leash tightened uncomfortably around my fingers. I winced, swallowed hard, and tried to maintain my balance as he dragged me forward. "You're invited to come any time after three." The words came out in a rush. "Ida said she didn't want help, but that way, since it's so close to post time, she can't very well tell the guests to leave, and she can make use of the spare hands."

"Good idea. It sounds like you're walking Maverick."

"I am." Maverick tugged, and I tripped over the threshold.

"I should let you get to it. Katie?"

I planted my feet and trapped the phone between my shoulder and chin to free up both hands and hang on. "Yes."

"Be careful."

My face flushed. My whole body heated in embarrassment. How could he have known?

"I know how strong that dog of yours is. Be firm."

"I will. Bye."

I braced myself for an obstinate pull. "Maverick, sit." Surprisingly, he did.

The need to look around overpowered the desire to leave. No bigger than a walk-in closet, I had merely to turn my head. The small, fusty room held a solitary chair next to a rickety wooden stand holding a tray, a filthy bedroll stashed in the corner on the floor, a pile of tattered quilts, a rusty bucket of water by the door, and an empty ceramic pot in the corner. Several pairs of dingy coveralls swayed from hooks near the ceiling. What didn't fit were the shiny keys dangling from the ring on a new nail by the entrance and the three-foot-high bookshelf, filled with pristine tomes.

"Someone is staying here. We're trespassing, Maverick." I had just stepped out when Maverick yanked the leash from my hand and spun back inside. I trudged after him and called, but my head scanning from side to side was the only thing that moved in the room.

"Maverick?" I cried.

I pulled aside the overripe-smelling overalls to reveal more of the grimy wall. I ignored the sour odor wafting from the bedroll, anxiously shoving it across the floor. "Maverick." I turned in a circle, searching for anywhere my dog could be hiding, and my voice squeaked again, "Maverick."

A shadow darkened the doorway and a voice bellowed, "Wrong place."

My heart pounded in my chest. I whirled and looked into the steely, intelligent gaze of Ole Severson. I blinked, and the gaze turned crazy. Severson hopped from one foot to the other. I recoiled at the grimace of yellowed and blackened teeth.

"Is this your place? I'm sorry. I didn't mean to intrude, but after the planks fell, my dog snuck inside." I saw what he saw as I looked around again. Panic gripped me, and I had to swallow hard before I could continue. "Do you know where he could have gone?"

Severson's eyes cleared again, and he pointed a bony finger to the rear of the lean to. A shiny black nose peeked from behind the bookcase.

"Maverick." I couldn't contain my relief. I rushed and knelt by his side, brushing grit and cobwebs from his dusty coat. I nuzzled his neck and tried unsuccessfully to sound like I was in charge. "You can't just go off all the time." He panted warm, wet air on my cheek, and I relented. Threading my fingers around his collar, I pivoted on my toes and began to utter my thanks, but Severson was gone too. People kept disappearing on me.

Only this time I knew Severson had really been there; no imagining—the crushed grasses bore the telltale sign of someone standing on top of them. I'd clearly overstayed … certainly not my welcome, but I felt I was close to understanding the note I'd found. I rubbernecked around Maverick and bumped my head on the doorframe. While rubbing the ache out of the spot, I debated my alternatives until a loud ringing caused me to jerk and bump my head again.

I fumbled with my phone, thinking it might be Pete. I

gazed at the unfamiliar number scrolling across the top of the screen and answered with a cautious, "Hello?"

I couldn't identify the snuffling and croaking at first. "Hello?" I said again.

"Ms. Wilk." The voice on the phone gasped.

"Kindra? What's wrong? What happened?"

She gulped air. "Patricia's gone."

SEVENTEEN

Kindra, breathe." I heard wheezing. "What do you mean Patricia's gone?"

Maverick reacted to my firm grip and equally firm voice. He wiggled from the hole in the wall, and we trotted outside and into the tall grasses.

"Dr. Bluestone came to pick up TnL." She fought to catch her breath. "But when he went to the barn, the horse was gone. I texted Patricia and …" She choked back a whimper. "Her phone buzzed from her room. She hates being tied to it, but since mom got rid of our landline, she always carries it with her. Now I can't find her. And I can't tell mom. She's worried about the horse and the farm and these crazy people and helping Dr. Bluestone look for the horse and—"

I broke in gently. "Tell your mother, Kindra. She needs to know." I took a calming breath. "Maybe she already knows."

"No, she doesn't. She asked me to get Patricia to help.

And I can't do that."

"Do you think Patricia and TnL are together?"

Kindra's voice rose. "Of course they're together. That's the worst part. I think he's been keeping her stable, what with the moving back from the deaf school and Dad and everything." She whispered, "What if she's run away? It'd kill my mom."

"I'll be there as soon as I can. I just—" She hung up, and with a tight grip, I carefully pocketed my phone. Then a terrible thought occurred to me. What if Severson wasn't as harmless as Ransam thought, and Patricia was in trouble? Tiny pinpricks of fear crawled up my neck as I scoured the countryside.

When Maverick and I hit the dirt, I had to drag him along. We neared the car, and I saw the activity at the farm. Anxious voices carried across the water. I opened the rear car door and unclipped Maverick's leash, but instead of hopping in, he bolted back the way we'd come.

"Maverick. Here." My ire almost blinded me to his alert. When I realized he was in finding mode, I took off after him.

Five minutes into his trek, he yipped and sat. To avoid barreling into him, I cut into the grass and tripped over a bulging root. My weakened knee took another hit, and this time I wasn't certain the pain would go away. I bit back my yelp, and my stomach clenched with the repressed emotions. I'd never forgive myself if I couldn't stop something from happening to Patricia. I hobbled to Maverick and eyed his singular focus. He centered his energy on a distant apparition—a young lady astride a tall horse, clopping down the road. I released a breath.

Patricia waved slowly, the dignified, ceremonial gesture of a public figure in a parade, as if she didn't have a care in the world.

When they were abreast of us, she pulled back on the reins and signed, "Hi, Ms. Wilk. What's up?" I only knew a few signs.

"Looking for you."

She furrowed her brow. "Why?"

"Kindra is worried sick. You and TnL took off without telling anyone, and you left your phone behind."

Her eyes grew round, and she patted her pockets. "Can you call her please? Tell her we'll be right there. I knew Dr. Bluestone was coming for him." She leaned over his mane and tenderly patted his neck. "I wanted to make sure TnL got his constitutional in today, and I needed horse therapy too. We're going to run. I'll see you there?" She loosened the reins and pressed her knees into his sides. They took off like a rocket.

Maverick relinquished his piece of turf. We speed-walked, as much as I was able, down the road again, and I redialed Kindra's number.

A whispering voice answered, "Ms. Wilk?"

"Maverick and I found Patricia on the other side of the pond."

Kindra's voice chilled. "What was she doing there?"

"You'll have to ask her. She didn't realize she didn't have her phone, but she should be right there."

"Is TnL with her?" she asked more loudly.

"Yes. She took him out for exercise before he's handed over to Dr. Bluestone."

"Thank you. Thank you." Kindra heaved a great sigh. "What are you doing over—She's here." Before her phone cut out, I heard the angry, yet frightened hiss, "What were you thinking?"

Maverick willingly entered the back and curled up on the seat. I started the car, and wrapped my hands around the steering wheel, forcing the tension from my shoulders and out my fingertips. Aware of the deep, cleansing breaths I took, Maverick sat up, unsettled, shifting from one paw to the other. "I'm good, my friend," I said to the handsome reflection in the mirror.

I reached to shift the car and checked over my shoulder for the nonexistent traffic but found Ole Severson instead, waving both hands before skipping into the undergrowth and disappearing. Could he be pretending craziness?

I slowly pulled out, my thoughts whirring over the sound of crunching gravel. What would happen to TnL? Where was Foggy Bottom? Why did the sisters really match everything? What was with Ole Severson?

I rolled down Halloran's drive. The yard looked like a parking lot. I inched closer, craning my neck, and counted Penelope's blue truck, two white dairy trucks, Gyles' red corvette, CJ Bluestone's veterinary truck pulling a horse trailer, a tan sedan, and Amanda's cruiser.

A cyclist flew between the long late shadows of the dairy truck and the trailer and bolted in front of my car. I slammed on the brakes. Angry dark eyes shot daggers through black horn-rimmed glasses and replaced all thought of pain in my knee.

The stout woman stopped her bicycle in front of my car. She swept back loose wisps of dirty blond hair, tucking the ends into a tight chignon, and shook her head with the grace of Demon Dancer. I blinked, and when I examined her again, I noticed her eyes were wide with fear. She balanced atop her bike with one thick-soled black sneaker touching the ground, the other on the pedal, and shrank away. She adjusted the long gray-and-white plaid dirndl skirt around her knees and the high collar of the frilly white blouse under her gray cardigan. She cowered, tentatively holding her hand up as if she could stop me.

I dropped my head. I guessed I'd misread her fear as anger. Maverick barked and reminded me I needed to connect with Kindra and Patricia. I turned off my car.

The door jammed. I shouldered it twice, and it clunked and crunched in protest before letting loose. I wrapped my fingers around the top of the window frame and hauled myself out, intending to apologize to the cyclist, but she shoved away and biked toward the house. Maverick bounded through the opening and was off before I could reattach his leash.

I found him nudging Patricia for a scratch. She cooperated absentmindedly, her eyes glued to her sister. Kindra mouthed her words carefully, and even I understood her. "Don't ever do that to me again."

Patricia signed her response which I took to mean, "Sorry," but her eagle eyes watched the adults circle the horse. Sadness billowed around her, and Kindra relented, taking Patricia's hand. They stood together, tightly wound spectators, ready for action at the end of the day.

CJ murmured calming words amid the nervous energy as Amanda accompanied him and TnL to the rear of the trailer.

Enzo leaned against his car, his arms folded across his chest. Fine curly dark hairs peeked out from the open collar of his crisp black shirt. One corner of his mouth turned up, as if he waited to be called upon to weigh in on the important decision.

Penelope held her hands up in despair. "It's my horse now. I should have the final word. This horse isn't showing any signs of mental instability. What do you think you're doing? Where are you taking him? Who are you?"

Amanda stepped forward and introduced him. "This is Chantan John Bluestone, Doctor of Veterinary Medicine."

He threaded the brim of a black felt hat through his hands. "Ma'am. I will board the horse until ownership is determined, and I promise to take good care of your animal."

Enzo unfolded his arms and shoved off his car, stepping toward Penelope. She lowered her voice but shook a paper in the air and punched her fists to her hips. "What in heaven's name is behavioral euthanasia anyway?"

EIGHTEEN

That's just it." I strained to hear the biker woman's soft voice. "That horse is totally unpredictable. Because of him, his owner, and my friend, lost her life. She's gone. He's alone in a relatively new environment. If he spooks again, who else might he mortally wound?" She pushed her glasses back up on the bridge of her nose. "I set the order to put him to sleep in motion."

"Just because you worked for her for a few years, Ann-Elizabeth, doesn't mean you know what she would have wanted." The volume of Penelope's shrill voice increased. She stepped forward. "My sister meant for me to take over if anything happened, and I'll just have to do that. I'll attend to Thunderbolt and Lightning."

Enzo said, "Of course, Mia would want what's best for the horse, darling."

Penelope cringed and spun on him. "Don't darling me.

I'm what's best."

In a breathy voice, Ann-Elizabeth said, with a hint of admiration, "Mr. Gyles, I think you've always had the horses' best interests at heart."

Enzo coughed behind his fist, as if to emphasize Ann-Elizabeth's astute observation.

Tony Relando stepped nearer. "I could sacrifice my current agenda and take the animal off your hands." His glinting eyes met fire from every quarter. He put both hands up in surrender and bowed from his shoulders.

TnL's head reared back. CJ stroked the horse's jaw and nose, letting TnL's massive head drape over his shoulder.

Kindra and Patricia sidled near and flanked CJ and TnL, a diminutive yet significant shield. Patricia said, "You're crowding him. Give him room."

Amanda stepped ten feet in front of the procession, and I brought up the distant rear. She gently patted the air in front of her. "Right now, we're all going to take a step back and give them some space. Dr. Bluestone has some tests he can perform on TnL to ascertain the horse's general health and overall mental well-being.

"Will you test for Coggins? Anemia? West Nile?" Penelope's voice hardened and she glared at Ann-Elizabeth.

"Only if the animal shows symptoms," said CJ. "I will take good care of this horse."

"I know from personal experience he'll take excellent care of the animal." Amanda took slow careful steps using her soothing demeanor. "Just calm down and wait for Mrs. Brown's autopsy results, and we'll know when and how she died. While we await the legal disposition of her assets, we're going to keep the status quo."

Patricia pulled an apple from her pocket and held it out on her palm in front of TnL. The snack vanished in two big bites.

"If I may have a word?" All faces turned toward the voice thick with Irish brogue—Liam's first speech in my hearing. "This horse is quite a plum in the industry. Look at his line, the musculature. He'd ride like a dream. There's so much potential. What can we do to help?"

Liam knew horses.

Penelope narrowed her eyes. "You said the tattoo and markings didn't match Foggy Bottom."

"The tattoo does not match because I believe someone went to great pains to modify the numbers, and his stripe might be covered with some sort of dye. I've seen it done before. Dr. Bluestone, is there a way for you to determine if the tattoo has been altered?"

CJ nodded. "Do you have the original number for identification?"

Liam turned the pages in his log back and forth, jotting and verifying his notes. Satisfied, he tore out a page and handed it to CJ.

"I will check and give the results to Chief West." CJ folded the paper and pocketed it before leading TnL, plodding slowly, in through the rear door of the trailer. The ramp came up and clanged, and the doors swung closed with a thud. A loud, long whinny filled the air, sending goosebumps up and down my spine. CJ took his place in the driver's seat, and Amanda banged twice on the side of the hollow-sounding trailer. The truck purred to life.

Tears spilled down Patricia's cheeks. Penelope said sympathetically, "It'll be okay, Patricia. The horse is not suffering from any behavioral disorder. He'll be fine." She nodded her head. "You'll see. We'll just pretend he's racing in the Kentucky Derby tomorrow. Where and what time did you say your celebration is taking place? I think we could all use a diversion."

Kindra said, fighting to put a positive spin on an otherwise glum evening, "Our gala begins one hour prior to post time." She answered Patricia's glare with the most remorseful expression I've ever seen. "Ms. Wilk, what's your address again?"

The tiny sly smile gracing her face led me to believe she didn't want to take the heat from her sister by herself. "3141 North Maple Street," I said. I tried to keep the corners of my mouth from turning down as my insides performed the perfect belly flop. Although Ida could handle any contingency, I was certain that her Derby party would bring out extremes in these guests.

Penelope's shoulders slumped. "Maybe we'll hear something from the attorney tomorrow. Living in this limbo is difficult."

Enzo added, "It would be nice to know where we stand."

Penelope jerked her head toward him and scowled. "I'm going back to Mia's."

"I'm sorry," said Amanda. "I can't let you in there until we've finished the investigation, and the final determination has been made."

Penelope sputtered, "But all my things are there."

Enzo tapped her shoulder. "I'm here now. I'll take care of things."

Penelope shrank from his touch and held tightly to the keys of her truck. He peeled the keys from her hand and tossed them to Liam. "Would you take her truck please? Penelope's coming with me." He whispered something in her ear, and he led her docilely to his sportscar.

Liam scrubbed the look of confusion from his face and headed for the truck.

Ann-Elizabeth eyed them all with malevolence. She huffed her displeasure and hopped on her bike, rattling the gears in a frenzied pace, and flew down the drive.

Tony smirked and slithered into his car, revved the engine, and spewed gravel as he lit out of the yard.

"Let's take care of the other animals," Kindra said. She steered Patricia toward the old red barn, nudging her to look at something other than the disappearing rear lights of CJ's trailer.

Maverick gazed at me. I couldn't praise him enough for not adding to the tension. I scratched behind his ear but stopped when I caught the look on Amanda's face. "What is it?"

"I have a favor to ask."

"Anything. You know that."

"Ida invited my officers to attend her dry Derby party. I think she wanted our presence, but we have so much to attend to, I doubt any of us will have the time. I'd like you to be our eyes and ears instead." Her brows lifted. "Not as Sherlock Holmes but simply keep a log."

Strange request. Usually, she'd want me to stay out of police business. "Why?"

"We have a lot going on this weekend. I have another pressing investigation, and we're down two men: one on medical leave and Officer Christianson is on desk duty."

I almost asked why again but didn't want to pry … much.

"Certainly. Do you have a specific agenda? Might I enlist the help of Jane? She knows these people almost as well as I do."

"Sure. Jane's naturally nosy enough. I'm not expecting anything drastic. I just want to keep my finger on the pulse of the …."

Amanda drew in a deep breath, closed her eyes, and let her head fall back. She sighed and seemed to contemplate her next move. She reversed the actions and said, "Dr. Erickson has the preliminary autopsy results, and they indicate Mrs. Brown's head trauma was delivered by horseshoe but most probably not by a horse."

What kind of awful person would try to frame a horse? How did they think they could succeed? Why would anyone want to kill Mia Brown?

"Katie?" She lightly touched my shoulder. "Are you okay?"

"Yes. Sorry." The pictures dissolved. "My mind went elsewhere for a second. So, the injury was caused by a person. You are investigating a murder."

"I don't think it can be accidental. Pete's going to need help keeping track, watching, and reporting what goes on tomorrow. There are guests who are not only possible witnesses but probable suspects." Amanda stared off into space. "It would be great for me to have more eyes and ears on the ground if anyone lets something slip. Just watch and report. Derby celebrations are generally short-lived, and I'm not expecting anything to get out of hand, but I don't know or trust any of these people."

"Ida invited Lance." Lance Erickson, the ex-chief of police and Pete's dad, had more than thirty years of law enforcement to draw on.

Amanda smiled. "He knows more ropes than I can tie knots in."

"Amanda, might I ask why Ronnie, Officer Christianson, is on desk duty?"

Blinded by brightness of the setting sun, I couldn't read her face but heard her words clear enough. "He's undermining my authority and seems to be after my job."

NINETEEN

Ida ignored the drizzly daybreak, shooing Maverick and me out for our morning walk.

"There'll be no time later," she said. "I might've bitten off a bit more than I can chew. I'll need a hand with a few odds and ends."

My chest swelled. Our surprise workers would be well received.

Dressed in workout clothes, Dad slid his arms into the sleeves of his rain jacket and crept to the door on his way to the gym.

"One hour, Harry. I expect your help too," she said.

"Yes, m'lady. Your knight in shining armor will return ready, willing, and able to do your bidding." He bowed. Ida swirled a dishtowel and flicked the tip in his direction. He grabbed my arm and whisked us out into the melancholy morning. "I think she worked through the night and has already downed two pots of caffeinated ambrosia," Dad said.

He saluted and trotted right on Maple Street. I led Maverick down his favorite path through the wildlife refuge around the pond where he'd found his first body. The discovery of the perpetrator of that violent crime had quashed my initial uneasiness to circle the pond again, but I still searched the water for unidentified floating objects, hoping never to find another.

Ida put me to work immediately upon our return, spreading three savory sandwich fillings on a variety of fresh, warm breads. She used stencils to cut out the special shapes of flowers, triangles, circles, and hearts, and placed the finished pieces on crystal trays. Next, we washed an assortment of fruit and whipped up a marshmallow cream dip so delicious I wanted to lick the bowl clean. She charged me with mixing mocktail ingredients in the clear plastic beverage dispenser, excluding the bubbly ginger ale.

Dad looked the part of a fancy server wearing a crisp white shirt, black vest, and sharply creased pants, ferrying platters of flaky pastries, tiny fingerling cakes, and pecan bites, tasty, sweet treats taunting takers from beneath a clear wrap. He thought he'd completed his tasks and dropped into a dining room chair, but rocked to standing as Ida wordlessly handed him collapsible trash cans to assemble.

"No rest for the wicked, Dad," I said, passing him on my way to the next assignment.

When I finished decorating the food trays with herbal greenery and edible flowers, Ida shepherded Dad and me into the huge tent—an otherworldly experience weaving through tables covered in linen and artfully decorated China dinnerware, crystal bud vases containing a single red rose and a sprig of baby's breath, satiny napkins in a rainbow of colors, hand painted glassware, and silverware polished to the ultimate shine—to sort the crafts covering a table at the far end. Dad wrapped pink satin in a turban around his head, struck a Mae West pose, and pursed his lips. In turn, he received a well-deserved swat from our hostess.

"Harry. Seriously?" Jane giggled as she rounded the pole elevating the awning over the entry. She swung the tent flap back but struggled to catch it on the hook.

Dad took the fabric from her, and being almost a foot taller, easily secured the corner. He made a point to look down on my petite friend. "It's about time you showed up, don't you think?"

She batted her large brown eyes and her laugh chimed. "Guests will be arriving, and you'll still be wearing yesterday's five o'clock shadow, handsome," she teased.

He glanced at his wrist, stuck out his chin, and rubbed the scruffy beard. "It'll have to do."

"You look smashing, Jane," I said and gave her a quick hug. "Of course, you always do." Her blond hair fell in waves over her shoulders.

Welcome sunshine had burned off what remained of the gray clouds. Dad hauled the cornhole boards and bean bags onto the lawn and came back for the ladder toss and the massive stacking block game.

Jane straightened her elegant floral mini shift, flipped the wide brim of her multi-layered red organza hat, and inhaled deeply. "The aroma wafting from your kitchen, Ida, dear, is divine." I'd forgotten how easily she slid into her relaxing Southern drawl, and it poured from her lips like blackstrap molasses. "Whatever is that remarkable scent?"

"That's the sauce I pour over my take on Hot Brown Sliders." Ida beamed. "They're a yearly staple."

Jane stared up at a long chalkboard and read the horse names and current odds aloud. She shimmied into the kiosk to test her space as bookie for the event, locating the eraser, chalk, back-up calculator, notebook, writing implements, and individual servings of chocolate and fruit flavored candies for wagering currency. Satisfied she could complete her assigned task, she ducked under the counter and sashayed under the trellis of red roses. She pursed her lips and posed for imaginary fans until I heard a soft wolf whistle.

"Drew, darling." Before she could wrap him in an amorous clinch I could see coming a mile away, Lorelei breezed through the entry, and Jane modified her embrace to a PG. Known for his outlandish neckwear collection, she straightened Drew's fabric rose petal tie.

Lorelei shook her head. "As if we don't already know what's going on," she said, picking imagined lint from the lapel of her iridescent lilac jacket. She checked over her shoulder and beckoned her mother to follow.

"This …" Marietta Calder circled the room, perusing every corner. She stopped in front of Ida and smoothed her charming white-and-black checked dress. "Is absolutely incredible. What do you have for us to do?"

"And us?" asked Danica Bluestone, herding Carlee, CJ, and Renegade. Danica wore a flouncy blue dress, and CJ's concession was a shirt of the same color, but he tugged at the collar, clearly uncomfortable. Carlee's sundress and the scarf knotted around Renegade's neck used the same fabric.

Ida furrowed her brow and glanced at her watch. "You're early."

"We don't want to miss out on any of the Derby doings. Duh." Carlee tilted her head. "Put us to work."

Ida glowed as understanding descended on her. This Kentucky Derby party would be one for the books, and she had the help she desperately needed but had been too proud to ask for. She dragged Lorelei and Carlee into the house. Minutes later, the rest of my impeccably dressed students showed up with one or both parents in tow. With her imperious manner, Ida intimidated those she had not met before, and soon she busied every pair of hands, tidying serving trays, straightening decorations, hanging mirrors, practicing yard games, and choosing horses.

At an hour until post time, Ida demonstrated her own hat making skill, replicating the elaborate headpieces she found in magazines and catalogs. Those who had not come properly attired bent to the task of adorning the simple hat forms with fabric, beads, buttons, feathers, and lace, using ribbons and hot glue guns.

After they completed their elaborate creations, the kids surrounded Jane as she gave a truncated but easy lesson on parimutuel betting and how the odds worked. She called me to the center of her circle and used me as her guinea pig. Several parents inched closer, trying to act as if they weren't listening just as intently as the kids.

"Ms. Wilk, you're going to choose three horses for the race prior to the main event, one each to win, place, and show. Since we are not using money, mete out your candy wager and we'll see how your choices pan out at the end of the contest."

I checked off my prospects and passed her all the wrapped green candies because, ugh, who likes the green ones?

"Really?" Jane whispered as she raked in my wager. I thanked her and stepped away as she completed her explanation about what my bet could net.

Brock and Galen turned on the three large TVs and finessed the screens streaming the Derby Day races, extending the arms and tilting the views. Anyone who wanted to follow any one of the remaining races would be able to watch it.

With forty-five minutes to go, Ida marched across the yard, in the company of Danica and Marietta, carrying her sumptuous sandwiches, announcing their significance to all. "They'll be ready as soon as I pour on the sauce. Be right back."

She returned brandishing a large ceramic kettle with a pour spout at the same moment the entire entourage, Penelope, Enzo, Liam, and Tony, tramped into the tent. Although their appearance took some of the wind from her sails, she graciously greeted the newcomers and invited them to join in the festivities, pointing out where to find the games, the betting window, and the food.

Ida stared for a short time and finally said, "You must be Mrs. Gyles. You remind me so much of your sister. I'm sorry for your loss. She was a delightful woman."

"Thank you. And, please, it's Penelope."

"What a lovely frock." Ida's brow furrowed. "Penelope."

Caught off guard, Penelope patted her hair and tut-tutted, disregarding the compliment to her sky-blue dress. "The invitation to your Derby celebration couldn't have come at a better time. We can celebrate the life Mia dedicated to horses. Let me introduce Tony Relando." Tony raised his chin in acknowledgment, adjusting the collar of a skin-tight light green dress shirt. "And Enzo, my husband." Enzo took Ida's hand and brought it to his lips as he bowed at the waist. Penelope looked away, seemingly embarrassed with his antics.

"That's Liam Byrne." Liam gave a two-finger salute and hooked the fingers in a belt loop. The crease in his khaki pants would have sliced a watermelon, and a too-big tan shirt bore the name Gyles Stables in red script.

Ida smiled broadly. "Welcome, welcome." She indicated the dispenser to which we'd recently added the carbonated infusion. "Mint Mocktails are on the green table along with assorted beverages."

"Where's the real stuff?" Tony Relando teetered and

appeared to have imbibed prior to his arrival.

Ida smiled sweetly, always an auspiciously scary occurrence, and said, "With all the impressionable children in attendance, *we* are not serving alcohol, though you may detect a few fumes in the sauce for the sandwiches."

"This ain't no Kentucky Derby party if you don't serve a real Mint Julep. I'm outta here," he grumbled.

Ida breathed deeply, centering herself, but before she blew her top, she threw her unencumbered arm wide, waving to Phil Ganka and Lance Erickson as they strode across the yard. The appearance of the two men made Tony step back, blustering and frowning, but he marched to the odds board, and it looked like he wasn't leaving after all.

Mr. Ganka said, "Ida, this is the best Kentucky Derby party I've ever seen. Thanks for the invitation. When do we get to pick a horse for the race?"

"Jane, I mean, Ms. Mackey is manning her post now."

Penelope muttered something under her breath, and Ida followed her gaze. Mia Brown's secretary, Ann-Elizabeth Tulis, parked her bicycle on the sidewalk in front of Ida's home. She stared at the ground, tugging at the cuffs of her long, light-gray knitted sweater and pulling the front panels together. She polished her glasses and reset them on her nose. Lifting her chin, she almost smiled when she caught sight of Mr. Gyles who nodded in her direction, but then her face hardened. She removed a hat from the basket on her bike and nestled it on her head before marching up the steps and stepping in front of Penelope. "Mrs. Clemashevski? Debora told me about this Derby party to celebrate Mia. She was the best. I just couldn't miss it. I hope you don't mind."

Ida welcomed her and introduced the newcomers all around. Lance eyed the strangers before extending a hand to shake.

In my conversations with Mr. Ganka, he usually sat behind his desk, but standing, he cut an imposing figure. He had squeezed his generous proportions into a fancy three-piece suit, and he tugged at the vest buttons straining across his middle. He followed Lance, reaching out to shake hands, when a clatter and smash made everyone turn.

TWENTY

One side of the table had collapsed, and our delinquent pups scarfed down as many of the open-faced sandwiches as they could, side-eyeing the reactions and slithering out of reach so as not to be caught. Multiple servings disappeared as the two dogs hurriedly vacuumed every morsel within reach.

CJ whistled, and the always-obedient Renegade hurried to his side and sat, gazing up in adoration.

"Maverick." My dog stalled at the unfamiliar harsh sound of my voice but only for a moment. I finally grabbed his collar, attached his leash, and held on as he continued to drag me through the remains of Ida's signature sandwich, inhaling the rest of the tiny pieces of savory turkey, bacon, and delicious cheddar cheese, until he heard a deep throat clearing.

Maverick licked the buttery evidence of his crime from

his chops and wiggled his backside, thumping me aside with his happy tail. My stomach flipped as Maverick pulled me close to Pete. He circled and wrapped the leash once around us. My heart picked up speed as I closed in on Pete's broad chest, and my hands landed on the lapels of his dark suit coat.

Pete's arms circled me, and I blushed when I realized he was disentangling us. I think I turned crimson when we finally stepped apart. Pete held the leash, and I knelt to collect the few crumbs left by my dog. Ida tramped close. I lowered my eyes and my chin quivered, "I'm so sorry, Ida. What can I do?"

I gazed longingly at the ravaged sight, and my stomach rumbled in protest to the hours since I'd had any real food. Ida laughed, waving the gravy boat of mornay sauce. "Remove your scalawag, and, Pete, please retrieve another salver from the fridge in my kitchen. I prepared for every contingency."

One tragedy averted, I dragged Maverick to the walkway. Jane hooked my elbow, walking with me, and whispered in my ear, "I need to find something more appropriate for you to wear." Only then did I remember my torn blue jeans, ratty sweatshirt, and dirty sneakers. "Be right back," she called over her shoulder to the line growing in front of her betting booth. Drew had taken her place. He stood straight as an arrow, looking utterly flustered. Sweat ringed his underarms, and his short white-blond hair stuck to his head. He, obviously, fared better using his crowd management skills as an officer of the law than a wager coordinator as he tried to make order out of chaos. Pete replaced the sandwich tray and joined Drew as Jane and I disappeared inside.

I rustled my dog's ears and said, "What did you think you were doing?" and received the same admonition from Jane.

"What did you think *you* were doing?" she chided. "Go fix your face and hair, and I'll choose what you have to wear."

We scurried up the stairs and twelve minutes later, my fancy blue togs met with her approval, and we rejoined the party.

"Looks like Drew and Pete could still use a hand." She released the vice grip she had on my arm and started a second line under the odds board, much to the delight of our guests. The lines rapidly dwindled down to Liam and Enzo trying earnestly to understand gambling with candy.

"Katie, dear."

"Yes, Ida? What do you need? I'll do anything."

She jabbed her fists to her hips and eyed me sternly. "I need you to wear a hat."

I gazed at the intricate creations surrounding me. My fingers raked my unadorned hair, and I sheepishly followed Ida to the craft table.

"I dismantled the hat we made on Monday, but we'll make another."

She lifted a white form and wound stiff, sky-blue fabric around the brim, pinning the edges underneath. The strings she pulled on the netting gathered it perfectly. She added peacock feathers and fronds with crystals shining at the ends and motioned me to bend down. She plopped her handiwork on top of my head and held the pearl end of a long hat pin between her thumb and forefinger. I squirmed. With an evil glint in her eye, she plunged it through the top and fastened her masterpiece. She tugged the mesh over my right eye and said, "Done."

I proudly examined all sides of the elaborate creation in the bank of mirrors and caught sight of an impossibly ashen Ann-Elizabeth pulling a stark black hat over her forehead. The thick lenses of her glasses magnified her pale brown eyes. Her wan complexion blended with her drab sweater and whitewashed her against the tent backdrop. She stood off to one side, wary and skittish, ready to skedaddle with the slightest provocation. I approached her slowly, and still feeling her accusatory eyes from the day before, worked up my courage to speak. "My condolences on the loss of your employer."

"I don't know what I'll do now. I'm truly going to miss her. Not like that sister of hers."

I made my eyebrows stay still, even though they wanted to inch up. "How long have you worked for Mia?"

"Almost five years. She was a wonderful boss." She shuddered. "Penelope said she'd take me on, but she's impossible. She treats everyone around her with disdain. No one lives up to her standards, neither her husband nor her sister. Oil and water. Nice and nasty. If it hadn't been an accident, I would've pegged her as the force behind Mia's death."

Holding back a bit of insider information, I held my breath for a moment, then asked, "What do you think of Enzo Gyles?"

"What a nice man. I feel sorry for him, fettered to the wicked witch." She removed her glasses, polished them, and put them back on the bridge of her nose.

"He seems pretty put together. Why would you feel sorry for him?"

She responded with a blank stare and turned to gaze at him. I guessed she was a woman of few words.

"Did you make your hat?"

"I wouldn't be caught dead …" She blushed and touched the hat brim. "Sorry, bad choice of words. I had my own lace percher created by Hood London to be worn by Ascot and Derby attendees. It's called a Garbo."

Duly scolded, I swallowed hard. "Mia was wearing a lovely hat from that shop when I met her."

Tears shone in Ann-Elizabeth's eyes. "She bought mine at the same time."

"Have you attended the Ascot or the Kentucky Derby?"

"Not yet. Mia planned to take me to the Derby next year. She had her eyes on a colt with a chance," she said, sniffling. "But that's not going to happen now."

She put her hand to the frames of her glasses and shrank into herself, curling her shoulders, and shifting her weight as someone closed in from behind us. I glanced over my shoulder at Liam and swallowed a gasp at his attempt to hide a faltering step. Dad did a similar jig when he didn't want someone to notice his infirmity. When I turned back, I caught Ann-Elizabeth scurrying through the kids playing games and disappearing around the corner of the tent.

"I wish I had a better eye for human faces," Liam said, staring after her. "I'm sure I've met that woman somewhere."

"Did you know Mrs. Brown? Ann-Elizabeth is … was her secretary."

"I met Miss Mia when she was studying economics, but I'm new to the Gyles' franchise."

"What do you do for Gyles Stables?"

"I'm just a stable hand. I take care of the horses. When we have a lead on Foggy Bottom, I check out the horse. I …" He caught himself but continued. "I have experience with equine disguises."

"How does one get experience like that?" I asked in jest, but the silence weighed heavily as I entertained the varied implications. To break the unnerving quiet, I asked, "May I interest you in a Mint Mocktail?" Liam nodded, and I poured two.

My curiosity about the wiry man bubbled to the surface. He accepted one of Ida's hand-painted glasses with a magnolia gracing the outside.

"Miss Penelope hired me not long after she lost Foggy Bottom. She was off searching for the horse, and I didn't realize the sisters' kinship until I laid eyes on Mrs. Gyles." One side of his mouth edged up. "It was fairly obvious."

I nodded. "How did Penelope lose Foggy Bottom, if I might ask?"

"It's a convoluted story, to be sure." I listened fixedly to his lilting voice. "Their father bred racehorses of fine stock. He didn't believe in female heirs but promised to equally split his successful stable after they both wed. One thought she married for love; the other married for the money. But in order to claim the rest of his estate upon his death, he charged his daughters with demonstrating their business acumen by expanding their enterprises through racing, siring, or whatever means possible. The one with the most financially sound business would inherit whatever remained."

Given Liam's sudden fascination with his footwear, I thought he'd finished his storytelling until he cleared his throat. "Foggy Bottom started winning, and it made him the most valuable of the horses. He belonged to Miss Mia. She tucked away quite a bankroll, and her ..." Liam's green eyes clouded and circled the air, as if searching for the right word, "husband," he spat, "sold the horse to Miss Penelope behind his wife's back for a goodly sum. Unfortunately, Mr. Brown took off with the money and died in a car crash. Miss Penelope didn't know the horse had disappeared as well until days later."

"Do you know how much money he collected from the sale?" And I wondered how it was wrapped.

"Miss Penelope blustered about losing one hundred fifty thousand dollars. Though she accused her sister of stealing the horse back, it appears she lacked a bill of sale, and she couldn't claim its loss even if we did find the horse. Miss

Mia denied the accusation. Miss Penelope had the stable searched, and they didn't find Foggy Bottom. Miss Mia left rather than face the ill will of her sibling. If Miss Mia had taken possession of the horse, with her gone, Miss Penelope wouldn't have a difficult time claiming him. Their father died last year, and she's the only one remaining."

"Who would have determined the success or failure of the ventures?"

"Good question. It would have been an impartial party, a racing disciple they both agreed to, or maybe the will specified an unbiased third party. The attorney would have decided, but Miss Penelope gets it all now."

"My friend, Jane, is a horse race devotee from Georgia." Liam stiffened. I sipped daintily. It was sink or swim time, and I elaborated on Jane's comment. "She might have seen you race."

He pursed his lips and squeezed his eyes shut. He dragged one open, probably hoping I'd disappear, and then the other. "Your friend was correct, but it was a long time ago. I had a fall which has prohibited me from riding." He placed the glass on the table and nodded. "If you'll excuse me." The warmth left his voice. "I believe they've called 'Riders up!'"

I watched him wander to the table where Enzo sat and engaged in an animated conversation. I placed a bet of fruit chews on the horse with the worst odds and asked Jane if they called him the under-horse as I mentally listed the snippets of conversation Amanda might find useful.

TWENTY-ONE

Get your beverages and load your plates, everyone." Ida beamed, extending a beautifully painted glass, clinking ice cubes around muddled deep green leaves, and swirling liquid with a tinge of color. A woman in her element, the center of attention, she winked her emerald eyes and her round, ruddy cheeks nearly popped with elation. "It'll be the best race day smorgasbord in Minnesota. And make sure you've selected your horse. Post time is in eighteen minutes." She swirled her caftan around her. Looking closely, I smiled at the beautiful simplicity. She'd transferred some of her abstract black pen-and-ink horse sketches to the silken fabric. "We'll lock in the odds with five minutes remaining."

"That's not the way it's done. I've been around tracks my entire life." Tony Relando swung his glass and the liquid sloshed over his fingers. "You can't just—"

Ida jerked her head so sharply, her newly freshened red

curls bounced around her face. "It's *my* tradition." Her steely spark shut down Relando's complaint, and he took a lengthy slurp from his glass to cover his magenta face. I imagined Ida's Derby rules differed from other venues, but she could set any rules she wanted.

Her guests crowded around the serving tables, balancing heaping plates of nibbles and bubbling beverages, gathering beneath the screens, and filling those tables with the best views. Horse names and current odds peppered the conversations.

I selected a multi-layered sandwich and took a tentative bite, circling the serving table and making room to stack more delicacies. My eyes closed as I bit into the soft bread and hummed in satisfaction. Ham salad with a touch of brown sugar on Ida's fresh rye, frosted with whipped cream cheese would win any cooking competition. Pete steered me to one of the folding chairs near the opening next to Dad.

A bugle sounded the familiar assembly, "Call to Post," and faces turned to the nearest screen, drawn like a magnet. Conversations died and the room quieted in the electric atmosphere. When the first lilting notes of *My Old Kentucky Home* floated in the air, a glistening tear slid down Jane's cheek, and she surreptitiously swiped it away. Eyes homed in on the nearest screen to analyze the spunky Thoroughbreds being led to the gate in regal pageantry, and we listened to the announcer describe each animal, the owner, the trainer, and the stable. The directory of horse names flashed across the screen, including the latest odds, and stated one horse had been scratched.

Jane called out, "Six minutes to post time. Final wagers should be placed now."

Tony Relando rose from his place at the table. With one hand resting familiarly on Ann-Elizabeth's shoulder, he said, "Save my seat, Annie."

She pushed her glasses up on her nose and shrugged off his touch.

Jane jotted down the final exchange, and Drew shut down the booth. They joined us, clenching their tickets with hopeful exuberance.

One horse stubbornly refused to enter his starting stall, and while we watched the jockey and handler marshal their charge, Penelope rose and tapped her glass with a spoon. "If I may have your attention, please." My students tensed, looking ill at ease with the unexpected disruption. Penelope puckered her lips, her earnest face so similar to Mia's. "My sister has been an ardent fan of horseracing. I'd like to dedicate the viewing of this race to Mia. The Kentucky Derby has always been her favorite." She raised her glass. "Thanks for the memories, sis. To Mia."

"To Mia," our voices echoed carefully, and we clinked our glasses.

I glanced out onto the lawn and saw an oddly familiar, tall man dressed to the nines in a green-and-white checked suit coat and dark green pants, standing at the edge. His Adam's apple bobbed above his shirt collar, and a sunflower yellow bowtie hung askew. He hooked his thumbs behind his ears and ran the fingers of both hands over the top of his head, carefully slicking back his mane of white hair.

Maverick's head came up and locked in on the figure. I turned to Pete. "Is that Ole Severson?"

Pete craned his neck. "Where?"

I pointed, but when I looked, Severson had disappeared. "I swear. He was right there." Pete's eyebrows couldn't have risen any higher. At that moment, I wanted help understanding the significance of the crumpled sheet containing the Knight's Tour I'd discovered and its possible connection to Severson. "I need to get something," I whispered.

"The race is about to start," said Jane.

"I'll be right back." I stood quickly to run inside and collect the geometric drawing, but my chair crashed to the ground behind me with a bang at the same time the bell rang the start of the race and the gate sprang open. My klutziness went unnoticed by all but a few.

Pete steadied me so I wouldn't topple. Drew re-stood my chair, and Jane patted it. I melted back into my seat, my eyes drawn to the screens and the breathtaking display of athleticism and effortless grace. The horses ran in pure synergy, a mesmerizing rhythm of hammering hooves marking time with jockeys gliding along the horses' backs. Rigorous training had paid off as the synchronous pairs ran in their biggest race of the year. Swept into the contagious excitement, we cheered for our chosen mounts as if we'd owned them. The announcer's voice increased in volume as his enthusiasm grew with each passing furlong.

And then it was over.

It didn't matter which horse won. Everyone in the tent hooted and barked for the opportunity to rewatch the thrilling photo finish and waited none too patiently for the announcement of the outcome.

After the judges analyzed the computer input and finalized the race result, my enthusiastic students and their parents exchanged high fives. Except Patricia. She escaped the frivolity by trailing Jane and Drew as they headed back to their kiosk to pay off a short line of winners. She pulled up a seat and watched the interchanges, frowning, wearing the same look she'd had when CJ took possession of TnL for safekeeping.

The race complete, Penelope and her retinue rose from their table as a single unit, not a smile nor a winner among them. I tried to commiserate with the losers as they made their way to Ida with thanks, but my heart wasn't in it. She shook hands and escorted them out of the tent. I wasn't unhappy to see them go.

Nor did Ann-Elizabeth's departure vex me.

"Hey, Doc," Drew said. "I could sure use some help here."

Pete gave me a what-can-I-do grin and began a third receiving line, judiciously doling out the sweet delights whether they were honestly won or not. The kids and their parents were busy collecting their winnings and finishing the fine food. I gave Maverick the sign for treat, and he raced me inside, pulling up short and sitting next to the cupboard, offering a paw. He wouldn't be denied, and he devoured the smelly salmon munchie in one gulp. I kicked off my shoes and took the stairs as fast as my swirling dress would allow. My stellar friends might have valuable insight to make sense of the Knight's Tour map and the GPS coordinates.

I retrieved my pants off the top of the week's pile of dirty laundry and peeled the paper from the pocket, unfolded it, and flattened it against my dresser top. The light from the window differentiated the colors of ink penned through the squares of the Knight's Tour making alternate paths. What could it mean?

My thoughts toggled back and forth as I walked back outside. The GPS coordinates on the back of the page took me to the shed where I'd seen Severson. Ransam had told us Severson played chess. Severson could have left the page for me. Preoccupied reviewing the pattern covering the squares, I was hip checked into awareness.

"Excuse me," I said. I glanced up at Ole Severson and back at the page in my hand. No time like the present to ask, "Mr. Severson?" I held up the paper. "Is this from you?"

His lips edged into a tight smile and revealed crooked,

yellowed teeth with large gaps between. He started to speak, but Ida called from the tent, and he bolted over the grass and onto the street.

I joined Ida. "Did you see him?" I asked.

She scanned the yard. "See who, dear?" she said, making motions as if to gawk down the street.

"Never mind." I folded and pocketed the paper, waiting for a quieter moment to ask my questions.

Ida put one hand on her hip. "Katie." My handwritten betting slip fluttered in the other hand. "How did you choose your horses for Jane's wagering exercise?"

Still searching for Severson, rubbernecking over her head, I shrugged and said, "The names spoke to me, I guess. Pythagorun, Sir Cumference, and Dogleg. Why?"

She turned up her nose as if she smelled something unpleasant. "Your method leaves much to be desired. Nonetheless, you won the Exacta for that race." She curled my fingers around the ticket and walked me beneath the red rose trellis. After she took about a thousand photos in every imaginable pose, she shoved me into Pete's shrinking line.

He smiled warmly. As he reached for my ticket, an angry buzz interrupted him, and he gave me an apologetic look. He wasn't on call, but he read the screen and shook his head. This ring needed an answer. He stepped away. I stood at the table and calculated my possible winnings. He returned, and as he dashed by, his lips perfunctorily brushed the top of my head. "Sorry, Katie, I've got to go. There's been a multi-vehicle pileup, and, with all the injured, Susie said they could use another set of hands."

Drew wrapped Jane in a quick hug and ducked under the counter. "Wait up, Doc. Sounds like you can use some help."

TWENTY-TWO

Rumors of the accident quietly circulated and subdued the energy. No one really paid attention to the last two races of the day, and the kids and their parents had places to go, people to see, and news to sort out. After snatching and snacking on just enough of the extras to assuage the unending hunger pangs of their bottomless stomach pits, my students helped Ida package the leftovers and divide the spoils.

The kids whisked the empty serving dishes inside. Moments later, Galen and Brock spilled onto the lawn, shirt fronts wet, sleeves rolled up, foam dripping from their forearms, hastily escaping a scathing reprimand from Lorelei who shook a soapy fist at them. They chuckled as she turned to go back inside.

Jane and I sat quietly under the cavernous tarp as we completed sorting and storing the craft supplies. We watched the golden sky fire up with bird song, bug sounds, and the rumble of distant cars. I prayed the victims of the accident would be okay and, selfishly, hoped I didn't know anyone hurt.

The paper in my pocket crackled when I changed position, and I extracted the conundrum.

"What do you have there?" Jane asked.

"I found this in an envelope on my desk yesterday after mock trial practice. I thought maybe …"

Her brown eyes opened wide. "Nope. Not me. But I'll take a look."

I smoothed the folded page. Jane turned it first ninety degrees, then one hundred eighty. "It looks the same every which way."

"I think it's a Knight's Tour." I explained the principle of the proposed problem, and she nodded.

"Who do you think left it?" She lowered her voice. "And why?"

I turned the paper over and tapped the numbers lightly penciled in the corner. Jane pulled the page close to her face and squinted. "Latitude and longitude?"

I shrugged. "That's what I assumed."

She snapped the lid on the bits and pieces of the flashy trimmings and dusted away any tell-tale traces of art supplies before jumping up and charging toward my ever-ready wheels resting on the cement slab next to the garage. Maverick loped behind her. "Let's go." She waved the grid page impatiently.

I glanced at Ida's front door, calculating the effect of our absence.

"The kids are almost finished. And we'll be right back," she said, opening the passenger door. I bit the inside of my cheek but wriggled the keys out of my bag and tromped to the driver's door.

Maverick jumped into the rear seat and snuggled into a

ring while Jane entered the coordinates into her app, and I gave a rundown of my first trip out to the dilapidated shed.

"You're certain you saw Severson out there when you found Patricia."

I nodded vigorously, but inside my head I wondered about my interpretation of all the recent visions. Maybe the conk on my head at the farm loosened some nuts and bolts. Maybe I was incorrect in my assumptions. Jane's never quiet, so her rambling eased some of my apprehension.

We closed in on the spot to Jane spouting, "Five hundred feet. Three hundred feet. Two hundred fifty … Stop. You passed it." She squealed. "We're going on a treasure hunt, just like searching for a geocache."

I shivered. I usually enjoyed the activity, but geocaching during spring break had led Jane, Maverick, and me to a body.

The knoll with its dead tree, tall grasses, and creeping vines hiding the shed looked less ominous with Jane's encouraging spunk. She popped open her door and hopped out almost before I stopped. Maverick soared over the seat to follow. I only shook my head.

Jane's app took us to the opening where the door had been. The fallen boards had not been replaced.

Remorseful, I hung back from the entry. "It looks like someone is living here."

"Then we obviously need to do a wellness check." She barreled through the opening, and Maverick and I followed hesitantly. "Hello. Anyone here? Are you alright? Do you need any assistance?" She circled the room and turned to me. "Do you think this is where Severson is staying?"

"He didn't say, but I got that impression."

Jane eyed her phone screen and headed toward the rear wall. "Dead end?"

Maverick pawed the floor in front of the bookcase. We

searched and saw arching scratches on the floor. I waved one finger, and Jane moved to the side. The bookcase screeched as if on rusty hinges before it swung as wide as Jane's eyes, revealing a dirt path down a dark tunnel.

She flicked on her phone light, and I did the same. "Come on. Let's go," she said with way too much enthusiasm and not enough trepidation.

"No one knows where we are."

She took a screen shot of the GPS coordinates and sent a message. "Drew knows now. Let's go."

Maverick raced the length of the short tunnel which ended at a heavy wooden door. Jane ducked and went after him, raising dust particles. I followed, sifting through sticky cobwebs and sending spiders skittering. Maverick shifted from one paw to the other and eagerly watched Jane's hand alight on the knob. Before I could issue a note of caution, she pulled on the door and stepped inside. An enormous room lit automatically, and I took a step back.

"Motion sensor," said Jane. "Come on, scaredy cat."

The room showcased the strangest solitary game display I'd ever seen. "Whoa."

"Look at this place."

Bright light illuminated two huge portraits in ornate gilded frames, hanging on opposite walls of an enormous space. In one painting stood a large, pinch-faced queen wearing a red frock with white frills and black trim, hovering over a diminutive and cowering king similarly dressed. The royalty in the second painting wore creamy white velvet with fur trim. The slender, blond queen smiled at us with warmth and held the hand of the handsome king who only had eyes for her. The mirrored ceiling reflected a black-and-white eight-by-eight latticework comprised of twenty-four square-inch, worn, pockmarked and cracked tiles. Yard-sized hollow copper-trimmed chessmen, green with patina, lined up along the perimeter.

Jane dashed up a short flight of steps and yanked on a heavy wooden door. "Padlocked."

Three armoires lined one wall, and she whisked open one set of double doors to reveal a wardrobe of creamy white, fur-trimmed costumes. She reached in and swished the hangers from right to left, examining the clothes. She jumped once and snatched a crown from the shelf above the longest dress, setting it rakishly on her head. She returned it and moved to the second set of doors. A similar collection of attire in a deep, dark red hung in a neat row. Ordered by length, first came eight or more plain shifts, and the array ended in one long robe and a festooned gown. The third and narrower cupboard held four partial suits of armor. Jane reached in and rattled the metal.

Laughing, she said, "This is a person-sized chess board." She snatched the grid from my hands.

"And it can be played with statuary or costumed people." I hefted a porous white stone pawn from the pieces surrounding the board. The fingers of one of my hands fit into a depression. As I lifted it, casters snapped out, and the pivoting wheels made moving the piece easy.

"This is awesome." Jane rattled the page and turned it around, her eyes lit with energy. She pointed to the different paths on the grid. "Do we follow this green part, the blue section, the gold, the red, or what? What do we do next?" She pointed at an arrow. "What does that represent?"

The completed grid presented one of trillions of possible solutions to an age-old problem, the Knight's Tour. "That could be where we should begin, and there are only four iterations so ..." I let my comment hang. One of the black squares on the floor around the outside, however, showed more signs of scuffing, scratched and discolored with use. I pointed to the tile on the floor and the coordinating square on the map, orienting the page to match the room.

Maverick panted. He minded well sometimes, but if we needed to stay true to the course, I hoped he would really listen. I gave him the hand sign and said, "Maverick, stay."

Jane and I followed the green-inked trek, two blocks one way and one perpendicular block, the movement a knight would make on a chess board. When we stepped on the final square matching the green path, the tile dropped an inch, and we heard a click.

Jane's smile fell and her face paled. "Do you think that's a trigger? Are we going to blow up?"

I had difficulty swallowing. "I have no idea." I checked my phone. No connection. We waited for a minute. And then two.

"We can't stay here all night. Maybe it's a locking mechanism, not a detonator." Jane raised one eyebrow and prepared to take another step. "I say we head onward."

Or upward, I thought. "Stay, Maverick," I repeated.

Together, Jane and I took a tentative step off the square, and when nothing happened, I breathed a sigh of relief. We heard a similar click at the end of the blue-inked path, and more as we took the final steps onto the blocks at the end of each of the other two paths. In addition to a snap at the end of the red line, tumblers rolled across the top of one wall, and we heard a low grinding sound. A patchwork of green moss covered the wall in front of us and was scraped away as the wall slid to the side, grating along the grooves at the ceiling and the floor.

Jane flashed her phone light into the inky black chasm. Dancing dust motes shrouded the view. When she leaned forward, Maverick launched himself between us and scampered into the darkness out of sight. Jane grabbed the molding to steady herself.

So much for 'Stay, Maverick.'

With my dog on the loose, I couldn't wait for the dust cloud to settle. I flipped on my phone light which penetrated only so far. I inhaled and sneezed, then stepped forward and gasped.

TWENTY-THREE

The narrow beam of light landed on Maverick. He sat tall and still, head canted, tongue lolling, panting happily at the top of a makeshift ramp—my makeshift ramp.

Jane waved her hand to clear the air, and she stepped into the space where I'd first seen the body. She gripped a metal bar and propelled herself forward. The portal closed behind her, and she quickly released the lever as if it were electrified, frantically grabbing at the sliding stone edifice. She inspected the now impenetrable wall and asked, with the first hint of unease, "Is this some sort of complex warren of underground spaces? Where do you think we are? This place is in shambles."

"We're under the horse barn on the Halloran farm, where I thought I'd seen Penelope. This is a secret tunnel to the farm I'm pretty sure Severson must have used for his unobserved access." Jane's gaze roved from the floor through the thick beams to the sky. Maverick began barking and playing tag, and I couldn't get him to settle down. "Would you please call Amanda?"

Jane nodded and punched in the number. Maverick immediately quieted, dropped onto his belly and hung his head over the opening, watching with furtive eyes. I reached up and caressed his chin. "Thanks, friend, I think."

Jane pocketed her phone. "Amanda will be right out. She said to wait where we are."

As Jane and I climbed next to Maverick, the flimsy metal made a wavering noise and sounded like hollow thunder, a portent of things to come.

We hung our legs over the edge and waited in the twilight, scratching and petting my pooch. Peeking through the rafters, I spotted fluffy, cotton candy clouds floating in front of the full moon and reflecting a fading orange, the exact opposite of what surrounded us. The sky darkened, and tiny pinpricks of starlight winked on and glittered against the purple sky, and everything around us seemed to run together in the dark.

We never heard her crawl through the barn and were startled when Amanda's silky voice said with a hint of irritation, "What did you find now?"

Amanda's powerful Maglite brought a hint of daylight, and I offered the mapped route for her to peruse, pointing out the Knight's Tour we'd taken which unlocked the door. She pulled on purple nitrile gloves.

"There is a passageway originating in an old shack on the gravel road across the pond and ending here, below the barn."

Amanda flashed her light around the hollow space.

Jane leaped gracefully into the pit. Before Amanda could stop her, Jane grasped the lever and heaved it down. The screeching sound initiated moving the wall and light from the game room flared through the opening.

"Whoa," Amanda said with a hint of awe. She gestured—*you first*—and said, "Katie, lead the way but don't touch anything ... else."

Although I'm taller by almost six inches, Jane smiled impishly at my inelegant, bumbling drop to the floor. Maverick's nails clicked down the ramp, and he pranced through the gap and onto the game board. I dusted my hands and took cautious steps. Once inside, we skirted the perimeter of the grid.

"What's in there?" Amanda asked, pointing at the locked door.

"We didn't open it," Jane said, sounding like we knew better than to interfere with potential evidence rather than being unable to release the lock.

Amanda tested the door anyway. The padlock held tight. She said, "Right."

Jane moved to the cupboards and reached out.

"Please don't touch. You'll leave more prints." Amanda opened each and peered inside, shaking her head. We made our way through the doorway and entered the rickety structure where we began the trek.

"The first time I came here, Ole Severson stood just outside that opening."

"The first time?" Amanda frowned.

I added hastily, "I think this is where he lives." I waited for a second and when Amanda didn't react added, "You should pick him up. He had the opportunity to kill Mia and move her body undetected."

Amanda sighed unexpectedly. "I don't have to pick him up."

I disguised the surprise in my tone. "You don't think he killed Mia?"

"I didn't say that. I don't have to pick him up because he's in the hospital. He was at the center of a huge pile-up."

Gut punched, my emotions cartwheeled, and I concentrated to articulate my thoughts. "Has he said anything? He still could've killed Mia."

"Anything is possible. But right now, he's in the hospital under heavy sedation."

"What caused the accident?"

Amanda turned her head and eyed me with suspicion. "Witnesses indicated a light-colored truck ran Severson down, ricocheted off the surrounding vehicles, and blew out of town, leaving a trail of crashed cars in its wake. It happened so fast with all eyes on Severson, no one noticed the driver, but it doesn't look like it was an accident."

She passed one pair of gloves to Jane and one to me and approached the volumes arranged carefully on the shelf. One by one, she selected a book, shook it, and passed it to our awaiting hands. When she gave the sign, we reshelved them.

"What are you looking for?"

"Evidence, however, I'm not seeing anything he wouldn't be willing to share outright. This shelter is crude, but I checked the records before I made the trip out here. It's definitely situated on part of the nonarable Severson property deeded to Ole and abuts the old farmstead. The chess board doesn't look new. It's been here a while, but it wasn't part of the public record."

Amanda rounded the room, looked under the mattress, around the honey pot, through the pockets of the coveralls. The only items she found without the grime of time were a thick tablet covered with black-and-white squares to record chess moves, some markers, a box of standard envelopes, and a sheet of stamps. She indicated a set of shiny keys.

"No idea. Never took them from the nail," I said, hoping

to stay on her good side.

She lifted the keys from the hook, and we followed her back to the grid. The padlock opened to the second key. "Stay," she ordered and disappeared beyond the door.

Seconds ticked away. Jane scratched the floor with the toe of her shoe, trying to contain her desire to snoop, because I had the same thoughts going through my mind, and we both snapped to attention when Amanda reemerged.

"It's a small storeroom containing antique barn paraphernalia and these."

"You found it," I said excitedly.

But the two-by-six-inch brick tightly encased in waxed paper she turned over in her hand didn't contain currency, but rather the news—newsprint roughly cut to the size of a bill.

"I don't understand. Is there more? Something else? I'm sure I saw cash."

"There are a few more bundles, but they're all the same. Sorry, Katie. Maybe wishful thinking?"

We marched back into the dreary abode. Amanda inspected the front entry and looked from Jane to me.

A confession spilled from my guilty lips. "I knocked, and the door fell apart. I know I should have put it back together, but that's when Patricia took off with TnL, and we went looking for her."

Without a word, we followed Amanda outside. She extended her right hand, palm up, like a surgeon. I scrambled and selected a board which she accepted and fitted snugly into the channels on the sides.

When she finished with the subsequent boards, and the rickety entry was re-blocked, she marched through the grasses toward my car. "I'll take a ride to Halloran's now, Katie."

I double-timed to keep up. "Yes. Okay."

Maverick and Jane took up the rear seat, and Amanda sat primly, her mind's gears whirring. We drove around the water and pulled into the drive behind Amanda's cruiser and between a Corvette and a sedan.

Patricia and Kindra stood under the yard light holding buckets and staring at us with a "now what" look.

Amanda raised her hand in greeting. "Hi, girls. I'd like to talk to your mom if I could, and it looks like she has company. Can you point me in the right direction?"

Kindra looked at Patricia before answering. "She's not in any trouble, is she?"

"No. Nothing like that. I have some questions about your property. Can I ask who's visiting?"

"You can rescue her from Mr. and Mrs. Gyles and that Relando guy," Kindra said sourly, leaning her head toward the porch.

"I'll do that, and I'll touch base with the Gyleses and Relando too. But neither the stable hand nor the secretary is here then?"

"Nope." Kindra interpreted Patricia's signing, and said quietly, "I agree. Mom's too nice for her own good. I think she'd like it if you had to drag her away for some reason as long as she's not in trouble."

"I can do that." Amanda took a step and stopped. "If you ever need help, you know you can call me, day or night."

Patricia threw her shoulders back and gave a quick nod.

We followed Amanda as she bounded up the stairs and rapped on the heavy oak door. Debora answered and hauled us inside. "Welcome. Come in. Sit down. Please, sit down. I have cookies."

TWENTY-FOUR

We waded through the palpable tension in the room, and it made me second guess having followed Amanda into the kitchen. Maverick sat. No tail swished, but his head swung back and forth in response to the glacial voices.

Relando leaned against the far wall, his arms crossed over his chest, scowling. "I'll pay top dollar for him outright, no matter what Ann-Elizabeth says. She doesn't have a say in what to do with him."

"You'll do no such thing," Penelope said.

Relando eased up. "He's an albatross to you, but I'll take TnL off your hands. He's exactly the horseflesh I need, and if it'll help settle your outstanding debt, so be it. I don't care what condition he's in."

"I have no idea what debt you're talking about." Penelope sounded frazzled.

Enzo said with ease, "I believe he's talking about the

money we lost to Mia's husband."

Relando bristled.

Penelope's face darkened and her voice took on a sharp edge. "That purchase was made in good faith, but the horse wasn't his to sell. Then he stole it back and died in a car accident. Mia knew nothing about the horse or the money, or so she said. But those occurrences aren't connected to anything happening here anyway. Dr. Bluestone is evaluating TnL and is helping Liam determine if TnL could be Foggy Bottom. Mia's will has yet to go through probate. I couldn't sell him even if I wanted to, which I don't."

She and Enzo appeared to have warmed to each other. He sat on the arm of her chair, his hand rested on her shoulder, and his fingers squeezed gently. Her edge softened. "I don't need to give up TnL, and I don't want to give him up. He's … part of my family, a reminder of Mia." She turned to Debora. "They're all a part of my family now, but I hope the horses can stay here, at least for a while. Patricia and … your other daughter have taken such good care of them. I'd like them to continue. Everything is up in the air, but I'll make good on the arrangement Mia promised. Ann-Elizabeth will continue to make payments on Monday mornings if that's okay, but I don't have any idea how long I'll, I mean, we'll stay in the area. Liam said the horses have been looked after well. I wouldn't want that to change. I trust his judgement."

"That loser?" Relando sniggered. "He fell off a winning mount and never got back on. Then he got in over his head."

Jane tapped my arm, and her eyes flashed an *I told you so.*

"You Gyles' plucked him from his penury existence and put him to work for a pittance because no one else would have him. And you believe the garbage he spouts about the horses."

Enzo stood abruptly. His piercing eyes shot daggers at

Relando. This time Penelope reached up and touched his hand, and he reluctantly returned to his position next to her.

Debora spoke as if Relando hadn't disparaged Byrne, Mia, her husband, and Penelope. "My girls love the horses. They are learning responsibility and earning a little spending money. Thank you."

Amanda stepped forward. "Mrs. Gyles, I didn't see your truck outside."

She pulled her jacket closer. "I rode with Enzo." She waited for him to confirm her statement. He nodded, urging her to continue. "Enzo gave Liam the keys to the truck. I was hoping he'd be here by now." Penelope looked down at her hands. "I wonder where he is. He had something important to tell us."

Penelope looked at Enzo with worry etched into her features. He smiled encouragingly, and she turned to Debora. "I want to apologize, Mrs. Halloran. I haven't been on my best behavior as of late, but I'm turning over a new leaf. Enzo and my horses are all the family I have left."

We let the comment sink in for a moment.

"Debora, could I speak to you privately?" Amanda said in a soft voice.

"I'm sorry we've overstayed our welcome." Enzo gave Penelope a hand to stand. "I don't know what's happened to Liam, so we won't keep you any longer. Thank you for your hospitality, Mrs. Halloran. Chief West, please let us know when Mia's body will be released."

Amanda nodded, and with that, Enzo and Penelope headed for the door. Relando shoved away from the wall, glaring at their retreating forms, and stomped after them.

Debora released a long sigh. "They've been here twenty minutes, and I still have no idea what they wanted. Penelope called earlier and asked that the girls carry on minding the animals so that wasn't it." She closed her eyes and shook her head. She dragged her lids open and said, "What did you need, Chief?"

"Did you know about the decrepit shack across the lake?" Debora's forehead furrowed.

"There's an underground passageway connecting an old, run-down outbuilding and your horse barn. It may have provided anyone, including Severson, an opportunity to easily access your land and make a clean getaway."

"That's how he did it. I suppose it's on the parcel of land his daddy left him." Debora grunted. "What did he have to say for himself when you brought him in?"

"He hasn't said anything. We didn't exactly bring him in. He was in a multi-vehicle accident earlier, and they don't know if he'll make it."

Debora looked stunned. "Is there anything I can do?"

"Can you tell me about the farm the way it was when you first came?"

"It's much the same as you see it now. Nothing has changed structurally. Just cosmetically. New siding. A little paint. A few flowers. We outfitted the equipment buildings to accommodate similar gear. The big change was tearing down a ramshackle storage shed but we rebuilt the barn for the horses on the same spot. We erected our organic milk operation from the ground up on newly acquired land, not part of the original Severson site."

Amanda nodded, mulling over the information. Maverick stood on all fours and barked, his tail waving like a conductor's baton. Amanda looked us over. "Would you mind terribly waiting outside? I'll finish up here, and I'd like a final word with you and Jane."

I urged Maverick with a gentle tug on the leash. "Come on, big boy. We'll take a romp around the yard and look for your buddies. Patricia might even have a *treat*." I cheated and used the operative word which always got my dog to listen to what I said.

When Jane and I finally lured him through the doorway and onto the lawn, he playfully danced a few yards down the incline, wiggling a happy dance, when his tale stopped wagging, and he jerked to a full stop. Every muscle in his body went rigid and hummed with energy. I could feel the strength building and shortened my hold on the leash, hoping I could stem the explosion of power and keep us in place, but it didn't help. Before I could begin to talk him down, he shot off like a cannonball. I clung to the leash and caromed after him down the driveway, to the pond's edge, and then ankle deep in icy water. Tiny waves lapped at my shins.

The off-the-chart decibel reading of Maverick's incessant barking roused Amanda and Debora from the kitchen and drew Kindra around the corner of the barn from the paddock. Kindra gestured to Patricia who slowly craned her neck to see what might be happening. Jane waded in next to me, intently staring at the moon's rippling, brilliant reflection on the water.

"Quiet, Maverick." My scolding went unheeded. "Maverick, are you merely howling at the moon?" I tried to lighten the mood, but I knew my question was moot as Jane grabbed my hand and pointed across the pond.

"Do you see that?"

I hadn't ever wanted to find anything in the water again. It could never be good, but I followed the end of Jane's pointing finger. Dread flowed over my head, down my shoulders, and onto the ground—a baptism by ice, and I shivered.

A straight, dark edge cut the surface of the water. Undulating waves darted over and under the static obstacle.

Jane reached down to pet Maverick, uttering soothing words. "Good boy. We see it."

When he determined he had completed his job, he turned and strutted onto the shore, accepting a ruffling of his fur from Kindra and a treat from Patricia.

"Amanda," I called. "Maverick spotted something in the water out there."

Her flashlight beam scanned the horizon, skimming over the wrinkles on the pool.

"There. Do you see it?" I called.

The light hovered when she found the spot. "Debora, do you know the depth of the water out there?"

"Ten feet is as deep as this pond gets, just enough for a kayak or paddleboard. Why?"

Amanda called for a backup team, and an hour later, a light blue truck had been towed from the pond and onto the shore under a bank of extremely powerful trouble lights. The team prepared for the worst, pulling on protective gear: gloves, boots, and masks. Water streamed from the cracks and crevices of the rust bucket. The officers took photos and carefully examined the outside, noting new dents and discoloration and calling in the license plate. They laid tarp on the ground below the doors.

"Ready," Amanda said. They backed away.

My heart thudded as Officer Daniel Rodgers secured the handle, took a deep breath, and wrenched the door. It opened with a blood-curdling squawk.

TWENTY-FIVE

Twigs and small leaves gushed with enough force Officer Rodgers jumped back. The foul water splashed onto the tarps.

Officer Rodgers peered inside the small cab. "Nothing, Chief. There's no one here."

It sounded like we exhaled as one.

"The truck meets the description of the one that caused the accident in town today." Amanda ordered the truck transported to the station for more analysis. Liam had been the last person known to have the keys to the truck and he was missing. She also put an all-points bulletin out on Byrne as a person of interest in the hit-and-run of Ole Severson.

Jane said, barely audibly, "Do you think Severson saw something like Liam killing Mia, and Liam attempted to silence him?"

"Could be. But Liam seemed so nice. It doesn't fit my

profile of him. He could have discovered something Severson did. Severson planned to take out the threat, and it backfired. I wish I had a better read on these people."

From our roost on the porch, Jane and I watched the personnel pack up and the cars clear the yard one after another. Maverick sat between Kindra and Patricia where they could both reach to scratch an itch or pet his side. The look on his face was at the same time pure bliss and a frightening deterrent to all but the heartiest of souls who might consider bothering them. Debora slowly rocked and eyed Amanda as she trudged up the walk, heavy thoughts weighing her down.

"Debora, I have to ask."

"Go ahead. You need to do your job, and I have nothing to hide."

"Do you have any idea how that truck made its way into your pond?"

Debora shook her head. "Ransam and our hired hands left around eleven to attend an organic milk production meeting in Minneapolis. They're not back yet. The girls and I left for Ida's Kentucky Derby party at two. We returned at half past seven. You arrived at nine with Ms. Wilk, Ms. Mackey, and Maverick. I didn't see or hear anything out of the ordinary." She forced a wan smile onto her features. "It does look like Penelope's truck though."

Amanda nodded. "The license plates confirm it." Her phone dinged. She gave a long, exhausted sigh and answered. "West." She listened. "Understood. Thanks." She slipped her phone into her pants pocket. "I've got to go. If you think of anything, anything at all, please don't hesitate to call." She turned to her car, slipped behind the wheel, and spun her tires.

"We should go too. Maverick, come." He licked the hands of both girls and hopped off the porch. "Get some rest, ladies. We'll see you Monday."

They mumbled responses but remained seated on the porch as we waved our farewell.

We'd traveled the road so often, I felt like my Ford knew its way, but when we reached the railroad tracks, we were halted by multiple sets of strobing lights.

"Isn't that Amanda?" Jane asked.

I pulled over to the curb behind a short line of cars before I took my eyes from the road and looked past four police cruisers and an ambulance. I let my gaze linger for a moment on the county coroner van, wondering at its appearance and hoping to catch sight of Pete, and finally found Amanda. The few minutes since we'd seen her at Halloran's had taken their toll. Her black eyes had a sunken look in a gray face. She stood stiffly but her shoulders drooped a bit. Her pale lips formed a straight line.

In contrast, Officer Ronnie Christianson strutted through the center of the light beams with a gleam in his shining eyes, smiling broadly, gesticulating to the emergency technicians and the surrounding vehicles. It seemed he'd taken the lead on whatever had happened and reveled in it.

We opened the door and joined the gawkers. I jumped, startled, when Drew materialized beside Jane, draping his arm over her shoulder.

"Probable accident," he said. "But Ronnie's investigating it as a possible suicide."

"Oh, no." Jane buried her head in his shoulder.

"Do they know the victim?"

"I guess you can never tell by looking." He tugged at his black bowtie. "The victim is Liam Byrne."

My stomach dropped. I'd liked Liam. "Why do they think it could be suicide?"

"The conductor witnessed the man accidentally trip and

fall, but the engineer reported the man came from nowhere and stepped out right in front of the engine. There was no way he could stop the train in time, and whether accident or suicide, that poor man will carry this tragic death with him for the rest of his life."

Maybe I'd had it backwards all along. If Severson killed Mia, and Liam figured it out, Liam may have sought revenge by running Severson down. He seemed a gentle soul, so I imagined him overcome by remorse and killing himself in turn. If Severson died too, we'd never know what really happened.

My dire thoughts were laid to rest as tall, dark, and handsome Dr. Pete Erickson joined our small circle. He wrapped his arm around me and tucked my head under his chin.

"It's late," he said. "We're just about done here, but you've had a long day and need to get some rest. The busybodies are coming out of the woodwork, and you won't be able to get through this way. Why don't you turn around, head to Atlantic Avenue, and take the back way to Ida's?"

I nodded. That would be easiest.

Pete kissed my forehead. "I'll talk to you tomorrow."

"Katie, with your approbation—"

Jane elbowed Drew in his ribs. "Not now, Drew."

"I'll get Jane home, if you're okay without a wing …" He carefully chose his next word, knowing Jane could engage more of her spitfire attitude over a sexist infraction. "… person." He bundled her off to his vehicle amid a growing crowd.

As I turned to leave, a newspaper van pulled up, followed closely by a car with our local radio station call letters detailed on the trunk. The journalists swarmed Ronnie like flies to horse dung. He stepped onto the short stack of pallets and puffed out his chest, and I navigated to Amanda's side.

A question that sounded scripted came from one of the journalists. "We hear you've wrapped up the murder of Mia Brown."

"Byrne worked for Brown until she fired him for betting on a horse other than the one he would ride in the same race," said Ronnie. "Working around racetracks, he would know how to weaponize a horseshoe. Brown was alive until Byrne visited the old Severson farm."

"The new Halloran farm," Amanda said under her breath.

"Motive, means, and opportunity." Ronnie gloated. "It's believed longtime resident Ole Severson witnessed Brown's murder, and Byrne was last seen driving the truck which hit Severson. Guilt-ridden and fearful after his failed attempt on Severson's life, Byrne committed suicide. We're well on our way to closing both cases."

Amanda leaned close to me and hissed. "They are believing his theory, but there's no concrete evidence. He's drawing conclusions prematurely."

"I'll take questions." He secured his thumbs in the belt loops of his pants and rocked on his heels. "Yes, I was manning the desk when the call came in." "No, he's not local. His license reads Kentucky, and he had outstanding warrants for crimes in Georgia."

Before answering the next question, Ronnie locked eyes on Amanda. "The call caught Chief West unaware as she was investigating the minor theft of a vehicle and was unavailable at the time of our discovery." He gazed over the crowd, not elaborating and lessening the importance of the discovery of the truck, and said with a kind of perverse pleasure, "I felt an immediate response was paramount. That's C-H-R-I-S-T-I-A-N-S-O-N."

With his mind made up, he had no motivation to look

into someone else, and he made it quite clear any further inquiry would be a waste of valuable resources.

Amanda hadn't moved a muscle, but her eyes were no longer dull and glassy. They were ablaze.

TWENTY-SIX

The rain forecasted by the glowing red sky at sunrise came in sheets at noon and brought Amanda to our door. Her eyes brightened in intensity, and her confidence had returned. Her skin glowed like burnished copper. She shook off the cold droplets and squeezed water from the long black braid slung over her shoulder. On a mission, she dropped into a chair at the table.

"I think Ronnie rushed to an incorrect conclusion, but as much as I'd like, I can't come right out and say it. It would look petty, and I will not give him the satisfaction of claiming I'm whining. I've heard he's been building an arsenal of accusations against me to support his assertion of being the better *man* for the job." She chewed on the inside of her cheek and went on. "I would, however, like some help quietly ticking off those final boxes and tying up loose ends. I want justice to prevail, no matter the outcome."

Maverick sat still, and I focused to equal his level of concentration.

"Confounding the evidence, Ronnie found twelve hundred dollars in Byrne's jacket pocket, confirming your statement about the cash you found buried in the wall the day Mia's body was found. The timing works. While you were out cold, he could have grabbed the money and moved the body."

"It felt like a lot more cash than twelve hundred dollars. While I was out, anybody could have grabbed it, and what happened to the gun?"

"No gun. Remember you were knocked unconscious. It could have been something else." I stared at Amanda as she watched the rain dribble down the window. She continued, "The train conductor has twenty-seven more years of experience on the job than the engineer. I think his interpretation of what he witnessed is more probable, but the clincher came after he signed his statement and mentioned one more critical observation."

I waited. Maverick nudged her hand.

Amanda looked right at me. "He said he could have sworn there were two people next to the track before the accident."

"Two? Then someone might know if it was suicide, or an accident, or—"

"Someone could have pushed Byrne onto the tracks. Ronnie's supporters would like the case solved, but I don't like it. It's too pat, especially when there might be another possibility."

"What can I do? Put me to work." Maverick woofed in concert with my offering.

"I need to learn all I can before I talk to Penelope and Enzo Gyles, Tony Relando, Ann-Elizabeth, and maybe a few others I'm not even aware of yet. I don't want to set off any alarms if one of them is guilty, but I don't want to put the investigation in rough straits either. I need incontrovertible proof."

She rubbed her forehead. "Daniel told me Ronnie's aiming for a vote of confidence hearing and is collecting as much data as possible against me. Unfortunately, his most eloquent detractor has taken a leave of absence; he's taking care of an invalid mother in Florida. The most verbal member of the City Council was originally outvoted in her quest to have a man replace Lance Erickson, and Ronnie wanted the job. If he gets it, he might want me out of the service area altogether, which could happen anyway, but I just can't let a murderer go loose if there is one. I'm wired to investigate, and I have to either disprove or prove the reason behind Byrne's death. Unfortunately, because he believes the case is closed, Ronnie released every bit of evidence. Everyone knows about the underground passageway, the chess board, Brown's murder, Byrne's death, and the probable connection to Severson."

"If you think murder's a possibility, so do I. We'd best make a plan." She looked as if she had a question which might make me uncomfortable. "Go ahead. I can take it."

"I am going to do everything by the book. But what did you do to uncover the identity of the murderers you helped put away?"

I thought back over my eight months in Columbia and snorted. "I happened to be in the right place at the right time, or the wrong place truth be told, and I believed my gut."

Dad stood in the doorway. "Amanda, why would you go to the trouble of getting Katie caught up in another investigation?" Their intense gazes met.

"She has an uncanny ability to discover and fit together tiny, disparate puzzle pieces of information, and I could use her help."

He pondered. "Wait here." Dad barreled through the adjoining door and returned with Ida in tow.

"Ronnie Christianson could stand a good ear twisting. I don't know what's come over him, but I baked brownies. Who wants one?" Ida used food to assuage any and all difficulties.

"Amanda, Jane remembered a bit about Liam as soon as she saw him. She'd seen him in a race. Let me give her a call." I didn't wait for an affirmation. Jane was also our best equine resource.

Fifteen minutes later, Jane, Amanda, and I sat behind our laptops. Amanda gave us an overview, and we began researching names associated with the case. Jane hit paydirt first.

"Listen to this from nine years ago. 'Even with three-hundred seven wins under his belt, the racing commission has charged twenty-four-year-old jockey, Liam Byrne, with betting on an opposition horse in his last race. As a consequence of his third infraction, Byrne will suffer a lifetime ban from Red Start Track and its affiliates. He maintains his innocence. "I was set up. Check the video. This time I didn't do it." His claim cannot be substantiated. Though the identity of the individual placing the wager cannot be confirmed through video records, witnesses have identified Byrne. One track devotee who wished to remain anonymous said, "I got an eye for details. It was him alright. A skinny little runt with all that red hair. Couldn't be anyone else." Byrne's employer, Zachary Brown, has released a statement. 'My fiancée, Mia …'" Jane stopped reading and shifted in her chair. "'Mia is most disappointed and has released Byrne from her employ.'"

"Byrne's acquaintance with Mia goes back," said Amanda.

"Byrne knew her when she attended college." In answer to the questioning glances, I told them the story Byrne had told me.

Amanda nodded and said, "I found a slew of articles about Tony Relando. They all say about the same thing. He has a keen eye for very successful horses, but his not-quite-strong-arm tactics aren't for the faint of heart. He buys well, but he doesn't bet well." She swiped through a few pages and stopped. She flipped back and forth. Her left eyebrow rose. "And he liquidated the partnership he had with Zachary Brown before Brown married Mia."

Goose bumps scrawled up my neck. "They've all been a bit close."

"What's the other name you'd like to research?"

"Ann-Elizabeth Tulis."

Keys clacked beneath Jane's nimble fingers. "Ann-Elizabeth hasn't made a very significant online footprint. Her social media exposure is minimal, and I have no photos of her,"

"Her job was to manage the dissemination of information and scrub Mia Brown's online presence after her husband's accident. She did that well." Amanda sighed. "Liam shows up in a very bad light. He's had years for his bitterness to fester. Maybe Ronnie was right after all."

"I didn't get that vibe from him, but that would mean Mia was the target from the beginning."

Amanda shrugged and continued typing.

I clicked on one link after another, following the reverse chronology of stories regarding Enzo Gyles from his current placement on the board of a recent investment, Therapy Thoroughbreds, through an editorial about his marriage to Penelope. I scanned articles applauding his success and return to his hometown, the speculation regarding his startup, praise for his graduating magna cum laude from Duke, and an account of some high school sports accolades. The easy-to-navigate trail of news made him out to be an all-around nice guy, though I'd witnessed firsthand his obsequious, slick toadying, and I could only take one more click.

The high school prom photo of a handsome couple elicited a smile and reminded me of the white king and queen in Severson's chess floor room. Enzo had the appearance of a much more mature male. And then I froze. The female in the photo couldn't be Penelope. It had to be Mia.

TWENTY-SEVEN

Are the days getting faster, or is it just me," said Jane.

We arranged the desks and chairs to resemble a courtroom for our mock trial practice. She hummed quietly, and I could tell she was deep in thought. She finally said, "What do you think Amanda's going to do with all the information we dug up? Although that herd of horse maniacs has a weird symbiosis, it still appears that Liam Byrne killed Mia. He had opportunity and motive. Maybe Ole Severson saw something, and Byrne tried to get rid of him as well. His failure resulted in having no recourse except suicide. Or maybe it was all an awful coincidence. Maybe Ronnie pegged this one."

"Maybe." A shudder crawled from the nape of my neck and down my spine. "I trust Amanda's instincts. If she wants to speak to everyone again, just to make sure she crosses her t's, the background information we discovered gives her insight to ask a different set of questions. I think there's more going on than we suspect." And I couldn't blindly support Ronnie over Amanda, especially if he was using this case to improve his chances at the chief's job.

I lined up the judge's gavel and block on the desk in the front of the room. "Do you believe there was a second person on the tracks? If Byrne was a victim too, there would be plenty of other unanswered questions."

"The conductor sometimes wears glasses and admitted to daydreaming. It could have been his imagination playing tricks on him in the dark. He wasn't as certain about another person near the tracks as the engineer was about Byrne hurling himself in front of the train." She rammed two desks together. "Oops. Don't know my own strength."

"I hope Amanda will keep us in the loop. She might need more help."

Lorelei swung around the entry. "Who needs help with what?" she said, trying to hold back a gigantic grin.

On the spur of the moment, I said, "Ida's thinking of perhaps hosting another event." I bit my lip, and Jane cleared her throat to hide a smirk. "Maybe for the Fourth of July."

"I can't wait for her next shindig. I'll help anytime. As soon as you let me know the deets, I'll make myself available."

More of the team filed in, saving me the embarrassment of opening my mouth again and getting me in deeper trouble.

The pall that hung over the kids last week had lifted, and they rehearsed with a rigor I hadn't noticed in a while. With the state tournament slated for Saturday, they decided a debriefing would help forward their performance. Although we would miss the teammates who had chosen to attend their final prom, they'd been asked to sit in as judges. We couldn't have secured more constructive criticism.

I read the valuable comments from the scoring rubrics, "'Make sure every word is enunciated clearly and said loud enough to be heard in the back row. Patricia, you had me spellbound by your portrayal of the widow, Maggie Murphy, and almost in tears.'" Patricia blushed magenta. "'All attorneys, but mostly Lorelei, you might catch someone unaware if you begin your cross with the tiniest hint of a smile.'" I looked up as Lorelei attempted the hint, but she came across as feral as a lioness.

"Or maybe not." Ashley said. "I take it back."

Even Patricia laughed heartily.

"'Galen, don't overdo Mauritz's Swedish accent so that it requires too much effort for the opposition to understand. You don't want them to ask you to repeat the marvelous words you've already delivered. Felipe, you rock as the *Titanic* lookout, Reginald Lee.'"

Felipe's dark eyes sparkled, but he squirmed in his seat. "I'm great with a definitive script, but what if my nerves take over? It's never happened, but I haven't done much extemporaneous performing." Saturday would be Felipe's second meet, and although an outstanding actor, just like in real life, no one knew precisely what to expect during court proceedings.

"You've prepared." I enumerated the salient points. "You are an actor. You know your part. See yourself playing the role. The audience will be physically closer than when you act on a stage so make eye contact with the attorneys, the judges, and the audience. You are playing a person and people make mistakes—"

"But not too many." Galen's comment brought out a few chuckles.

With all the seriousness I could muster I said, "Remember, this is supposed to be fun." Then I cracked a smile. "If you're still nervous, try exercising before the trial begins. Jumping jacks. Pace a bit. While waiting to be called to the stand, concentrate on your breathing. And for goodness's sake, don't listen to Lorelei."

"Ex-*cuse* me." Lorelei's left eyebrow raised.

Felipe's head jerked up. He'd only been involved in a handful of rehearsals, and he wasn't sure if I was kidding. I wasn't even sure I was kidding but smirked. "I just wanted to know if you were paying attention."

As I shuffled through the remaining pages, the kids scrawled notes on their legal pads. I donned a scowl for the final remark and read, "'You're going to knock their socks off.'"

It took only a minute for the team to bulldoze the furniture back into the semblance of a classroom, the screeching of chairs sprinkled with excited chatter comparing dresses and costumes, bus versus limo rides, dinners out in contrast to cafeteria food, upcoming athletic contests, heavy-duty assignments, and final exams.

I clapped my hands for attention. "Rehearsal Wednesday. Final dress. Now git." And everyone disappeared.

Stuffed with assignments from two classes and tests to be corrected from three others, I dragged my bulky briefcase out to my car and tossed it onto the passenger seat. Before putting the car in gear, I checked my phone for missed calls or messages and found none. I put my car in gear and headed home. "Maybe if Maverick could use a phone," I said to the air, "I'd have proof someone missed me." I moaned, half in jest.

The short drive gave me just enough time to plan my night and organize the rest of my jam-packed week. Late last evening, Pete released autopsy results revealing death by a blow to the head and concluded the body had been moved. No surprise there, but Amanda would be hard pressed to examine the clues much further since Ronnie had apparently wrapped the entire crime up in a package with a neat bow, laying the blame entirely on Liam Byrne. Penelope Gyles intended to hold the memorial for her sister in Columbia. We'd hold our last full mock trial practice on Wednesday, and Friday we'd run over the schedule for Saturday's meet, discuss courtroom decorum and any last-minute reminders, and pack up our paraphernalia. As I maneuvered onto my cement parking slab, out of the corner of my eye, I saw a dark shape dash through the kitchen. "Maverick."

I loaded my arms with all I could carry and traipsed up the walkway. Hoping Dad would be in residence, I rang the bell, but after the third ring, I intuited he wasn't home. I inserted my key, but the knob turned freely. "Dad?" No one answered. I sniffed a faint floral scent. "Ida?"

"Maverick? No use hiding." He'd show himself for a treat. I kicked the corner of his mat into place and rummaged in his drawer. Palming his favorite stinky salmon-flavored cookie, I said in a sing-song voice, "Maverick, I have a treat for you." Nothing. Perhaps I'd seen a curtain instead or a shadow caused by headlights shining through the window, and Maverick was out on a walk with Dad, but that would mean I couldn't trust my senses—again.

My phone rang. I read the screen and answered with a bright, "Hello, Dr. Erickson."

"Hello, Teacher Wilk. Are you up for dinner tonight? After a weekend from Hades, the admin hired two locums to take the calls. I'll have an eight-to-five job, for the first time in my medical career, lasting fourteen glorious days."

I ignored my briefcase and tossed my plans to the four winds. "I'd be delighted."

"I'll be there in thirty minutes, and we'll do Italian. I haven't seen Romano in a long time."

As we disconnected, I grinned remembering our first

dinner date at Romano's, then raced to touch up my lipstick, draw a brush through my light-brown hair, run a magic mascara wand over my lashes to accent my baby blue eyes, and change shirts, which still gave me twenty minutes of time to work. A crisp knock sounded as I finished recording the final corrected test.

I opened the door and drank in the tall, lithe, insouciant man on the stoop. His dark hair curled at his collar and his distractingly attractive eyes twinkled with mischief. "So, this is how the rest of the world feels when not worried about being yanked away from dinner with a beautiful woman. Our new doc can't begin soon enough."

"Come in for a sec. I haven't seen hide nor hair of Dad and Maverick yet. Let me give him a call." I punched in his number and heard his phone ring from his room. A lot of good it did him there. We'd have to have a long talk. I knocked on Ida's door. No answer there either.

"Do you want to wait?"

"No. I'll just leave a note and let Dad know where I'll be."

In large block letters, I wrote, 'Out for supper with Pete. Love you.' After Dad's traumatic brain injury, he insisted he did better when we were consistent. Sometimes walking my dog required both hands, and we needed a convenient location while removing or outfitting Maverick's harness to stash incoming and outgoing mail or anything else extraneous we carried. The top cubby in the cabinet by the back door met the parameters. Every time he entered, he opened the door and swept his hand through the cupboard, removed the mail addressed to him, and returned the rest. Sometimes we exchanged messages. He never forgot, and he'd discover my note.

But I'd been remiss. I hadn't yet checked the cubicle

today. I opened the cupboard and a white legal-sized envelope drifted to the floor. I picked it up and eyed it suspiciously. It was addressed to 'K Wilk' in a distinctive, thick pencil scrawl and didn't include a return address.

"Aren't you going to open it?" Pete asked, one eyebrow arched quizzically.

TWENTY-EIGHT

Pete held his crystal goblet up to the light, gently swirling the gleaming garnet liquid. "Let's take a look at your message again."

Reaching to extract the black-and-white checked pages, I spotted Enzo Gyles nursing a martini at the bar, half-heartedly listening to the animated, curvy brunette next to him. When Penelope tapped his shoulder, the girl pouted as they moved to a table in the corner farthest from the counter. Tony Relando slithered onto the seat vacated by Enzo, but before he started up his conversation, the girl flipped her long locks over her shoulder and packed up. She shimmied her very short skirt into place and scurried out the door.

"Do you know her?" I pointed to her retreating figure as I oriented the grid so the outlines of the chess pieces faced him. I slid my chair closer.

"No." Pete's eyes never left mine.

I puckered my lips and shook my head. "I feel like I should."

We examined the pages top to bottom, side to side, and upside down while we dug into two helpings of the sky-high decadent lasagna Romano Santino was known for.

"You have no idea what they mean or who sent them?" Pete asked between bites, wiping drips of sauce from his chin.

"This is the second message I received on paper identical to that unearthed by Amanda in the shed owned by Severson. He hasn't regained consciousness, has he?"

"No, but he could've sent the envelope before the accident."

I nodded. "Why would Severson or anyone else send these to me? I only play rudimentary chess, and I don't openly share that fact. The glyphs are adequate representations of white and black chess pieces, but they seem to be haphazardly placed on different squares on the grid."

"We'll have to play some time." When his eyes met mine over the rim of the wine glass, he winked. My heart leaped in my chest, and I momentarily forgot all about the game.

I reluctantly broke his gaze, and his lopsided grin slid to one side.

"No one admitted to seeing Severson on Saturday, but I saw him and asked if he'd sent me the Knight's Tour, the map Jane and I used to find the passageway under the barn. He laughed at me and vanished. I suppose he could have moved Mia's body, but just because he moved it doesn't mean he killed her. And anyone who discovered the tunnel could have moved the body unobserved. That entire horse entourage was in Columbia at the time."

"Including Liam Byrne."

"Admittedly, including Liam Byrne." I shook my head. "If I remember correctly, Penelope and her assemblage left immediately after the big race. Any one of them could have driven the truck involved in the accident that put Severson in the hospital."

"Katie." Pete's honeyed voice held the tiniest reproach. "Let Amanda handle it."

"But that's just it." The words tumbled from my lips. "She has misgivings, but Ronnie convinced the city muckety-mucks that he solved the case. Amanda doesn't think the investigation is complete. She's not convinced all the facts have been uncovered." I inhaled deeply. "Ronnie Christianson wants your dad's old job. I just don't know if he's the right person to be chief."

Pete covered my hand with his as a shadow passed over our table.

"Good evening, Dr. Erickson. Miss Wilk," the man snorted. "Lose any more bodies?"

"Have you, Ronnie?" Pete said with a smile as he squeezed my fingers ever so slightly.

"Nope. I only need to see them once," Ronnie's voice took on a sardonic edge. He snickered and tipped his bottle of soda. "Wilk, I know the conk on your head might have scrambled your memories, but for what it's worth, we discovered who murdered Mrs. Brown, tampered with the body, and found your money." He took a swig from his bottle and sauntered across the floor, glad-handing the restaurant patrons.

There wasn't much of the delicious lasagna left, but even that was too much for my lost appetite. I pushed my plate to the center of the table and turned away from Ronnie Christianson. My eyes drifted to Enzo and Penelope Gyles, and I was caught off guard. I hadn't known them long, but it was out of character for them to sit so close together.

She plucked a bright ripe strawberry from a glass serving

bowl mounded with whipped cream and fed it to him. When she caught me staring, she blushed and bowed her head. I looked away, but seconds later I snuck another peek to make sure I hadn't imagined what I'd seen. Enzo pressed his card into his server's hand, but Penelope had disappeared. My face flushed. I hadn't meant to intrude.

Romano approached with a big smile. "Dr. Pete, Miss Katie, tiramisu?"

Pete noticed my discomfort and kindly said, "No, thank you, Romano. Just the check, please."

I knew Pete supported Amanda, but on our way out to his car I worked up the courage to ask what he really thought of Ronnie. They'd both grown up in Columbia. They'd known each other forever.

"He's been a good officer, and when Dad had his heart trouble, he stepped up to the plate. His strengths lie in knowing the community and reading the faces of the folks he's known his entire life." He gave me a hand up into the cab and clambered around to get into the driver's seat as a metallic green vehicle with beefy wheels gunned its engine and roared out of the lot, with Penelope behind the wheel.

Momentarily losing concentration, Pete said, "Wow." He shook himself back into the conversation at hand. "But you have to have leadership skills as well, and therein lies his deficit. He's more militant, ordering people around rather than encouraging cooperation. There are city members with an agenda, however, who believe they'd have an in with the police department if he were chief." He shook his head and pulled onto the road. "They aren't necessarily bad people, but they want to have a little influence over the one in charge of local investigations, just in case."

"Don't you think he jumped the gun, naming the killer and declaring his death a suicide?"

"Technically, the case is still open, but he covered his bases with his claims, and his supporters want this in his win column."

I chewed on my lip. "I trust Amanda. I think she's right. When I met Liam, he was affable, though guarded, and seemed kind."

"The operative word is 'seemed.' In any given situation, people can be driven to do strange things. Maybe he was threatened or snapped. Maybe he stole money to pay off a long-standing debt or gambling loss. Maybe he contracted a life-ending illness. We'll likely never know the exact prompt."

Ida's rambling Queen Anne appeared, lights on in every window of the front apartment. "Would you like to come in for a bit?"

He tapped the clock on the dash. "You, my lovely lady, have school tomorrow, and I have a regular eight-to-five shift. But I'm open for supper again."

His car didn't move until I closed my apartment door, secured the lock, and blinked the light, telegraphing I was safely inside. Remembering only the new invitation to supper, I pressed my hands to my chest and slid to the floor, sighing, where I was met with a warm tongue swathing my smiling face and a sleek tail swishing dog hair into and out of a pile by the door.

The pages containing the chess grids crinkled, and I pulled them out again, laughing and turning my face away from my furry friend. "Okay, okay, Maverick." I climbed from the floor and sat at the kitchen table, smoothing the pages flat.

Dad sauntered into the room, rubbing his eyes.

"Sorry," I giggled. "I didn't mean to wake you."

"I wondered what message the flashing lights sent." His

lips formed a meaningful smile, and he filled the hot pot. "Chamomile tea?"

I nodded as my giddiness abated, and I postulated sending the dots and dashes of a Morse code message via lamp light, on/off switches, binary patterns of zeroes and ones, and black and white. I sat up, ramrod straight, as the realization dawned on me. The message on the grid was in binary code. "Take a seat, Dad. We've got work to do."

CHAPTER TWENTY-NINE

An hour later, Dad and I were no closer to solving the riddle of the black and white chess pieces. I dragged my eyelids up and blinked a few times to avoid seeing double.

"You're not doing any good rehashing what you've already determined doesn't give you an answer," Dad said. "Get some rest and try again tomorrow. Maybe something will come to you."

Horses and numbers, queens and kings, pawns, and bishops came to me all night, waking me over and over, and when the alarm sounded, my dry gritty eyes urged me to pull the covers back over my head for another ten minutes, but Dad's voice boomed up the stairs. "Katie, Penelope Gyles is here to speak to you."

I hauled myself out of bed and threw on some sweats. It would be a short conversation. School awaited.

I smoothed my unruly flyaway hair and pasted on a face

I hoped looked wide awake. Penelope sat comfortably at our kitchen table, sipping from a cup of Dad's tremendous brew. I gratefully accepted a mug for myself, and as I inhaled the fresh aroma, my eyes drifted closed in anticipation. I dropped into the seat opposite her and slurped greedily.

"Morning," I croaked.

"I'm sorry to visit so early unannounced, but you've been so helpful. Can I rely on your discretion?"

I lifted my heavy eyebrows, partly to keep my eyes open, partly to emphasize my assurance.

"Enzo and I have mended fences." I'd already figured that out for myself but didn't say a word. "And we've attributed our reconciliation to the support we've had in this lovely little village. In light of … Mia's murder and Liam's death, we've come to realize life is simply too short. The Hallorans, your students, and you have been so kind and understanding, we'd like to invite you to Mia's memorial service Wednesday evening at six o'clock in the downtown funeral home chapel." She glanced over my shoulder. "You too, Mr. Wilk. And your darling little landlady and anyone else who would like to pay their last respects."

I almost laughed out loud, visualizing what Ida would say in response.

"We're hosting a light supper as a thank you and allowing a moment to share any vignettes of encounters you might have had with my sister." With that, she sniffed and rose, nodded her head, and, before I could process her revelation, she exited.

"Darling little landlady? Are you going to tell her?"

"Absolutely not, but I feel like I should go. They can't have met too many people in the short time they've been in Columbia. I'll inform the kids, but I'm sure the high school gossip tree is all lit up, and they already know." The cuckoo clock chimed the quarter hour, reminding me I had just enough time to get ready for school. "Dad, did it feel like Penelope had something else she wanted to say?"

He cleared the cups, pondering his answer. "I don't rightly know."

I prepared for the day, wondering if I'd imagined Penelope leaving words unsaid. By the time I'd arrived at school, it seemed the invitation not only made the rounds among my students, but among the faculty and staff as well. Jane's foot tapped an anxious rhythm while she ranted about the convoluted emotions prompted by attending a memorial for someone known for only an hour, but of course she'd be there. Mr. Ganka emailed, promising he'd attend in support of the kids. Even ZaZa said she'd lower her impossibly high standards and attend the service for the poor departed soul.

It seemed everyone knew, therefore the onslaught of students descending on my classroom after school shocked me.

"We don't have practice or a meeting, do we?"

"No, Ms. Wilk," Carlee said. "But we would like to visit an equine therapy facility today. We came up with the idea on Saturday while we were finishing up the dishes."

And while Jane and I were investigating Severson's area below ground. "Horses. Today?"

Jane rounded the corner, waving signed permission sheets and swinging the dreaded van keys. "It's all taken care of. The kids talked to Mr. Ganka yesterday, and here we are. You driving? Or am I?"

I couldn't disappoint the glowing faces. When Jane drove, I knew in her mind a stop sign was merely a suggestion, so I swiped the keys and led our troupe to their waiting chariot.

When they were all buckled in, I said, "Tell me about this facility."

"I read up on the ranch," said Lorelei.

"Of course, you did," Brock smiled indulgently and earned a tap on his knee.

Carlee said, "They offer horse therapy to individuals with disabilities and children at risk. I think I want to volunteer there. The benefits to the kids with a wide range of challenges is profound."

Lorelei nodded her head. "Riding a horse can help improve flexibility, balance, and coordination."

"They've seen improvement in non-verbal as well as verbal communication skills."

Patricia nodded. "And, as I well know from Mom's repeated remarks, you learn how to be responsible when you care for an animal."

"Are they expecting us, or is this a surprise visit?"

Jane wriggled in her seat and sat up straighter. "I verified the appointment this afternoon."

"Traitor," I whispered under my breath.

Although I'd conquered my terror of the four-legged animals, I still found the towering half-ton hoofed bodies worrisome, and the steering wheel became slick with sweat.

Ten minutes out of Columbia, Jane said, "Turn here."

White fencing bordered an enormous dirt paddock in front of an even larger enclosed arena. A cheery blonde wearing a white cowboy hat shoved the doors apart and waved. I parked under the visitor sign and before I removed the key, the van doors rumbled to the side and the kids piled out. Jane's hand landed on my forearm. "It'll be great. You'll see."

I nodded, and she dropped to the ground, gravel crunching as she took off after my students. I inhaled slowly and looked up as the woman jogged to the entry gate where she met them, her effervescent vitality palpable from even this distance. She lifted the latch and waved them through. In my haste to catch up, I fumbled with the seatbelt. Not a good way to begin my tour. I took another deep breath, and successfully pressed the release.

Six pairs of worried eyes waited for me. I beamed but when Jane overacted being afraid—a sign I might have overdone the grin—I tempered my toothy smile. She relaxed and nodded.

"I'm Lisa, general manager, and we're so happy you've come out to visit. Before our two young riders get here for their afternoon lesson, I have time to give you the A plus tour." A happy light shined in her blue eyes. "Follow me."

We filed through a door on the far side and the earthy warm smell undid me.

"This is called ..." She waited for someone to finish her sentence, getting a sense of how much or how little our group knew.

"The tack room," Patricia offered, gazing lovingly at the line of gleaming bridles, halters, harnesses, and reins hanging from hooks on the wall. Polished saddles and stirrups lined racks for the length of the room. She opened the cupboard filled with blankets, brushes, combs, towels, and grooming supplies.

The smell of leather, wood shavings, and hay with an overlay of liniment took me back to my first riding experience, and I heard Lisa's voice as if it came from a great distance. I wanted to laugh with the exhilaration of sitting high in a seat, rocking in time from front to back with the forward movement of my mount, Abacus, and cry with loss of my first riding partner, Charles.

Lisa detailed the use of each piece of equipment. We followed her into a second room. "Here's where we take care of the horses' hooves with a pick, a spray, a soak, and oil. This is also our first aid room." She pointed to another door at the far end of the room. "Through there you'll find our cleaning supplies. Any takers for wiping down the directional cones?"

Patricia and Carlee dragged the other four behind Lisa and listened intently to their instructions.

My phone dinged and I lifted a finger to Jane, excusing myself to read a text from Amanda.

A neighbor overlooking the tracks read the *Sentinel* today. She saw the article concerning Mia Brown's murder and memorial and the accompanying photos. She swears to have seen two people walking. She remembers yelling to them, telling them they were too close to the tracks for a midnight stroll. Ronnie is not entirely happy. It's not over yet.

I responded. Do you need me for anything?

I'll let you know.

Jane tilted her head, and I whispered, "Amanda."

THIRTY

The two grinning youths adjusted their helmets and climbed the mounting blocks, eagerly sliding into the saddles. I watched in wonder as six volunteers guided two behemoth equines through a course defined by orange cones, red barrels, long wooden dowels, and standing white PVC posts. These special kids made it look so easy, and their smiles almost chased the apprehension out of my system. Almost.

Lisa fielded questions and escorted us out of the arena. "We'd love to see you again," she said, distributing the pages she'd been fluttering in her hand.

Back in the van, the volunteer forms made the rounds. Carlee and Patricia filled in pertinent information, leaving blank the line for parent signature.

Lorelei said, "Ms. Mackey, what did you think of the horses?"

Jane answered and entertained us with stories of her

glory days of riding during the short trip back to school.

Jane and the kids emptied the van, but before she rolled the sliding door closed, Carlee said, "Thanks, Ms. Wilk. I know horses aren't your thing, but I'm glad I joined your after-school activities."

"I am too, Carlee."

The door slammed. Wanting to leave the van at least as clean as when we acquired it, I ambled through the seats, picking up the few pieces of trash and two volunteer applications. The parent company name, Therapy Thoroughbreds, caught me by surprise. I sat quietly in the driver's seat for a minute or two, contemplating Enzo Gyles' support of the worthwhile endeavor before remembering Dad's comment about sending a message with flashing lights. On/off, black/white, and a possible solution to the chess grids presented itself. Not only were there black and white pieces. There were also black and white squares on a board.

I tore through the vacant halls of the school and into my office, digging through my canvas tote for the checkered pages. My finger followed the spines of my reference books, alighting on a narrow volume and set to work.

Although I was no longer fluent in Morse Code, I knew I had the correct source of the message, dots and dashes. I'd previously used the color of the pieces rather than the spaces they occupied so I attempted to unravel the communication using black squares for dots and came to an abrupt halt, stymied by a dash, dash, dash, dot. There was no corresponding letter or number. Flipping the colors for dots and dashes, the first line displayed three dots—an 's.' The rest of the lines produced twelve letters, but no words.

I crumpled my solution page in frustration, packed up, and hauled myself home to burn off whatever emotion blocked the answers I attempted to conjure by walking

Maverick. His lolling tongue, cocked head, and jaunty step calmed my nerves enough so when my phone rang, I didn't bark at the caller.

"Dinner at Thai Fyre?"

"You know eating out every night can't be healthy."

In mock pain, Pete said, "You walk Maverick every day. Doesn't the delight of being with me count for something?"

I chuckled. "Of course. What was I thinking? What time?"

"I'm parked in your drive now."

I caught sight of the big royal blue truck and broke into a light jog.

* * *

Pete told engaging stories about growing up and his youthful indiscretions. The healthy laughing was great for my heart, and my cheeks hurt, stretched so far from side to side through courses of steamed vegetable dumplings, Pad Thai, and crispy duck. Over the small table with the last bite of a shared lip-smacking fried banana eggroll and coconut ice cream to top off the meal, Pete said, "You're unusually quiet."

"Still pondering the chess grids."

"Did you bring them with you?" I nodded. "Let's take another look."

I gingerly pulled the pages from the envelope and handed them across the table, making light of my quasi-solution. Pete buried his nose in the pages in front of him. Sighing, I stared at him and watched him work. What a delicious view. And from my vantage point, the letters appeared upside down, and in reverse order, the deciphered letters spelled out 'deadPenelope.'

I snatched the papers and wrote out the letters for Pete to check.

"They are definitely meaningful words."

"Dead Penelope or Penelope dead, but how could that be?"

"Unless it means exactly what it says. Penelope's dead." Pete caught my eye. "This is a terrible message with horrible timing. Because we'd shared our observations of their personalities, Amanda thought Penelope had been the intended victim all along. Was this a foreshadowing, a prediction, a confession, and a mistake was made? When was it sent?"

"The postmark is faint, but I think it indicates Saturday, definitely after the body was identified and before Severson was run down. Who identified the body?"

"Her sister." Pete shook his head.

I called Amanda and was instructed to leave a message. "We may have new information about Mia Brown's murder. Call me."

We drove home, pointedly avoiding talk of Penelope's death. When he stopped, Pete got out and lent a hand. I felt like a princess stepping down from her carriage after a lovely evening. We could see Dad sitting at the kitchen table, playing solitaire. After a light kiss, Pete reminded me to leave the investigation to Amanda. "Tell her what you're thinking and let her do her job. And say goodnight to Harry."

With my safety in good hands, Pete backed down the drive.

Without missing a beat, Dad said with a slight rebuke, "How was your second dinner out this week?"

His stern face broke into a smile and his eyes lit as I presented him with a white cardboard carton filled with his favorite Thai food. "I'm taking Maverick for a walk around the block. You don't have to wait up."

At the mention of the 'w' word, Maverick stretched his

paws out front and quickly made his way to the hook holding his leash. Dad mumbled, "Bye," around a mouthful of tasty shrimp fried rice.

We took the short route, just for a breath of air. I wanted to determine what happened and began picking at the threads, enumerating my points to Maverick.

"Being the prickly sort, Penelope accused her sister of being in cahoots with her dead husband, stealing Foggy Bottom and the money. Her harassment could have driven Mia to murder. But then Mia would have been suspect. Instead, Mia was the victim. Maybe Penelope did more than just accuse her sister."

Maverick ignored me.

"Mia released Byrne after an investigation found Liam placing bets on horses which he couldn't legally do. If Byrne did hold a grudge, it would still be directed at Mia."

My head ached.

"And then there's Tony Relando. He claimed Penelope owed him, and he acted as if buying a winning racehorse from her would wipe out her debt, but Penelope didn't act like she owed him and wasn't willing or able to sell anyway. And what we read online hinted Relando didn't have the funds needed to buy a horse right now. Money again. People have murdered for less. In addition, he had dissolved his partnership with Zachary Brown, but why? Was that also required by Mia and had he resented it?"

Maverick picked up his pace. His ears flopped and his tail wagged. Just another walk on another evening.

"At the onset, Enzo Gyles was at odds with Penelope— not a particularly amicable marriage. As her husband and beneficiary, he'd do well if she were out of the picture, but of all the suspects, how could he mistakenly kill Mia instead of his wife. And the last time I saw them, the geniality between them had warmed."

The secretary came to mind. "Ann-Elizabeth. Mia hadn't wanted to be reminded of her dead husband's perfidy, stealing and selling her prize Thoroughbred and dying in a car crash. Mia said she didn't have the money, nor did she know the whereabouts of the horse. She wanted a low-key existence and moved to Columbia where Ann-Elizabeth worked hard to keep Mia Brown's name out of the public eye. And now Ann-Elizabeth's livelihood, to keep Mia's footprint small, has ended. She needs to begin anew. I wonder what she'll do. She didn't seem to mind Enzo but didn't like Penelope the least bit. Could she have mistaken Penelope and Mia?"

I shook my head, getting pretty far afield.

"Instead, Mia's disappearance made Penelope believe she took back Foggy Bottom. That would make her all the more determined to get even with her sister. Maybe Mia was the intended victim."

A car purred behind me and turned at the corner. "And what on earth would Ann-Elizabeth gain by the death of TnL? How could she justify the euthanasia? I'll have to see what CJ has discovered."

Maverick glanced over his shoulder but kept walking. Maybe it was a little weird talking to my dog, so I let the rest of my thoughts simmer quietly.

Liam worked for Mia before Penelope hired him, but Mia believed her husband's accusations of Liam's illegal dealings. Liam lost his career as a jockey and his future jobs in horseracing. Although Penelope treated him with disrespect and continued to dangle the horses he loved just out of reach, at least he could see and be with them. What could have grated on him to such an extent that murder would rid him of a threat or menace or impediment to his future well-being?

And what was it Liam said about one sister marrying

for love and the other for money? I wondered which was which. Zachary Brown sold a horse that didn't belong to him, took the money, and the horse disappeared. Though he died, maybe he should be investigated more thoroughly?

And therein was the crux—a mix-up in victims and motives.

Lights swept the street in front of me as I turned onto Maple Street. I could have reached out and touched the hood. "Hey. Watch it."

Maverick picked up his pace, and we returned to a cleared table. The door to Dad's room was closed so I'd have to continue my discussion with Maverick over tea and a snack. I grabbed two bitesize pecan tarts, leftovers from Derby day, and I retrieved two of Ida's savory homemade sweet potato chews for Maverick from the cookie jar on the counter.

"Here you go, Mav." He scarfed them down and settled on his cushioned mat.

Amanda did not reconnect, and I felt the end of the day weighing down on me. My last thought before drifting off to sleep returned to the words on the chess grid. 'Penelope's dead' could simply mean what it said, but when I woke, it didn't make any sense at all.

THIRTY-ONE

I regarded hump day as either the hill to climb in the middle of the week or the slide on down to the weekend. This Wednesday presented a mountain of things I needed to complete.

Our once-a-month department meetings required attendance. The department chair circulated recording forms and recommendations for next year's duties. We plugged final exams dates into the schedule and shared plans for end of the year cleaning, collection, and storage of texts. And one of our cohorts asked for a volunteer ticket taker for the next home baseball game to fill in because his wife planned a surprise weekend away without telling him.

"That's why it's called a surprise," ZaZa whispered, rolling her eyes, and for just a second, she seemed to consider me an ally. But I could have been wrong.

The morning dragged. Many of my students claimed

to have attended the track meet the day before and hadn't understood nor completed their assignments. I slogged through lunch and had been remiss in reading the history field trip notice. More than half my last hour students had opted into a day long trek to visit the *Titanic* exhibit at our local history center, but it made a great math game day for those who remained until Justine accused Kindra of cheating.

"No, she didn't, Justine," said Patricia.

Justine turned her back. "What do you know?"

"I know you said something. Your jaw moved, but I can't hear. Would you face me so we can talk?"

Patricia tentatively reached out her hand, but Justine jerked out of her way. She turned slowly, looked hard at Patricia, and said, "No."

Intervention time. "Justine, I don't tolerate rude behavior. It's unacceptable in my room or anywhere else for that matter. Let's work this out."

Her cold eyes found mine. "You're such a problem solver. But you don't even know when you're being studied."

The bell rang. She stalked out of my room, and the remaining students scattered like confetti in the wind. Flabbergasted, I could barely catch my breath. Why would she scrutinize me?

"She's just not at home here." Patricia shook her head. "Been there. Done that." She had gone away to a school for the deaf, hated it, got herself booted out, and returned home, only to face similar difficulties. "At least I have friends. Poor kid."

Patricia rarely showed her generous side, but when she did, she helped put everything into perspective. Before I managed to put away the dice and cards and come up with any words of wisdom, however, Galen and Carlee rushed into the classroom.

"Ms. Wilk," said Galen. "Ashley left the costumes in her car, and water seeped inside. There's damage on some of the clothes. My white shirt needs to be cleaned and pressed before Saturday, and I think I can do my own, but some of the others are ruined."

Carlee said, "Maggie Murphy's shift is stained, and the shoulder pads of the vintage jacket we had for Molly Brown to wear need to be replaced after the seams are reinforced. The pea coats smell like mildew. They'll never work the way they are. How are we going to get all the repairs and cleaning done before the competition?"

Ashley's tear-streaked face peeked around the corner. "I'm so sorry. I had everything in a plastic tub under a tarp, but my trunk leaked." She sobbed lugging a huge plastic box onto the desktop. "I found an inch of water in the bottom of the tub this morning and I don't know how long it's been like that."

"No problem. We'll get everything fixed or replaced. Having the period pieces was beneficial but only to help you get into character, and you're perfectly able to do that without the extraneous clothes. They didn't add that much to your overall performance. Maybe just a little feeling of an edge." My students had fun dressing up, but they'd be just fine without these specific clothes. However, I knew Ida could work her crafting magic, and I'd definitely ask for her help.

Ashley sniffed, "It was fun to dress up. The clothes were so helpful, and today was going to be our final dress rehearsal. I'm sorry."

"Let's pull out the costumes and see what we can salvage. You did without the little extras when we began mock trial this year, and with all the experience you've gained, you can certainly do it again."

The kids drew sodden fabric from the box and managed

to wring out the clothes, laying them flat across the desks, dripping water everywhere.

A subdued practice, replete with serious, distracted faces, proceeded until Lorelei launched into another out-of-character pep talk.

"We've been up and down and all around. We know this trial inside and out, as both the plaintiff and the defendant. As plaintiff, *Titanic* survivor Maggie Murphy is …"

She dragged the completion of her sentence from Brock, who said in a monotone, "… suing the White Star Line for negligence and maybe even wrongful death of the love of her life, Connor Robert Mitchell." Lorelei prompted him by rolling her hand. "The plaintiff witnesses are …"

Carlee exhaled and filled the dead air. "Captain Rostron of the *Carpathia* and the magnificent Molly Brown." She started to laugh. "And no one, not even our team can predict what she'll say." She began another thread. "The defendant is the White Star Line, and its witnesses include …"

Ashley snuffled. "… Second Officer Charles Lightoller, lookout Reginald Lee, and Swedish military attaché—"

Galen jumped in using his well-rehearsed Scandinavian accent, "—first-class passenger, Mauritz Håkan Björnström-Steffansson."

"We're competing at state, and that in itself is a great achievement." Lorelei looked at each of her teammates in turn. "I'm looking forward to having a good time on Saturday, so no pouty faces. It's been a rough week, but we've been through tough times before and that has made us stronger and adaptable. For those of you attending the memorial tonight, I propose we meet outside the chapel at five-fifty and enter en masse. We can stick together."

"Don't feel like you have to attend, but I'll be there with you," I said, lifting one of the costumes to my nose and trying not to react to the sour odor.

"And so will I," Jane said, the first words she'd uttered since practice began. "Go home and rest up for a bit. Mrs. Gyles said they are providing a light lunch so be prepared for anything. You just never know what light lunch means."

Galen grabbed his shirt, intent on cleaning it for the meet on Saturday. Someone else picked up a white shirt and a vest. Jane helped me collect the remainder. We commiserated for a bit—our students had relished taking on different personae enhanced by period clothing, but they'd acted well before we'd found the pieces. They'd do so again.

"I'll take the coats to the dry cleaner and ask for a rush job. Any ideas for the jacket?" I asked.

"Ida's creative. If she can make hats out of paper, she can probably whip up new shoulder pads," said Jane. She looked preoccupied.

I carefully folded the soaked fabric and slid it into a plastic tote. "I'm going to drop these off at the cleaners. See you at the chapel."

"Sure." She made a move toward the door and turned back. "Katie, I think someone's been following me."

"Why do you think someone is following you?"

"It started on Monday on my way home from practice. I couldn't spot anyone, but I've been feeling uneasy ever since. It's creeping me out. I haven't done anything differently, so I don't know why Monday would be the turning point, but—"

"Why don't we go to the memorial together? I'll pick you up at five thirty-five."

Some of the uneasiness left her face. "It's probably nothing, but that sounds like a good plan."

The dry cleaner, a card playing partner of Ida's, promised to have our costumes ready by late afternoon on Friday—one of the many perks of small-town life.

Molly Brown's costume would require a little more tender loving care. I pinned a note to the vintage jacket and left it on Ida's kitchen table where she couldn't fail to notice it. I crossed my fingers, hoping she'd have a plan for makeover magic.

Maverick and I had time for a mini walk and any number of steps with him were better than none at all. When we finished, I still had time to change into black pants and a gray patterned shirt, subdued and, I hoped, just right for the service.

Jane waited on the curb outside her apartment. She slid into my passenger seat and said, "Did you see anyone suspicious? I still feel like someone is watching me."

I glanced right and left, fore and aft, and Jane said, a little manic, "Don't let them catch you."

"No one will notice *my* curiosity. I'm behaving like a careful driver." I flipped on the blinker and glanced over my shoulder again. "I don't see anyone, but that doesn't mean there isn't someone there. Why do you feel that way?"

"I'd say it was all in my head, but since Monday I've been ultra careful and when I got home today, I noticed one corner of my rug was turned up. It's a little thing, but I think someone was in my apartment, looking for something."

My blood ran cold. Monday, when I returned home, I thought I'd seen Maverick rush by the kitchen window. The door had been open, and I hoped Dad had been the culprit, but what if someone else had been in my kitchen?

THIRTY-TWO

No one could fail to see the huge reminder sign placed next to the funeral home entry, 'Respect this Celebration of Life. Please turn off your phones.'

I wasn't the only attendee fumbling with the phone buttons as we walked into the gathering space outside of Mia Brown's Visitation Suite before signing the guest registry and selecting a program. Carefully curated photos of Mia's cheery face graced the front: a bouncing baby, a cheery toddler atop a huge horse in the arms of a man who might have been her father, a graduation photo, Mia and Penelope dressed startlingly alike, Mia as a lovely bride with most of the groom cut off, and a photo of her in her Derby hat perched on her head. Inside, in a very small font, I read her detailed obituary and was surprised by her age. She appeared if not older, then much wiser than thirty-four years jam-packed with school, races, horses, marriage, widowhood, an equine business, and finally a brutal murder.

Small groups congregated inside, speaking softly to one another, examining the pictures and items on the memorial table and watching the video tribute containing twice as much footage of horses than of people. A larger-than-life recent portrait of Mia occupied the space on the easel at the front next to the lectern. With dark hair, her head tilted at that angle, and barely smiling from the gilded frame, it was easy to see how she could be mistaken for her sister.

Jane and I took seats on the benches next to Dad and Ida. I scanned the remaining faces. Sadly, the turnout was minimal, and I realized I knew everyone attending the memorial.

The somber director began with a moment of silence to remember our sister. When the guests began clearing their throats and shifting in their seats, he called upon the first eulogist.

Patricia threw her shoulders back, held her head high, and walked to the podium. She took a deep breath. "Mrs. Brown allowed Kindra and me the phenomenal opportunity to work with her stellar horses. I don't know what my future will hold, but I do know, I've found satisfaction dealing with animals, and I'm volunteering at Therapy Thoroughbreds as soon as I complete the training." Enzo could hardly contain his smile, and Penelope patted his hand. "If we can continue helping out, Mrs. Gyles, please let us know."

Debora Halloran opened with her great appreciation for Mia. "Though ultimately destroyed by the tornado, our partnership succeeded in building a functional horse barn to Mia's curious but exacting specifications, on an organic dairy farm no less." A few guffaws made their way around the room. "I, too, learned about a different herd animal and hope Mia's dreams for each of her horses can still be brought to fruition." She stammered, searching for more words. Not finding any, she looked around the room, blushed, and took her seat.

Ann-Elizabeth stood behind the tall desk and honked into a hanky too many times to count, unable to put together any words to honor Mia other than, "She was …" She stumbled back to her seat on the bench in the first row but as far away from Penelope as she could.

The director asked for other speakers to honor Mia. Penelope stood and took a step off to one side, waiting an interminable amount of time for further contributions until the rustling and restlessness in the crowd finally coaxed her to give her short tribute. She extolled Mia's strengths as a sister, virtues as a horse lover, and acumen as a successful businesswoman. She spoke a few words about their desire to please their father who taught them the basics of the equine industry. She explained the need to wait for the body to be released at which time she would take Mia home and have a proper burial service, and we were all encouraged to attend.

I cast a sidelong glance at Jane's implacable face. She blinked twice, a hard *no*.

After a few more words, Penelope finally thanked everyone and invited them to break bread.

The light lunch turned out to be a bona-fide smorgasbord and would have fed an army of starving high school wrestlers like Galen. Juicy steak, baked potatoes with all the fixings, lightly salted, crisp *haricots verts*, buttery garlic bread, cut seasonal fruit and a sweet dip, a Columbia staple—pistachio salad with miniature marshmallows, and angel food cake with fresh strawberries and whipped cream completed the menu. My students ate their fill and hung together in a group, staring around the room. After a polite and proper ten minutes, Lorelei snuck a fingertip wave, and my students retreated to the back of the short line to pay their last respects, extend their condolences to Penelope, Enzo, and Ann-Elizabeth, and bid a final farewell.

I envied their easy escape, leaving Jane and me at the wrong table to get away unnoticed, seated between ZaZa and Tony Relando.

"ZaZa, I've been meaning to tell you," I said quietly, so Mr. Ganka might not hear the interchange. "I found two girls in your room watching the storm during the tornado. They'd gone to the restroom and snuck back in, passing by you in the hall. One was Cecilia and the other name I didn't catch, but she wants to be a storm chaser. Did you know they were missing?"

The look of contempt she gave would have burned a more tender heart. When it came to ZaZa, I'd grown almost immune, but I broke eye contact first.

On the other side, Relando ignored Jane's attempts at small talk. Instead, he pointed across the room at Penelope, pacing the back of the dining area, wringing her hands and shaking her head. Enzo walked with her, occasionally speaking softly, but only further agitating her.

Mr. Ganka didn't hold with impropriety and continued to attempt a normal everyday conversation. He tried to do what Jane could not and draw attention away from Penelope's plight. "Tony, what kind of horses do you own?"

Relando answered with a curt, "Winning ones."

ZaZa pounced. "You are rude," she said, thus ending any future dialog. At that moment, I envied her forthrightness and ability to hit just the right buttons, at least when aimed at targets other than me.

Amanda finished her circuit of the room and sat, rounding out our table, eyeing our disquiet with suspicion. The suspicion seemed warranted when we heard Penelope hiss at Enzo, "I have to do it now, or I might never get the opportunity or have the wherewithal."

"Pardon me." Some of the visitors ignored Penelope's soft words. She lifted a coffee cup and tapped it with a spoon. "Excuse me, please, but may I have your attention. I have an announcement to make."

Amanda's phone dinged, and the double doors behind her opened. Officer Daniel Rodgers stepped in first, effectively curtailing Penelope's announcement. He answered Amanda's confused gaze with a tiny shrug and an apologetic look. Two more officers joined him. They stepped off to the right and left, forging human brackets around Penelope and Enzo.

Amanda rose and tilted her head in a question. "Officer Rodgers?" When no ready answer came, she prompted, "Do continue, Mrs. Gyles. Sorry for the interruption."

Officer Rodgers tapped the cell phone carrier on his belt. Amanda stepped off to the side and extracted her phone, pressing buttons and reading. Her face darkened.

Penelope's chin dropped to her chest, and she looked at her shoes as if she could find the words there.

In the quiet, the ornate old grandfather clock in the lobby chimed, heralding another entrance. Ronnie Christianson barreled through the doorway, reaching past his firearm to the shiny handcuffs dangling from his belt, saying loudly. "The prints on the corpse were not on file, but we have since discovered they are not those of Mia Brown, but of Penelope Gyles."

The room inhaled as one, sucking the sound out of the air. As the cuffs snapped around her wrists, Penelope, or rather, Mia groaned. "That's what I was trying to tell you."

"Sure, you were," sneered Ronnie. "You're under arrest for the murders of Penelope Gyles and Liam Byrne. You have the right to remain silent. Anything you say can and will be used against you in a court of law." He tugged a card from a sharply creased shirt pocket and continued with the Miranda Warning as the room erupted.

She said more loudly, "I am Mia." Ronnie continued reading. The chaotic noises rumbled. She looked from one stricken face to another. "Penelope and I had not been on good terms." She tried to drown out the Miranda warning. "But we put aside our differences this week and decided to play the game we played as kids. We wanted to see who could spot the difference."

Ronnie completed the words from the card and directed her toward the doors.

"Listen to me." She shook him off. "It's been a long time since Penelope and I had fun looking so much alike and trading places. Even our dad sometimes couldn't tell us apart. When I found her body, I panicked. I was supposed to be there first. Someone must have thought Penelope was me. I feared for my life. I didn't know what else to do."

THIRTY-THREE

Thursday dragged until Jane joined me after school. "Have you heard anything?" She plopped onto the corner of my desk. "I can't believe it. Well, I mean, I do, but what a mess. Do you think Mia really killed Penelope?"

I chewed on the inside of my cheek, slowing my retort so I wouldn't say something I'd regret later. I carefully chose my words. "Ronnie has made mistakes before. I'm finding it hard to believe."

Jane's eyes lit up. "But this time, I think he might be right. Mia had every reason to want her sister out of the way. Her husband took her fabulous horse and sold it to Penelope, who paid a hefty sum of money—"

"Supposedly."

"He stole the horse back—"

"Allegedly."

"And died before he could share its location. Suspicious.

Penelope really thought TnL was going to be Foggy Bottom."

"That hasn't been ruled out, just not proven yet. Remember CJ was going to examine the lip tattoo and determine if it could have been altered." I exhaled with defeat. "If it was changed, there is another strike against Mia. She knew about the horse and willingly changed the tattoo."

We liked Mia, and the thought she might be guilty of murder silenced us, but not for long.

"So, if Mia didn't kill her sister, who did?" I could almost see the wheels turning in Jane's mind. "Did you see the way Enzo looked at her?"

"I think he knew who she was, maybe not right away, but I saw them at Santino's, and they had that lovey-dovey look in their eyes."

"I suppose Mia could have killed her sister in aggravation. Penelope had a way of irritating me just by the way she stood against a wall." Jane shrugged. "Or maybe Mia killed her in self-defense?"

"Mia said she found Penelope's body. Penelope was already dead, so she's not claiming self-defense. I should have guessed at her identity when she could remember Patricia's name but still couldn't remember Kindra's. Remember when we met her the first time, she had trouble and referred to Kindra as the 'sister.' I don't know why, but she cannot keep that tiny scrap of information in her head. Jane, you have to see what I found." I opened the file I'd saved regarding Enzo Gyles and clicked through the set of photos from his high school days.

Jane peered closely at the screen. "Well, I'll be. Mia and Enzo were a couple before Penelope and Enzo. I wonder how that happened."

A deep voice sounded from behind us. "Let me tell you how that happened."

Enzo Gyles stood in the doorway with blood shot, red-rimmed eyes, mussed hair, and wrinkled clothes, on the verge of collapse. "I loved Mia. I love her still. I should have said something. I know everything about her, every crease in her face, every expression, every movement. I knew who she was the moment I laid eyes on her but played along with her charade."

Jane hopped off my desk. She grabbed a chair and rolled it behind him. He dropped into it and his head fell into his hands. "Can I get you something to drink?" she said.

His head came up partway. "That would be very kind."

Jane pushed out of the math commons door and returned shortly with a bottle of water.

"Thank you." He cracked the top and swallowed a good portion. His snobbish self-centeredness had melted away. "Mia never would have killed Penelope, but she had plenty of reasons to do so, and I don't know what to do to save her."

I sat dumbfounded. Jane leaned in and said, "We're listening."

"Their mother died unexpectedly when they were toddlers, and their father brought them up the only way he knew how. He thought he knew what was best for his daughters. All outward signs indicated he kept them in line with an iron fist, the same way he cared for his horses. Mia was careful, thoughtful, and tempered her father's harshness. She asked for little, and he denied her nothing. Penelope asked for the moon, and he denied her nothing as well. Spoiled and selfish, Penelope got everything she asked for, including a sister who would do almost anything for her.

"Mia and I dated in high school and the first two years of college. We both had a love of horses and a love of cars, but her father never liked me and gave me an ultimatum. If and when I got a solid job and made good money, enough to take care of his little girl, he wouldn't stand in our way. I had big dreams and told Penelope, making her promise to keep it a surprise, but the surprise was on me. As soon as I took off, their father made that ridiculous patriarchal deal with his daughters. They would never inherit his stable until both were married. Mia absolutely loved the horses and hoped she could rescue them from her father's exacting training, and Penelope absolutely loved the cachet that came with the money and the lifestyle the horses brought with them."

He cleared his throat. "My first successful endeavor gave me enough collateral to purchase Foggy Bottom. I sent the beautiful colt to Mia's father as a peace offering, a promise to uphold my end of the agreement."

Enzo's eyes darkened and his voice took on a hard edge. "Meanwhile, Penelope lied and told Mia that I hadn't want to be saddled with a woman I was tired of. I'd left for good, but, though the horses might suffer longer if they stayed, she'd endure along with Mia if she chose to wait for unrequited love." His eyes flew to the ceiling.

"Mia believed everything Penelope told her; they needed to marry to secure their future interests and protect the horses. As soon as Mia married and was taken care of, Penelope would also wed, and they'd both be set for life. Penelope told Mia she was fortunate to have found Zachary Brown who loved Mia with all his heart." Enzo's voice cracked. "And of course, Penelope helped uphold the lie that their dad only had their best interests at heart."

Enzo's head dropped back. He dragged it forward. "Liam Byrne had a gambling problem but had been working on it, and with Mia's help, he was breaking the habit. Zachary Brown was jealous of any relationship Mia had—human or animal. Weeks later, after they married, Zachary confessed to Penelope he'd dressed like Liam, even used some bills

Liam handled in case more evidence was needed, and placed the bet to get Byrne banned to keep him away from Mia. Penelope supported Zachary. She worked on Liam, asserting the staged production was Mia's idea, and destroying their tenuous relationship. At the same time, Penelope led Mia to believe Liam had succumbed to his problem and she should stay far away from anyone who could damage the reputation of her stable."

"You realize that gives Mia reason to get both Penelope and Liam out of the way, don't you?

Enzo held up one finger and finished the bottle of water. "Mia and Zachary had been married two weeks when I returned the first time. I ..." he stammered. "I couldn't believe it. I tried to sway her, to tell her I never gave up, to make her admit to the mistake she'd made, but divorce was off the table. Her dad made sure of that. Divorce from husband equals divorce from the animals. She had her half of the horses, Foggy Bottom among them. She wouldn't give them up, and I'd left her. She didn't have any reason to trust me. She wouldn't even believe the horse came from me and not her dad." He shook his head. "You should have seen the hurt in her eyes and the victory in her father's and sister's eyes."

"If she discovered the truth, that would be more ammunition against Mia, Mr. Gyles."

He went on as if in another world. "I couldn't stick around and watch someone else live the life I'd envisioned even though I could see Brown only loved what Mia could give him." He snorted. "I found my niche. Business was good. I threw myself into work since I had no hope. Then Penelope sought me out. She comforted me and promised she'd watch out for Mia, but she needed a husband too. I wanted to make sure Mia was happy, even if from afar. I thought I might grow to love Mia's sister. By that time, I had amassed enough money that her dad, uncharacteristically, didn't object, though our prenup clearly spelled out how my money could be used. I could watch out for Mia, but I would not give Penelope a leg up on her sister. I would take care of Penelope, but she'd have to maintain her equine business venture on her own."

The plastic bottle crackled when he twisted it into an hourglass shape. "The only horse hobby I have is supporting Therapy Thoroughbreds. I love helping to provide gentle horses for special needs individuals and have earmarked funds to continue their work long after I'm gone."

"It sounds like you had just as many reasons to kill Penelope."

"I'd take the heat. I'd confess if they'd let me, but I have an iron clad alibi. I was speeding on the backroads of Monongalia County, being followed by Officer Ronnie Christianson. You have to help her." He looked out the doorway with sad eyes. "Liam had been trying to correct the injustice for a long time, but the closest both he and I could get to Mia was her sister."

Our dumbfounded silence was broken when Carlee Bluestone raced into my classroom. "I'm sorry, Ms. Wilk. Dad's finished examining the horse, and you won't believe it."

THIRTY-FOUR

Iburst through the door and found my dad and Ida at the kitchen table, staring at the glasses in front of them, picking at a mouth-watering dinner of meatloaf, fluffy mashed potatoes, and shimmering buttery carrots. The yeasty scent of freshly baked bread filled the air. I inhaled before saying, "TnL is really Foggy Bottom." I tossed my jacket and briefcase on the bench near the door.

"Yes, dear, we heard." Ida inadvertently nudged the handle of a pitcher with her fork, rotating it back and forth. The fork clattered to her untouched plate, and she pushed it to the center, cupped her chin in her hands, and rested her elbows on the table. "They have more irrefutable evidence against Mia Brown."

"Poor CJ." Dad lifted his glass, stared through it, and set it back on the table. "The paperwork for both TnL and Foggy Bottom still names Mia as titleholder, and there is no one to dispute the ownership." He lifted his glass again and tossed the contents back.

"Why poor CJ? What's wrong?"

"No one knows what will happen to the animals with neither sister able to care for them. CJ is returning his charge to Debora and the girls who are doing their best to mind the horses, but they don't know for how long. With Mia under arrest, Ann-Elizabeth no longer has access to funds to pay for the boarding, and Penelope's attorney indicated all her equine assets were bequeathed to her sister, unless, of course, it can be proven Mia committed the murders and benefited from the crime, in which case, they have no idea where the unfortunate horses will end up."

I took in a deep breath. One more strike against Mia. "Maybe Enzo will step in."

Ida sipped her drink and watched me over the top of her glass. She gestured for me to join them. "Would you like one, Katie?"

"One what?"

"A Mint Julep made the old-fashioned way," she said with a smirk. She muddled dark green leaves in a short glass, added ice cubes, and poured the tinted beverage to within a hair's width of the top.

I reached for the lovely, light, minty drink, remembering the one she'd fixed before. The first sip almost brought me to tears the bourbon was so strong, but I barreled through, and the smooth second sip was easier to swallow. Over Ida's shoulder, I saw a ruffly white collar peeking out of the neckline of a maroon satin jacket hanging on the portable clothes rack, cleaned and pressed. "Oh, Ida. Thank you. The kids will be so happy."

My phone buzzed. The screen read "West." I set my glass on the table and accepted the call.

"Hi, Amanda. What's going on?" When Amanda didn't answer right away, I rose from the table and said again, "Hello?"

"Katie, I just can't get a handle on the latest turn of events. Maybe I'm not the right person for this job after all, but I don't see Mia Brown as a murderer, and around here I'm definitely in the minority."

I could maybe have used another sip of the Mint Julep and looked longingly through the condensation dribbling down the side of the ice-cold glass, but said instead, "Why don't you stop over, and we can talk it through?" She didn't have a ready comeback, and I added for good measure, "You can say whatever you want. You don't have to give me specifics about the case."

"Ronnie hasn't held back any of the particulars, so you probably know everything already. I'm sure Ida does," she added with a snicker.

I looked over my shoulder thinking about what Ida said, and although Amanda couldn't hear my answer, I nodded, then said aloud, "We're having Mint Juleps."

She hummed. "I'd like that. See you soon."

As I disconnected, Pete's ring tone started up. "Katie," he said. "What are you doing tonight?"

"Amanda is stopping by for a Mint Julep, a real one—"

"Ida's Juleps?" His voice lowered and he said slowly, "Be careful."

"And to discuss her future," I went on, sipping the cool cocktail.

"If it means anything, she has my backing, but right now Ronnie thinks he has the support he needs, and they're planning on holding a vote of confidence hearing on Monday." That was news to me. "I know he doesn't have the backing of all the city council members, and I hope Amanda speaks to some of the undecided. Assures them. Lets them understand the steps she takes to ascertain guilt or innocence. Dad and I have discussed all the good she's done. She's meticulous, careful, and honest—really good at her job. He'll be there to offer support."

"Having the old chief of police on her side must carry some weight. Do you want to have that conversation with her? She might take it better from you than me."

"And suffer your company? Absolutely."

When I disconnected, I found Ida at the stove already replenishing her store of simple syrup, humming a happy tune. The table was cleared but for a slab of tasty meatloaf I finished off in seconds. I'd just wiped the sweet and spicy sauce from my lips, and the bell rang.

I opened the door to Pete and Amanda. Amanda said, "You didn't tell me you were expecting company. I hate to barge in on a date." Her dark skin took on a rosy glow.

Pete's eyes glinted with mischief and set my heart to pitter-pattering. "Come in, both of you. We need to talk." I grabbed Amanda's hand and dragged her through the doorway before she thought to get away.

She was dressed more approachably, in civilian clothes. Her ebony braid hung down her back and she wore the lightest touch of lipstick. Ida handed her a glass of her mixological perfection and after the polite first sip, Amanda's approval came freely. "This is the real deal."

Pete's small sip and knowing smile indicated he'd tasted Ida's special cocktail before. He set to work immediately convincing Chief West of her value. "Amanda, you need to get ahead of Christianson on this hearing." Her eyes challenged his command. "I've heard it on the best authority—my dad— you are very good at your job. You've done phenomenal work in your first five months, and he's looking for a lifetime of more Amanda West."

One of her eyebrows arched, emphasizing her disbelief. "Lance is a good guy, but—"

"Lance was chief for most of my life, and he was darn good at his job, even if I do say so myself. If he says you're the real deal, I won't dispute it, but you need to talk to the right people."

Dad and I filled glasses and circled the table as Ida and Pete gave Amanda their liege advice, pointing out individuals who might not yet have made up their minds, people who wouldn't be swayed by any characteristic other than being a great lawman or lawwoman.

"Now, tell us why you don't believe Mia Brown killed her sister."

Amanda blew a wisp of hair away from her face. "It's just a feeling."

"I always trust my gut. What do you need us to do?" Pete's intensity acted like a magnet, and the five of us brainstormed for thirty minutes, random thoughts, going down rabbit warrens of ideas and alternatives.

A pounding on our door brought the discussion to a complete stop. Dad opened the door and CJ entered, leaning heavily on his cane, his limp more pronounced than usual.

"I returned TnL to the farm, and now Patricia has taken off with the horse again. This time Carlee and Kindra went with her."

<h1 style="text-align:center">THIRTY-FIVE</h1>

The sky turned blaze orange as the sun dipped below the horizon in the west. Pete glanced in the rearview mirror, keeping track of Amanda's car behind us, as I smoothed the wrinkles on Maverick's forehead. "Debora said Patricia has ridden TnL almost every day since Mia began boarding the horses. She's come to rely on its stability and strength to help steady her life. Debora and Ransam are scouring one of her favorite paths around the farm and into the fields abutting it. We'll search down the maintenance road that runs behind the pond at Halloran's. That's where Maverick and I found her the day CJ came to get TnL."

"Ann-Elizabeth checked on the horses earlier today, and TnL nipped her. She was rather put out. She told Patricia the horse was crazy, and they should cease taking him out, but Patricia said the horse had been cooped up all day and just needed exercise. CJ said Carlee came to help the girls take care of the horses tonight—one more set of eyes and an additional pair of hands. I'm sure they're together, but none of them are answering their phones."

"Patricia turns off her ringer to have a more peaceful ride and not startle the horses. She probably convinced the other two to follow suit."

He snuck a glance my way. "Do you ride?"

"Have I ridden?" The moment of truth had arrived. "The first and only time I rode a horse I …" *What had happened?* "I discovered more about myself than I ever thought possible. It was rather complicated and traumatic. But would I ride again? Possibly at some date in the distant future." For a fleeting moment, I remembered when I sat high in the saddle it had been exhilarating. "How about you?"

"One of my best friends and I competed in barrel racing through six seasons, beginning when we were ten. I loved it, but neither of us owned horses after we turned sixteen." He sounded wistful. "I've relied on friends for my fix ever since. Maybe someday we'll try it together."

I took shallow breaths so I wouldn't give away my abject terror, but he could read my mind. He covered my trembling hands with his, and we followed the road in silence.

I gestured as we passed Severson's shack, and Pete nodded. "He hasn't regained consciousness, but I sure wish he could talk. He might be able to clear up a few questions."

We'd slowly driven another half mile down the bumpy road when Maverick stood on all four paws and barked. He continued howling until Pete rolled far enough ahead his headlights caught three tall horses standing by the side of the road.

I opened the door before the truck came to a full stop, slid from the seat, and dashed next to Carlee. We cast long dark shadows into the night. Caught in the headlight beams,

Kindra and Patricia stood in the scrubby grasses doing their best to calm Demon Dancer who pawed the ground and whinnied. Patricia ran her hand from poll to withers, trying to massage out what might be pain. Maverick circled the six, shepherding his girls and the horses, keeping them safe and together.

CJ came from behind me and tapped Patricia's shoulder. Relief washed the fear and pain from her features when she recognized him. She stiffly climbed to standing, and he took her place, laying a calming hand on the horse's leg, whispering quiet words.

"I kept thinking someone will come for the horses soon. We came out to ride possibly one last time, but Demon Dancer tripped." Patricia wiped tears from her eyes. "I didn't want to continue to ride him, hurt him more, or maybe make him lame. Will he be okay?" Her strident voice pierced the dark. "We've been down this path fifty times and we've never encountered terrain like this."

Pete shined his flashlight over the topography, moving slowly, stopping on a mound of freshly dug dirt. He spoke softly, so the girls wouldn't hear him. "It almost looks like a grave. Something's certainly buried here."

Amanda slipped her phone into her back pocket. "Debora and Ransam will be waiting for you at home."

Patricia took a small step back to give CJ more light and room and staggered, favoring her right leg. Pete tossed me the flashlight and reached her in time to break her fall, gently lowering her to the ground. I spotlighted his workspace as he palpated her foot, ankle, and shin. "Where does it hurt more? Here? Here?"

When she involuntarily jerked away from him, he stopped and examined the joint more closely. "Katie, can you get the first aid kit from my truck? It's on the floor behind the front seat."

I dragged the bulky case across the rough ground and knelt at his side in the scratchy brambles, trying my best to approximate Nurse Susie, but since I couldn't identify what he wanted by the medical terms he used, I ended up waiting for him to point rather than waste time trying to guess.

He finished wrapping her ankle, lifted her, carried her across the field, and swung her up into the truck's cab. "I'm fairly certain it's a bad sprain, but after we check in with Debora, we'll get it x-rayed to make sure. You coming, Katie?"

Kindra gave me a look of such desperation and I waved her close. "You don't need me. I think I'll stay here and help CJ and Amanda, but Kindra should go with you. She can help."

Pete nodded, and Kindra soared into the back seat.

I slammed the door and tapped its side, indicating it was safe for him to pull out. The red tail lights receded, and I turned around. As Amanda returned from her vehicle, the look on her face cemented my feet in place. One spade had materialized in her hand, and she held out another. I grabbed it and followed her lead.

She dug around the soft hill, sifting small amounts of loose dirt, and tossing it off to one side until she hit something hard. With a small brush, she fastidiously unearthed a metal truncheon with a horseshoe crudely attached at one end. If looks could do damage, Amanda's would have lit a bonfire.

She stepped close to me and said in a low voice, "Pete will need to examine this with the wound in mind, but to me, it appears to be the weapon used on Mrs. Gyles' skull. Someone wanted it to look like a horse did it, but Pete knew better."

I held the flashlight, and by the time she carefully slid the club into a large evidence bag and secured it in her trunk, CJ stood and led Demon Dancer out of the ditch and onto the gravel road. "A small strain we will watch. I have given the animal a temporary feel-good fix, but I will need to walk him back to the farm."

Remembering his noticeable hobbling from just a short time ago, I said, "You ride with Amanda. Carlee and I can lead the horses back, right Carlee?"

She beamed. "Right. No back talk, Dad. You do your thing and …" The smile on her face grew tenfold. "I'll do mine."

He harumphed but picked up the helmets and folded his long, powerful body into Amanda's passenger seat.

Carlee wrapped the leads of Demon Dancer and TnL around her hands. I retrieved the reins of the quarter horse. Maverick sauntered near us, staying just outside the beam from the flashlight, and with his escorting, I had no doubt our procession would be seen safely to the Halloran farm.

THIRTY-SIX

Fridays were inherently chaotic. My students used the proximity to the weekend to rationalize all kinds of unusual conduct—more tardies, cutting class, excuses, less concentration and completion of homework—and those days closer to the end of the year threatened to become even more so.

At the start of the day, I prepared my to-do list, organized my lectures so as to utilize the most productive minutes, fashioned my quizzes to be quick and to the point, and added the plethora of May events to my calendar—banquets celebrating the academic and athletic accomplishments culminating at the end of the year; choir, orchestra, and band concerts; and tournaments for spring activities. I'd already received a few graduation party announcements and couldn't wait to revel in their achievements. I also verified the mock trial bus would be on time, bright and early, inspected our supply tubs, restocked the snacks, and arranged to collect the dry cleaning after practice, but I couldn't prepare for every contingency.

Patricia brought up the rear in the straggling line of my last hour students, and with her iridescent smile, I almost didn't notice the crutches. "Ms. Wilk, what fun do you have for us today?"

My mouth gaped, and though I pulled myself together, the class behavior had rapidly devolved to throwing wadded up paper and epithets at one another. Usually, I could quell the bad conduct with a look, but this time I needed to employ my standard cheer whistle. I stuck my thumb and forefinger in my mouth and let out a screeching tweet.

The welcome laughter opened a discussion about expectations, applied mathematics, realistic cost of health care, and concluded with fifteen minutes to complete an assignment. Patricia pulled herself up and hobbled toward the front of the room. She brushed by Justine, who growled, "Watch it—"

Another word followed. Though I couldn't make it out, Kindra's verbal comeback came on within a second. "You take that back you rich, spoiled brat."

Justine slithered out of her seat, lithe and predatory, narrowing her eyes to slits, and as I moved between them, the bell rang. At first, everyone sat perfectly still, waiting to see what might happen. Justine grabbed her pack and spun on her heels, and my students peeled after her, with the exception of Kindra and Patricia.

"What's up, Kindra?" I asked.

She mumbled, "Sorry."

"Who cares if she calls me a klutz," said Patricia.

"I care." Kindra's head jerked up.

"I read lips, remember. She can't say anything to hurt me.

I just pretend I don't hear. It drives everyone crazy. Ask my sister." The laughter bubbled from her, and one corner of Kindra's lip curled up.

Disaster temporarily averted, I asked, "What's the diagnosis, Patricia?"

"Just a sprain, like Dr. Pete said, but it's still pretty swollen, and it's going to hurt for a while. The crutches help me get around. Otherwise, I'm pretty much toast. But don't worry. I'll be there tomorrow."

"Do you think we're ready, Ms. Wilk?" Kindra said, biting her nails. "We'll be up against the best teams in the state."

"You earned your spot. You're ready." I shoved together desks and placed chairs to make the space resemble a court room. "No matter what, it'll be a great experience."

The rest of our mock trial team streamed in, nerves simmering. "What do you say we talk through aspects of the trial instead of acting it all out for the billionth time. That way you'll be fresh tomorrow."

The excitement grew every minute they spent together, and by the time Jane popped in, it sounded like a party. They weren't sure if eliciting sympathy for Patricia would work in their favor or to their detriment, so they brainstormed ways to lessen calling attention to the crutches, discounting decorating them with blinking mini lights.

Jane's phone rang and she put it on speaker.

"Hey gang, are you ready?" Our attorney-coach, Dorene Dvorak, could be relied upon to pump up even the most dour of souls. "I said, are you ready?"

They answered with whoops and whistles, cheers and hoots.

"Great," she said. "Get rest tonight, eat a hearty breakfast, and I'll see you at the meet tomorrow."

We pulled together for our team cheer, gathering in a

circle and throwing our fists to the center. We pumped up and down with each word, "One. Two. Three." And raised our fluttering fingers to the ceiling when we shouted, "EsqChoir."

I finished returning everything to its rightful place when Pete phoned.

"Almost half the locum time has been used up, but I still have the freedom to join you and Maverick in a long walk, a light supper, and a lazy night with no call. What do you say?"

"That sounds wonderful. I'm sorry your first relaxing week has been so hectic. I'm on my way out the door now. Give me twenty minutes, and Maverick and I will be ready to hit the road."

The rocky week had come to a close, and I had hope for the start of a better weekend. I couldn't seem to wipe the smile from my face, until I ran into ZaZa. "You know they're going to get crushed tomorrow. You have prepared them, haven't you?"

"Actually," I said, "although they might not come away champions, they're already winners. I don't know why you have to be so negative."

"I'm just realistic. One never knows what the future will bring, does one? *C'est la vie, n'est pas?*"

It's a good thing I hadn't time to amp up my happy gene yet. That was the same line she used when she heard about Charles and me getting together. It quashed a tiny speck of the promising feelings I had for a good weekend. She spun on her sky-high heels and clip-clopped out of the math commons, sounding a lot like Demon Dancer.

I stopped at the cleaners and couldn't praise them enough. Only one of the jackets still wore the telltale stain, but they had to point it out. Under a very bright light. And magnifying glass. Aiming with a hatpin. No one else would find it.

"Thank you. You don't know what this will mean to the

kids. How much do I owe you?"

"Pshaw. It's free. We'd do anything for Ida. She's the best. She supported our Joey when all he wanted to do was paint. She even provided supplies when we couldn't afford them. We owe her big time, and we'll never be able to pay her back. I wish all teachers were half as thoughtful and understanding." She helped me hang the clothes on the hooks in my car and gave me a mischievous grin. "She has hope for you too."

"That's a lot to live up to."

By the time I left the cleaners, my grin was back in place. All was right with the world.

Pete stationed his truck on the street outside Ida's and leapt from his vehicle as I pulled in the drive. I clattered up the steps and met Maverick who held the leash in his mouth, giving me about thirty seconds to get ready for our constitutional before his displeasure would rise to the forefront. Pete snapped on the lead, and we were off, meandering through the wildlife protection area.

Walking quietly side-by-side allowed me to recharge my personal battery because we didn't have to fill every second with idle banter and mundane chit-chat. We could just be. Having decided to dine at Thai Fyre, mostly because Santino's was closed for a private party and there weren't too many other choices, we returned Maverick to the house and headed downtown.

The after-work crunch mob had finished eating supper, and we beat the dining crowd. We slipped into a booth near the front windows, scarcely noticing the scattered pockets of patrons dotting the usually bustling rendezvous. Gazing at Pete's scrumptious eyes made me hungry for dessert first, but I held out and ordered my next two favorites—hot jasmine tea and Pad Thai.

The smile that launched a thousand heart palpitations sat

across from me, and I chuckled at Pete's next words. "Are you ready for tomorrow?"

"You're not the first to ask that question today." I thought for a moment and a smile inched its way across my face. "Jane and I don't do much, but Dorene is the greatest mentor we could have asked for. She—"

A chair clattered to the floor at a table on the other side of the room. Enzo Gyles leaned back in his chair, hands raised in surrender, looking up at a dark-haired woman. She jammed her finger at him a few times. "Admit it. It was you. How could you?" She threw down a napkin and stormed from the restaurant, but I couldn't see her face.

Before I could ask Pete if he recognized the woman or what Enzo could have admitted to, his phone buzzed. "It's Dad," he said, quizzically. "Excuse me." He rose from the table and stood in an alcove near the kitchen, speaking animatedly, combing his fingers through his thick mane. I sighed as I imagined tangling the tousled curls around my own fingers.

I shook off the reverie and checked out the table where Enzo had been. He left before I was able to find out more, but a presence at the bar caught my eye. Tony Relando leaned against the rail. One cowboy boot dangled on the rung of the chair next to him, and he tipped a glass of amber liquid my way. His smug smile gave me the creeps, but I nodded in response and wondered what made people turn out the way they did.

His eyes shifted to the entry and a shadow dropped over his face like a veil.

THIRTY-SEVEN

I followed Relando's slitted eyes to the doorway and cocked my head. I didn't want to draw attention to myself so without moving a muscle, I watched as Justine marched assuredly across the restaurant and halted in front of him. Although all I could hear was an angry sizzle, her body language told much of the story. Every sharp movement emphasized her fury, from the set of her jaw and the carriage of her shoulders to the stamp of her foot and the jerk of her head.

I watched her hostility grow, particularly when the adult in the dialog appeared to disregard those feelings. Relando's facial expression morphed from laughter and jeers to weightiness and ire, and Justine's feelings intensified. I wondered how she knew him.

Justine needed support. Pete remained locked in a deep conversation with Lance, so I had time to run interference. I slid back my chair and gathered my wits to confront the scary guy.

"Sit down, Justine," Relando ordered. He pointed to the stool next to him. She shook her head violently.

"Justine," I said breezily, approaching the bar all friendly-like, "I thought that was you."

She whirled on me with malice in her eyes. And then they softened a touch. "Ms. Wilk. What are you doing here?"

"Having a delightful, delectable supper with my ..." Did I really want to share my love life right now? "... friend. This is the best Thai restaurant in the entire city of Columbia."

"It's the only Thai restaurant in the entire county," said Relando. He took a long swig from his tall glass, finishing the beverage, and waved a finger at his server to deliver another.

I ignored him. "I highly recommend the Chicken Pad Thai. It's my fave. And I always finish with a dessert. Their sweets are to die for." Probably not the best choice of words given the most recent happenings, but I had to make certain she was safe. "What are *you* doing here?"

Her animosity came back full force, and she seethed. "I'm making my argument to get out of this hole in the wall and go home." She glared at Tony Relando. "Ms. Wilk, meet my deadbeat dad."

My head turned, facing one and then the other.

"Yeah. Sometimes I find it hard to believe too," said Relando. "Fortunate for her she takes after her mother."

"Tony," Justine said, dripping with sarcasm. "I can't do this anymore, and you can't make me. I'm not good at being anyone's toady. Do your own dirty work."

"Calm down, my little Rusty Justy." Relando reached out to touch her shoulder, but she shrugged him off. "I just want what's best for you."

"You want what's best for you, you mean. And don't call

me Justy. I'm not a child, and you haven't so much as called on my birthday for years. Suddenly you're all concerned about my welfare, my living in Chicago, and my plans for the future. Well, my immediate plans are to leave here."

"Your mom needed a break," he said as if it was a foregone conclusion.

"You mean you paid her. I don't know which of you is worse. I called Gram."

"I need you, Justy … Justine."

"You know, it's a good thing I can vouch for you being on the phone and driving when that lady died. The police chief was checking alibis." Tears pooled in her vivid eyes. "You only want me to do your dirty work so you can get what you want, like always. I won't do it anymore." The tears spilled down her cheeks. "I can't."

Her sorrow filled eyes met mine. "Sorry, Ms. Wilk." She brushed past Pete as she ran from the restaurant.

"She's your daughter? Whatever could you expect her to do that would cause that much angst?"

I'll give him credit. He was a good actor. He bowed his head and twirled the glass in front of him. "I thought having my daughter make friends with the Hallorans might make it easier for me to talk to Penelope's sister."

"You wanted to use her to get close to the horses, but she didn't want to help you. That's why she was so mean to Patricia and Kindra. You're a despicable piece of—"

A warm protective hand braced my shoulder. "Let's go, Katie. Whatever you say won't make any impact whatsoever on this paragon of virtue." Pete's fingers caressed my arm as he steered me to our table and my fried banana dessert. "I never liked that guy. Do you want to tell me about it?'

I brought my clenched fists to my forehead, warding off the headache threatening to close in from just outside my line of vision. When I dropped my hands in my lap, the explanation exploded. "The young lady, Justine, is a new student in one of my classes, and it turns out, Tony Relando is her dad. He was using her, I expect, to help him get his hands on TnL. That's why he came to Columbia, and that's why he brought her here too." I stuck my spoon in the ice cream. "She's been simply awful, discontented with everyone and everything in Columbia." I licked my spoon and swallowed the sweet goodness. "She singled out Patricia and Kindra Halloran, but I think she was doing everything in her power to thwart his nefarious plans, whatever they might be. Why would her dad do that to her?"

"Is there anything we can do?"

"It sounded like her mom won't be there for her right now either. But she has someone she calls Gram. I'm assuming that's her grandmother. She needs her. I'll talk to Justine."

"We can help her if she wants."

My spoon clattered in an empty bowl, and I wondered what happened to the ice cream. "What's up with your dad? Lance is doing well, isn't he?"

If possible, Pete's eyes went from concerned to even more concerned. "Dad's health hasn't been this good in months, and he's been discussing the case with Amanda. She believes Ronnie's reckless disregard for accuracy in lieu of checking and double-checking clues, canvassing witnesses, and exploring the truth and trying to secure the job of Chief of Police is blinding him, hogtying him to the easiest answer."

"Is he checking out the statement by the witness who saw two people at the railroad? Or Enzo's alibi?"

"Ronnie checking? No. Amanda? Yes." He puckered his lips.

"What? What else is going on?"

"Dad also said he thinks Ronnie might have the number

of votes he needs to oust Amanda at Monday's meeting. Some of the undecided want a smooth-running department and any dissent is seen as a failure. Having Amanda gone might seem like an easy fix, but the truth should win out. In this case, although everything points to Mia Brown as the perpetrator, if Amanda thinks more suspects need to be addressed in the murders of Penelope Gyles and Liam Byrne and the attack on Ole Severson, I'm with her. If Ronnie is sheriff, we might not ever find the truth."

Pete had thoughtfully placed a takeout order for my mock trial tournament lunch and Dad's noon repast. He paid the bill, and we strolled to his truck, both so deep in thought when the apparition named Justine materialized in front of us, I nearly took off running, but Pete steadied me.

"Justine. Are you all right?" Dumb question. Of course, she wasn't all right. She gnawed on her lower lip and swiped at her puffy eyes. "What's wrong? What can I do?"

"Gram put some money on my debit card. I'm getting out of Dodge. That's Columbia to you." A hint of the tough Justine glinted in her eyes. She hiked the strap of a carryall up on her shoulder. "Would you apologize to Patricia and Kindra for me? Gram said I need to do that. I tell Gram everything, and we decided more bad stuff happened here in the last two weeks than happened in Hinsdale in the last two years." My jaw dropped. "Kidding." Her calculated gaze almost colored with amusement. "Seriously, Ms. Wilk, can you be any less transparent?"

Pete waited for her to take a breath. "Is there anything you need?"

"No. Thank you. I've stayed with Gram before. She knows what to do. I just need to get there." She held up her phone, displaying a bus ticket.

Pete's smile stripped away her defenses. He pointed his

key fob, and his truck chirped. "I think we can help out there. Hop in. We'll give you a ride to the station."

As we settled into the seats and belt buckles clicked, I said, "You don't have to leave, you know. The school would do anything it can for you. So would I."

Her reflection in the rearview mirror pulsed under the streetlamps. "No. That's okay. I've got a lot to figure out. But thanks anyway."

"You're always welcome in Columbia."

"Yeah. I couldn't ruffle Patricia's feathers no matter what I tried, but it was fun to see her sister in action."

The bright lights of the bus station acted like a beacon, calling all travelers.

"Do you want us to wait with you?"

She almost smiled. "No. I've got this. See him?" She pointed to the security guard at the door. "He's my new best friend, so don't worry about me, but Ms. Wilk, this place is crazy. Watch. Your. Back."

THIRTY-EIGHT

Although our departure time was dark-thirty, the kids came prepared and bounded up the steps in high spirits, ready to take on the world, or at least that part of it that would host the best high school lawyers in the state. If they won the first three duals, they would compete in the finals—a dream come true.

"What do you have in that duffle bag?" I asked as Carlee banged first the door, then the railing, and lastly my shoulder.

"Sorry. We're a little overloaded." She dragged the case down the aisle, followed by Galen. "Lorelei sent us an up-to-date screenshot of the weather app this morning. She suggested we come prepared."

"Of course, she did," said Brock as proud as a peacock.

The look Lorelei gave him would have frozen a streaking meteor in the sky, but Brock continued to show his pride.

Carlee spoke as if she wasn't in the middle of a growing

tiff. "With raincoats, umbrellas, sweaters, hair dryers, brushes, makeup—"

"Right," Felipe kidded, batting his long, dark eyelashes.

"Everything we might need for the unpredictable *weekend weather*. We packed our performance clothes in case we have to walk in the rain. This way, after we qualify for the finals, and if we finish in time, we can also get partially ready for the Grand March." She blushed. "Just in case we make it that far."

"You will." Jane paged through the tournament manual. "If the schedule runs on time, and this isn't their first rodeo, you know, we should definitely finish and return with seconds to spare. I hope we do. I'd love to see you all spruced up and ready for a night of fun. But right now ..." She tucked the papers back into her satchel and nestled deep into the plastic seat. "I'm going to try to take a nap. We have a two-hour bus ride ahead of us." She pulled her jacket tighter, crossed her arms, and closed her eyes.

Justine's words had kept me up half the night. Why would I need to watch my back? I couldn't sleep. Instead, I read up on the most famous racehorse, Secretariat, record holder for all three races in the Triple Crown, most winning jockeys, Eddie Arcaro and Bill Hartack, with five victories each, and most successful trainers, Bob Baffert and Ben Jones, with six successful Thoroughbreds apiece. I read about doping horses, high scoring bets, and tried unsuccessfully to tamp down thoughts of an innocent Mia Brown.

Two hours and fifteen minutes later, we roused the sleepers, passed through the security checkpoint, registered for the tournament, took over our assigned conference room, changed into our mock trial duds, polished shoes, filled water bottles, unpacked lunch bags, and theoretically sharpened our swords by checking our writing utensils.

Dorene breezed through the door, all business, in a three-piece, navy pin-striped suit and matching pumps. She tossed back her head of short hair, flashed blood-red nails, curled her fingers to draw the kids together, and said as she gripped her hand in a tight fist, "Let's get this done." Her contagious conviction brought a smile to even the most nervous of us.

Our jittery first opponent did an adequate job, and against most other competitors, they'd have fared well, but it was obvious from the onset of Lorelei's well-rehearsed introduction, Columbia had done its homework.

She nodded as she addressed the room. "Good morning, Your Honor, members of the jury, opposing counsel, members of the gallery. My name is Lorelei Calder. I am lead counsel for the plaintiff. I'll be conducting the direct examination of Maggie Murphy, wife of twenty-three-year-old victim, Connor Robert Mitchell. She is claiming negligence by the White Star Line in its operation of the R.M.S. *Titanic* and is seeking damages for breach of duty of care and causation of fatal injuries, having suffered tragic loss of life, forfeiture of wages, incomparable pain, and unparalleled mental anguish. I will cross-examine forty-one-year-old Reginald Robinson Lee, the sole surviving lookout aboard the luxury passenger ship, and I will summarize our case-in-chief at our closing statement. Thank you." She held out her hands. "Let me introduce my co-counsel."

After each student had described his or her job as attorney or witness in the case, the judge entertained pre-trial motions. The defense tried a relatively new tactic, requesting the statement of one of the plaintiff's witnesses be disallowed due to her star status around the globe.

"Everyone in the world has heard of the unsinkable Molly Brown," the young man argued. "There is no way to get an unbiased jury pool of her peers, and therefore we beseech the court to have any evidence she might give excluded."

Kindra argued in favor of retaining our witness, citing the excessive recognition as futuristic, happening in our current time, not reflecting the time of the court proceedings. "Margaret Brown, better known as Molly Brown, has a first-hand attestation of the occurrences of the day. Before the events of April 14, 1912, she was but a socialite, however, her evidence is crucial and her truthfulness, impeccable."

The court denied the defense counsel's request. Kindra reveled in her success.

That trial progressed even better from then on, and we moved to the quarter-final round.

During the first trial, Maggie Murphy, aka Patricia Halloran, had time to move unassisted to the witness box, sliding her hand along the railing opposite the jury. But the greater distance in the second trial prohibited that successful maneuver. As unobtrusively as possible, she navigated the room with only one crutch. It apparently didn't make much of a difference. The announcement after lunch informed us we'd edged into the top four.

We never knew what bizarre but possibly truthful answer Felipe would give in his role as Reginald Lee. Our consummate actor with years, literally three, under his belt, never knew what words would leave his lips either. Felipe's answers stumped the semi-final plaintiff attorney for a moment, and the noticeable time taken before making an objection showed indecision. The objection was sustained, but it was difficult to unhear Felipe's comment and impossible to unsee the lawyer's flustered moments.

At the conclusion of our third head-to-head, but before the results were posted, Lorelei's confidence waned.

"We are so much more in control when we're the plaintiff.

This time I just couldn't get a feel for the outcome." She chewed on her lip for a split second then rounded up her teammates and said, "If I don't get to make this pronouncement any other time, I want you all to know how much fun I've had and how much I've learned from all of you." Her teary eyes surprised even Brock. "You're the absolute best."

She was our granite. While we waited for results, the entire group sat in our ready room, thoughtful and subdued.

THIRTY-NINE

Some of our students needed a breather when the wait stretched on interminably. Jane and I split the duties. She declared she'd rather not brave the drizzle, so I grabbed a granola bar for my lunch-on-the-go, took my four charges, and exited the building, stepping briskly, trying to dodge the sporadic raindrops.

Carlee and I brought up the rear. She tore off a section of a peanut butter and jelly sandwich and stuffed it into her mouth, and I regretted not snagging something more nourishing. From under the hood of a plastic poncho, she said, "I wish TnL and Demon Dancer could stay in Columbia, but if Mia Brown is found guilty, Dad said whoever gets custody is going to move the horses. Her secretary wants control of the animals, citing her past work with them, and her understanding of the expectations of each. Patricia will be crushed, of course. She talks to TnL as if he's a real person."

"She has her friends now. The horse may be easier to talk to but certainly not the only one." I smiled.

"Do you think she did it?" She took another big bite.

"Do you mean, do I think Mia Brown is guilty? I really don't know."

She polished off her salty sweet lunch. We hugged the curb as an ambulance passed, siren wailing and lights flashing, and we picked up our pace, burning off a little extra energy.

Before reentering the building, I tossed my trash—the remaining tasteless dried-up bar in its wrapper, vigorously shook water from my hood, and meticulously wiped the bottom of my shoes, biding my time and preparing words of consolation if we hadn't survived the grueling third case. But according to the tournament bracket hanging in the entry, the decision still hung in the balance.

As I neared our room, I heard raised voices and dashed inside to find Kindra nose-to-nose with Justine.

"I said stay away from my sister."

"Sheesh. I just wanted to apologize. My gram says I owe you an explanation."

"What's going on?" I said calmly as I stepped between them.

"She thinks she can waltz right in, say she's sorry, and do anything she wants, and I for one am not going to let her get away with it." Kindra trembled with fury, reaching around me to shake her fist.

Lorelei's fingers locked onto Kindra's elbow, and Brock stood poised to either add his support or act as a deterrent.

Justine gazed at her feet. "I didn't want you to like me when my dad wanted me to get on your good side. He's always scheming, trying to manipulate circumstances in his favor. I just didn't know what he planned to do." She looked up at Kindra. "I still don't, but Gram is helping me figure things out, and she said what I need to do first is tell you I'm sorry for the way I behaved."

"How did you find us?" asked Lorelei.

"In my life, you have to pay attention to your surroundings and be prepared for any contingency. I listened to the announcements and sat in the math commons during your last practice. You're pretty good. And, by the way, the state tournament information is plastered all over social media and Minnesota news, so anybody can find out if they want to know."

"I assumed your gram lived in Chicago. Is she here?" I looked around the room and only saw familiar faces.

"Gram has an apartment in Inver Grove Heights. She met me at the bus station this morning, and we had a long talk. I'll turn eighteen in September and graduate next year. She said she could put up with me as long as I follow her rules. I've already lived with her in the past so we shouldn't need to involve any legal beagles with all their red tape. Whether you like it or not, Gram and I are going to be sitting in the audience, front and center, cheering for you."

"I'd like to meet your gram." Kindra relaxed her shoulders, and Lorelei released her arm. "Just don't be a jerk again."

Justine crossed her heart, spit in her palm, and extended that hand to Kindra who never even questioned returning the gesture.

Patricia sauntered in as if she'd waited outside the door for just the right moment. "I'm glad that's settled." She signed, "friend" and Kindra interpreted. Justine copied the sign and wished them luck.

I shook my head, gazing at these young adults. There were moments when I second-guessed what I could offer them, but I loved my job.

The edginess had been replaced with concern for a team

member, and before the nervousness reared its ugly head again, Felipe stuck his head in the doorway. "They're posting the semi-final results."

Everyone watched Lorelei to see what they should do. She shrugged and said, "It's now or never."

En masse, my students traipsed after her and slowly approached the registration desk. Brock's hand rested on her shoulder while her eyes followed the lines down the master list posted on the wall. After a few groans, members of another team peeled away, and our kids, more worried about Lorelei, watched for her reaction. When Brock squeezed her shoulder, all eyes stared at her face. It was a mask, but only because she had them eating out of her hand. As a smile snaked its way across her lips, they erupted in delight.

"We have one more trial to prepare. Let's go see what Ms. Dvorak has to tell us," she said in a light and airy tone, as if it was just another day at the courthouse. She turned, and the kids paraded back to our room for a last-minute pep talk from our marvelous attorney coach.

The head of the welcoming committee beckoned me to his table. "I'm sorry to inform you, Dorene Dvorak had an adverse reaction to something she ate." He leaned close and whispered. "Broke out in hives and it became a bit difficult for her to breathe, so we called an ambulance. The EMTs gave her a shot from an EPI pen. They think she'll be fine, but they didn't want to release her so she's under observation. She said to tell your kids, if they got into the finals, 'Go get them.'"

My stomach clenched. "I will. Is there anything else you need from us? Will this count against us?"

"Not at the state level. All the judges are ... well, acting judges. Attorneys are needed for the kids, but we don't use them like they do at some meets."

"Thank you." I swallowed hard, contemplating the difficult job I'd have of informing the kids.

The room was awash with excitement, Jane re-tying ties and finger-pressing jacket pleats, Lorelei pacing, her lips moving a mile a minute, Galen guzzling water from a bottle, and Felipe jumping up and down. I hated to put a damper on their excitement, but the decision was taken from me.

FORTY

"Ms. Wilk, where's the number one attorney in the state? Does she know yet?" Brock asked, standing with his neck stretched out while Jane knotted his tie.

"She doesn't know, and we might have to call her. You know that ambulance that passed us? Ms. Dvorak was in it." All movement halted. "She ate something that didn't agree with her, but the EMTs assured the host she would be fine. She's at the hospital under observation."

Lorelei said, "If she'll be okay, can we call her? We have to tell her."

At the same time, Kindra dropped a bill as if it were toxic. "Ms. Dvorak ate *your* lunch, Ms. Wilk. She left this ten in its place for you to buy some food at the cafeteria."

She ate *my* lunch?

Jane acted fast, drawing her phone like a revolver and punching in Dorene's number. Dorene answered the video call after the first ring. She wore a drab green gown, and her hair had a spikey unkempt look. "Hey, kids. I'm so sorry. I don't know what happened, but they won't let me out for fear I'll sue them, and I'd win. I might sue them anyway for false imprisonment, but that one might not fly. Well? What's the news?"

Everyone wanted to talk at once.

She gave one giant, "Quiet." And they listened. "I love you all, and I assume your excitement means you've made it to the finals. I always knew you would. Now for the nitty gritty."

For the next five minutes, she gave a precise and thorough pep talk to each of our competitors. While she spoke to the students, I called Dad. When he didn't answer I called Ida. She picked up with a cheery, "Hey ho. How's the meet?"

"Great, Ida. Um. Dad isn't answering. Do you know where he is?"

She lowered her voice. "He probably forgot his phone in his room again. He's right here. We ate lunch together, and he's helping me with dishes."

"How's he feeling?"

"Same old grumpy self." Her tone became more serious. "Why, Katie?"

"Can I talk to him?"

After sounds of swishing and scraping and a little laughing, the phone changed hands and Dad said, "Hi, darlin'."

"Dad, you really should hang on to your phone." He laughed. "Seriously, I wanted to warn you. Something might have gone bad in your Pad Thai. Dorene Dvorak ate my lunch and had some issues. They took her to the hospital. I grabbed the paper bag …" I stared at the bag with my name written on the front in a handwriting I didn't recognize. I saw a sack in the fridge and grabbed it this morning on my way out. Could it go bad overnight, or did it have help?

"Katie? You there?"

"Yes, Dad. I'm here."

"Sorry I missed you this morning. You were leaving too early for me to get up, but I hope you do well today."

"Can you ask Ida if she's heard anything about food from Thai Fyre causing illness? Either way, you might want to toss the takeout we brought." I heard a shuffle and muffled voices.

"Nope. Never. But if you think it's not good, I'll get rid of it. And while you're on, next time you're to give Ida a heads up. She'll make special bars for the kids."

"Thanks, and I wanted you to know we made it to the finals. Keep your fingers crossed."

As I pocketed my phone, I wondered if and how someone could have tampered with my food. No sooner had I shaken the thought out of my head, and it crept back in. This room was open all morning. Anyone could've walked in. Justine did.

But why my lunch?

Dorene had a few final words of advice for the kids. "There is nothing more I can teach you. You're on your own, but you are so ready. Call me on your way home, and we'll figure out how we're going to celebrate your victory."

"Our victory," Galen said with the flicker of a smile on his face and dancing eyebrows.

"Hey kids, may I have a quiet word with your coach?"

"Good luck, team," she said.

I took her off speakerphone. "Dorene, I think you should be thoroughly examined."

"Katie, I absolutely detest hospitals."

"The lunch you ate—my lunch. There's something weird about it."

I didn't hear a sound. "Dorene?"

"Yes." Her voice was low and gravelly.

"I think you might have been poisoned."

She waited a few seconds before saying, "I'll take care on my end. Katie, watch yourself. If that lunch, which, by the way, was awful—I threw half of it away—was planted for you, someone is not kidding around."

It only took a minute of thoughtful reverie for Jane to rev up our students and get them back on track. She continued her housekeeping duties, reminding them to speak clearly, stand tall, make eye contact, and believe in themselves.

Patricia hobbled close and nudged me. I smiled, and she nudged again, discreetly holding her phone so I could read the screen. Our opponent had competed at the state mock trial tournament for seven years and won the last three meets. She slid the display to a photo of a relatively handsome, dark-haired young man raising a trophy the size of Jane. What I didn't like was the look of superiority on his face—a sneer of contempt for other kids.

"We're bringing him down, Ms. Wilk. No fear." She swiped the screen to black and thumped to the table to collect what she needed.

The students, my kids, secured ties and straightened hems, neatly squared up the edges of the stacked notebooks they carried, and took one more swig from their water bottles.

I waved them together for my last bit of inspiration. "People, no holds barred. If you have a crazy idea, this is your last shot. It may work. It may not. But have faith in your ability and have a great time doing your thing today because you've earned it." I threw my fist out and they joined me in our chant. "One. Two. Three. EsqChoir!"

Brock threaded his fingers through Lorelei's, and she glanced at him with a shy smile. She hung on though, as the team filed out of the conference room with the pair in the lead, marching tall and quite professional. There would be no second chance. This was it. They had to bring their A game. But they'd shown their winning colors all year by deep diving into history, listening to Dorene, giving up free time to practice mock trial, and supporting each other under all sorts of circumstances. I nearly burst with pride.

Jane pulled the door closed behind us. She wrapped her arm around my waist and squeezed with just enough support to liberate the breath I hadn't yet released. "They're going to do great. And if not ..." She shrugged and dropped her arm. "It's been a real trip, and I'm glad we made it together."

We sat in the gallery, and I imagined every emotion I read in Jane's face was reflected in my own as the case evolved. When one of Patricia's crutches knocked a table leg and the opposing counsel hopped up to pretend concern, Jane brought her knuckle up to her face, and I held my own in place on my lap. She stretched the kinks out of her neck when Lorelei finished the direct examination and leaned forward to listen to the cross, but Patricia was nonplussed.

Carlee as our Molly Brown was boisterous, a little loud, full of righteous indignation, supportive of survivors, but not rattled in the least by any question posed.

But the clincher, in my view, was Arthur Henry Rostron, captain of the famed ship, *Carpathia*.

"Please, Captain Rostron, tell us how the events progressed."

"On the night of April 14, 1912, I was awakened when our wireless operator told me—"

Opposing counsel jumped to her feet. She'd been waiting to pounce. "Objection. Hearsay."

However, Galen was at the helm of the direct examination and countered immediately with a cool head. "The statement is not being offered to prove the facts asserted, only that Captain Rostron had a response."

"Objection overruled. You may continue."

"I learned of the *Titanic's* distress signal and set course, negotiating through fifty-eight nautical miles of ice fields and praying we'd reach the ship in time. The *Carpathia* rescued only seven hundred twelve survivors and returned to New York where the full horror of the event was revealed." Felipe's succinct direct testimony caught the defense off guard.

She rose again, more slowly, prepared but not expecting to be examining the witness yet. She attempted to gain ground by disconcerting Felipe with random but not altogether peripheral questions. Unfortunately for her, as a method actor, Felipe knew Rostron's birthdate and place of birth, experience before the tragedy, length of service, and even his wife's name, information not provided in the trial transcripts but true, nonetheless. History was Jane's bailiwick and details were mine.

"And everything you've told us is above board."

Felipe sat back. His eyes brightened. He saw a pun. "Everything I've said is anchored in the truth."

FORTY-ONE

We won. My intelligent, empathetic, kind, enthusiastic, thoughtful, strong kids won the state tournament, and we would represent Minnesota at the National High School Mock Trial competition slated for early June in Atlanta. Our first call had gone to Dorene, and although we had to leave a voicemail, I'm sure she'd be ecstatic. Jane called her dad, and his elated voice boomed throughout the auditorium and was echoed by a thunderstorm raging outside.

But happiness acted as its own umbrella. Even squeezing raindrops through their hair and peeling sodden fabric plastered to their chilled arms as they hopped onto the bus, the kids' smiles blazed across their faces as they fired up their devices and sent messages to family and friends.

News spread like wildfire. Phones rang with congratulatory calls, buzzed with excited emails, and dinged with laudatory texts. And to top it off, our teammates who chose prom rather than taking a wild stab at the Saturday competition only shared delighted celebratory accolades.

I hadn't made any contingency plans. I maybe hadn't really thought we could win, so I hadn't even begun to investigate how we'd get across country but get there we would. Fortunately, Jane's dad promised to subsidize any financial obligations.

Amid pride ringing in my ears, animated chatter, myriad phone sounds, the back-and-forth thwack of the windshield wipers, and water splatting the sides of the bus, I almost missed a call from Pete. "They won," I answered breathless.

"Did you really have any doubt? Don't tell them yet, but Dorene and I are placing a half-page ad in the *Columbia Sentinel* to give the kids their due."

"You've talked to her then. How is she?"

"She wanted a few words of medical advice from a friend in the business. She's feeling better already. She reacted to noodles she'd nibbled laced with betamethasone—your noodles."

I blinked. "Jane said that drug was used in a horse doping scandal."

"It's not likely to have been an accidental exposure. I've told Amanda. Let her do her job, Katie."

I mumbled my answer.

"Dorene'll be fine, but tell Jane, and watch yourselves." I could feel the reprimand that didn't come. "And can you send me a nice photo from the meet?"

I thought my students were brilliant, and Dorene Dvorak, their attorney-coach, was the icing on the cake. Jane and I provided transportation, snacks, practice space and time, historical data, and our reasonable observations. Dorene gave them perspective, insight, critical formulae, correct legal procedures, comprehensive answers, and unlimited support.

"I have pics of the team on stage receiving their trophy. That piece of hardware is almost as tall as Ida." I chose three shots and sent the message.

"Got them." I heard tapping over the phone line. "Done."

"Are you going to the Grand March?"

"Already here. Last year, two young women decided not to eat the day of prom and fainted as they passed through the auditorium during their introduction. This year, I volunteered as doctor-in-residence, just in case. I'll be backstage."

"I'll have my trusty canine companion in tow, so we'll meet you after the Grand March."

"Good. Afterward, we'll go out for a celebratory cocktail. Congrats, again." With a sloppy grin on my face, I slipped the phone into my bag.

Although they'd missed out on a swanky dinner, our swift ride home afforded Lorelei and Brock, Carlee and Galen, and Kindra and her new beau time to dry off and change, and still make their spectacular entrance at the Grand March. Their teammates assured them they'd be there with catcalls and whistles. They couldn't wait to behold the boys out of their sweats and ill-fitting suits and into rented tuxedos and Lorelei wearing makeup for fun.

By the time I dropped Jane at her apartment so she could attend the Grand March with Drew, the rain had lightened to a fine mist. I grabbed a rain poncho and picked up Maverick.

Late to arrive, we parked as close as possible but still at the end of the long line of cars. Standing under Drew's golf umbrella, we observed prom attendees queued up under an extended narrow blue awning, dressed in their finery, strutting down the royal blue carpet, giggling, and posing for photos as the endless line of couples funneled forward. Our kids joined the throng near the end, but nothing could dim their elated grins.

"It's going to be another thirty minutes before they're through," Jane said. She huddled under Drew's arm for warmth.

I glanced around and found all my students but one. "Have you seen Patricia?"

"Not yet," Jane said. "She told Kindra she wouldn't miss the Grand March, but she needed to check on the horses. Felipe gave her a ride home."

I spotted Felipe, standing with a band of sophomore brothers making plans for their own prom initiation next year, laughing and enjoying the spectacle.

"Katie?" Jane said, but I'd quickly passed into the massive swarm of observers, dragging Maverick, and I didn't hear anything else she might have said.

Felipe's smile faded when he saw the look on my face. "What's wrong, Ms. Wilk? You don't look so good. Did they take away our first place?"

"No, nothing like that. Felipe, where's Patricia?"

"I gave her a ride home and—"

"Thank goodness. Where's she now?"

"She should be here shortly."

"She didn't come back with you?"

"No. The lady wanted to say goodbye to the horses before she left town, and she said she'd make sure Patricia got back. Patricia told me I could leave."

I concentrated. Penelope was dead and Mia was in jail. Who would want to say goodbye?

"Did I do something wrong?"

"No, Felipe, you did nothing wrong," I said as I turned. I purposely made my feet step calmly, but being almost last to arrive, I'd parked a distance from the entry door, and trotting didn't look too worrying. I slid into the driver's seat and Maverick bounded over me to the passenger side. With trembling fingers, I inserted the key and maneuvered the car toward Halloran's. I didn't want Patricia to miss her sister's date, but I didn't trust her to some woman. I had a bad feeling, and I'd learned to trust my gut.

If the police hadn't been assigned to direct traffic for the stream of cars at the high school, I'm sure one of them would have pulled me over. I couldn't jettison the feeling of alarm and maybe drove a bit over the speed limit. Usually, Maverick covered the back seat, wrapped in a circle, but tonight he stood up front on all fours, head erect, eyes alert until we passed the pond.

Apart from the few dim rays from the yard light set up on a pole behind the utility barn, the farm site stood in darkness. It felt vacant. Debora and Ransam would be attending the Grand March, but where was Patricia?

I pulled in around the side of the house and leashed Maverick. We trudged up the steps and tried the bell. No answer. From there, I canvassed the other buildings, watching for movement, listening for sounds, and flashing my phone light. She wouldn't hear me, but she might see me.

Maverick pulled the lead taut, and we stopped. I heard stomping followed by horses whinnying, and Maverick took a few quick steps toward the horse barn. "Maverick," I hissed. He stopped. His shoulders hunched, and he employed a stealth I'd only witnessed in nature films. He was the embodiment of a panther—black, silent, and lethal.

I flashed my hand-held light, holding Maverick motionless so I could hear any other sound, but there wasn't one. I gave him the hand signal to go ahead.

He moved through the wet grass with the assuredness of a veteran searcher, one paw forward at a time, stopping to sniff the air redolent with spring scent. He ignored the house and the outbuildings and led me to the ravaged horse barn. I could still hear the whinnying, but it originated in the secondary shelter. I used all my strength to redirect my dog, but my shoes could not find purchase and I skied behind him to the aperture the horses had made in their escape earlier that week.

The overwhelming void made me cringe, but I knew Maverick had a sense I didn't. Slowly, carefully, painfully, I shunted the piece of metal siding out of our way, and we slipped underneath and inside.

Some of the debris had been removed, but it hadn't changed otherwise. The structure appeared unfriendly but stable. Sturdy support timbers held up what remained of the roof, and Maverick wound his way through the maze to the open pit and waited. I furtively peered over the lip. We couldn't get around the dead end.

Nothing. "She's not here."

I reacted to the sounds of hooves thumping against a wooden wall accompanied by muffled animal noises. I yanked Maverick out of the horse barn and tugged him toward the makeshift substitute shelter.

The closer we got, the louder the sounds, and the horse didn't sound happy. Then I heard Patricia scream, *"Help!"*

FORTY-TWO

Sounds came at me from all around. I couldn't pinpoint her location, but we raced the last twenty-five yards to where I thought she might be. Maverick stood on his hind legs and pushed forward with both paws. I pounded on the door. "What's happening? Who's in there? Let her go." I rattled the latch and crashed my shoulder against the door. It wouldn't move. Though slivers peeled away from the soft, rotting wood, it hurt like the dickens.

The wind shrieked. Rain pattered against the roof. Patricia's voice raised in pitch. "You can't take him."

"Patricia," I yelled. I knew she couldn't hear me, but maybe she could feel my energy and my presence. I aimed the beam around the building, searching for an implement to break down the door. Light glinted on a dingy tool—a shovel, and it seemed like my best bet. I dropped the leash. "Stay, Maverick." I hoped with all my heart he would listen.

The shovel clanged when it connected with the metal latch, and the excruciating reverberations thrummed through my fingers and up my arms. I hit it again. And again. One of the screws popped loose. The noise echoed. I made my aching arms swing again, and half of the latch fell to the ground. I pulled on one side of the heavy door. It opened, and a wind tunnel blew into my face.

Maverick dashed inside. I stepped gingerly but quickly over the assortment of items on the floor of the utility building, on the lookout for Patricia and the horses. The wind howled in the cavities of the empty makeshift stalls, throwing noises to the far corners of the farm. I inched through the improvised reuse of space until I reached the back wall where one of the quarter horses stood tethered to a ring dangling next to an opening. Splintered wood swung, oscillating, squeaking, and hanging precariously from the jamb.

Did Patricia and the horses crash out of the shed, or had someone broken in the rear door and taken them away?

Maverick caused me to jump and drop my phone when he brushed against my knee.

"Oh, Maverick."

I retrieved my phone, and the dimming light beam leaped in small circles as we crept across the yard.

Maverick alerted. I couldn't recognize anything; I had to guess what he'd scented. His tail wagged, so I imagined a friend rather than foe. "Find," I whispered.

Within seconds, Maverick led me in through the back of the ruined horse barn. TnL appeared, standing tall and majestic in front of us, snorting and pawing the ground. Maverick sat and I tentatively reached up to take the leather strap hanging from the horse's mouth. A wooden cudgel sliced the air in front of me, and I reflexively jumped back, dropping my shovel. I withdrew my hand at the same time a disbelieving voice squeaked, "Ms. Wilk?"

Maverick had been right all along. Patricia leaned heavily on TnL. Urgent words, spoken softly, tumbled from her lips. "I thought you were her. She's already taken Demon Dancer, and she's coming back soon. We've got to get TnL out of here. She kept repeating, 'I did it all for nothing. Now they'll all pay.' She's going to …" She cried out.

"Who?" I asked. "Who is she?"

She swiped rain from her face, and I saw pain etched there. Patricia's leg crumpled beneath her, and she slid down TnL's side to the ground. "Look at the cannon," she croaked. She pointed at the beginnings of a white sock on the horse that hadn't been there previously. "This *is* Foggy Bottom. Dyed." Her eyes rolled to the back of her head, and she collapsed into a heap. I reached for her, took in the unnatural bend in her leg and gasped.

I yanked out my phone to place an emergency call, but the screen wouldn't light up. It was out of juice.

I brought my hands inches away but didn't touch Patricia, afraid I might invade the invisible forcefield and hurt her even more. She moaned and grabbed my fingers so tightly I cringed, and with a high, piercing voice, she cried, "She's coming back. Get TnL out of here. He's in danger." Her pleading eyes searched my face for an affirmation, and she squeezed.

"Okay. Okay."

"Promise," she hissed in agony, signing what I assumed was the same word, and tossing me her white knit cap.

"I promise I'll take care of TnL."

She released her grip and fell back, unconscious.

I couldn't leave her where she lay, and I couldn't move her. I scanned the space, rapidly flipping through one bad idea after another when I spied a pile of dusty horse blankets.

I shook the top one and stretched it over Patricia, gently tucking in the corners to secure the ends. She whimpered, but I shook two more, and sloppily mounded them on top of her, hiding her from view. I ran toward my car when headlights bounced onto the driveway.

I snuck back to Patricia and knelt next to her. In reaction to the slamming door, Maverick's head whipped around. I whispered, "Quiet," and gestured *down* and *stay*.

Someone discovered the broken door, and I heard angry growling. The wind carried the voice clearly. "I'll find you. I know you can't have gone far. It won't do you any good. Nothing can save TnL now."

I listened intently. *Did I recognize the voice?*

The voice calmed. It chortled and said, "You can't hear me anyway. I don't know why I'm even talking, but maybe it will make me feel better to say everything out loud. Love isn't blind. It blinds people."

Boxes rumbled, shifted across the floor. The voice had a lilting quality. "I loved Enzo Gyles the first moment I laid eyes on him in high school. Years later, I finally found him alone in the lounge at Churchill Downs, nursing a fourth Mint Julep, and he bared his soul. I'm a good listener."

Glass shattered. She muttered an oath and nearly screamed the next words in irritation. "He said the love of his life had needed someone with money and horse sense, and he set off to make his mark in the world, but he'd never shared his plan with her. With some of his earnings, he bought a promising colt from Tony Relando as a gift for her and sent it to her dad." Her cackle stood the hairs on my arm on edge. "In his quest for success, he was gone too long, and when he returned to claim the horse and his bride, he discovered she'd married a philandering leech." More grating of something along the ground. "To add insult to injury, Foggy Bottom had been included in her dowry and she never knew the horse's provenance. That colt started to win races, and Enzo had been content as long as Mia was happy. He watched from afar. What a crock. I knew I'd be the one to set him free from her spell, and he'd know I was the right one for him." I winced at the sounds of metal chunks hurled against a distant wall. Patricia didn't react. "Where are you, you little brat?"

TnL's head reared up, and it took all the strength I had left to lift my hand against my fear and stroke his silken nose. "Quiet."

The wrath-filled voice continued, punctuated by thuds and bumps. "No one recognized me in disguise. I became Mia's assistant. I watched and waited, but Penelope moved fast. She'd planted seeds of discontent between Enzo and Mia, lying about who said what and why they could never be together. Mia was married but Penelope trapped my Enzo with empty promises. I never thought he'd fall for her deceit, but she sank her talons in deep. He never loved Penelope, but he married her.

"However, he loved Foggy Bottom almost as much as he thought he loved Mia. I plotted. If neither Mia nor Foggy Bottom were in the picture, I could break Penelope's fragile hold and get Enzo back, so I enlisted the help of Zachary Brown to get rid of the horse. What a mistake that was. Zachary wanted control of everything, and when he figured out Foggy Bottom's connection to her old flame, he stole the horse, and since Penelope could pay more than I could, he sold it to Mia's sister. To. Her. Sister. When I found out what he did, I fixed him good. His brakes never worked again." She started throwing things around, banging against metal and thudding against wood. She screeched, "Come here."

A light beam flashed across the yard through the cracks in the old wall. "I'd altered the tattoo and dyed the legs, but before I could get rid of it, Mia saw him and fell in love with a horse I'd *found* and she hoped to use as a sire. She said she'd pay almost as much as Zach got from Penelope. Then I convinced her to leave the toxic proximity of her sister and move to this godforsaken place, hoping to put distance between the sisters."

The snickering came closer. "I collected on Foggy Bottom twice—once from Penelope and once from Mia, and every Monday morning, after I paid this stinking farm for taking care of my horse, I touched up the dye job on his markings. No one would have noticed … until Byrne showed up. He told Penelope, and she waited. She caught me touching up the dye just before the tornado struck and threatened to expose me. I lashed out, but I had to make it look like an accident."

When she reached the destroyed doorway, she waved what looked an awful lot like a gun and keened, "Where are you?"

The breeze carried the familiar odor of dung, hay, and lilies, taking me back to my fall in the barn. My fingers went directly to the bump on my head. I'd been purposely knocked unconscious by someone intent on keeping the body, the money, the gun, and the horse a secret.

FORTY-FOUR

Pummeled by sharp icy pellets of sleet, I squinted at the stout figure emerging from the rear of the utility shed. She removed glasses from her nose, slipping them into a back pocket, and scoured her face in her hands. She took a fistful of fabric from her chest and tore off a puffy midsection. The look of disgust on her face morphed to a sneer as she threw it to the ground, losing thirty pounds. She ripped off a mousy almost-blond wig and shook out a head of lustrous brown hair, catching it in a hair tie. Dumbfounded by the transformation, I mopped my face with my sleeve and almost didn't recognize the woman from Santino's.

"The first time we met in ninth grade, Enzo said I was beautiful." Ann-Elizabeth Tulis would have been gorgeous but for the fuming set of her jaw. "I knew he and Mia wouldn't last. She'd never trust Enzo again. But then Penelope worked her black magic. I needed to get Penelope, the conniving witch, out of the way, and then help Enzo through his imagined grief. I knew all about the tunnel, but I didn't know the old coot still lived there. I caught a glimpse of him when I moved the body."

Ann-Elizabeth peered into the dark recesses of the farm, seemingly right at me. "I was almost crushed when I thought I killed Mia. She put on a good show of being such a kind soul." She raised her hand to the sky and shook it, screaming, "I would have given Enzo everything, but when I approached him at Santino's, he didn't recognize me. He only had eyes for her, and when I saw them, I knew I had it all wrong, and Mia was no better than her sister. She couldn't fool me any longer. She was luring my Enzo back. But I'll show them. I'll show them all."

She lurched two steps one way and two steps another, her eyes assiduously scanning the ground. "I'm going to find you, and you'll regret taking my horse."

Patricia's hand clutched mine. "Promise," she signed and fell back against the ground. Maverick crawled close to her, stretching his full length and resting his nose on her shoulder. I repositioned the blankets and tucked the ends under a cement block, hiding them both. I signed *stay*, and put my finger to my lips, praying he'd keep watch.

I yanked the cap down over my ears. Maybe I could make Ann-Elizabeth think I was Patricia.

Ann-Elizabeth closed in on our location with more assurance in each step and an evil glint in her eyes. When she lunged at the entryway, I did the only thing I could. I stepped onto the pile of blocks, hugged TnL's neck, and threw my leg over his back. Clinging for dear life, I clutched his mane, lowered my head to his neck, and squeezed my thighs together. His ears twitched once, and he bolted in front of Ann-Elizabeth, knocking her aside.

A shot rang out and the zing close to my head made it clear she'd taken aim. TnL bolted and galloped across the open field. He picked up speed, and the terrain blurred. My heart beat a rhythm in opposition to the pounding hooves. His ears lay flat against his skull, and he breathed loudly. His nostrils flared. The flowing mane whipped my cheeks. I could only take shaky, shallow breaths and couldn't swallow. My bones slammed together, and my teeth clacked. As we gobbled up the ground, we spit out a trail anyone could follow, and I risked a glance over my shoulder, hoping to have drawn her away from Patricia.

Against the yard light, I could see the silhouette of Ann-Elizabeth sitting astride the young quarter horse, accelerating rapidly, an arm raised. My only hope was that she bounced as forcefully as I did, and she'd miss her target.

I turned back just before we exited the open field and entered a dark void. Attacked by an onslaught of branches and brambles, I ducked, laying close to TnL for protection. I tried to locate the origin of the bullet thwack in a tree off to my right. If she shot enough, maybe she'd run out of ammunition. A whump struck the ground, close enough to hear but not to see. I tightened my grip on TnL's mane, pressing his sides, mentally urging the stallion to stay ahead of Ann-Elizabeth.

We brushed through stiff, sharp vegetation that tore at my pants and jacket, scratched my face and the backs of my hands, and poked at my scalp through Patricia's thin cap. TnL slowed and battled his way up small mounds and down steep ravines. He vaulted over obstacles in his path, barriers I couldn't see and hadn't time to prepare for, and my body folded and unfolded with every jerking movement, but I took solace in the fact we continued advancing forward, farther from Patricia.

"I won't let you take my horse. You can't escape." The words bellowed from behind me, but too close for comfort. I mentally coaxed the handsome ride to move faster, but not so fast I'd plummet from his back.

The seconds ticked by and felt like hours. The wind howled. The heavens opened and rain fell in sheets. The hooves churned up the muddy earth. My teeth chattered. Goosebumps crawled up and down my back and neck. TnL lost his footing, and to keep my seat, I shifted from one side to the other, trying to redistribute my weight.

I wiped an eye to see ahead of us and tightened my grip in panic. A thick fallen tree blocked our path, but rather than slow or stop, TnL soared over it. My tired, rubbery legs couldn't keep me in the seat, and while airborne I wondered how much longer we'd stay connected. I clamped my eyelids shut, and as I slammed into his back, I hung on to TnL with every ounce of strength I could muster.

The rapid bouncing slowed. I had no idea which direction we'd taken. He advanced onto a gravel path and the cantering morphed back into galloping. The wind whipped my face, and I kept my eyes closed against the hammering rain.

I hugged the warm neck and prayed.

And then TnL stopped, nearly tossing me over his head. I ventured to open my eyes and almost wept. To my horror, we'd circled back where we'd begun to the Halloran farm. TnL returned us to our starting point and put Ann-Elizabeth too close to Patricia. The second horse clopped behind us.

"No," I whispered. "This can't be happening."

"Get off my horse. Now."

I sat up and slid my leg over TnL's rump. I wrapped him in an embrace. "You tried." I widened my stance, putting more of my body in front of the horse.

"Step away from Foggy Bottom. You're a lousy horse-woman anyway."

I turned to face her and whipped off the cap. "No," I said with authority, or at least I tried to hide the fear raging in my chest.

Ann-Elizabeth turned a dark purple and she screwed up her face. "You. I saw Severson talking to you, but I didn't know if he'd had time to tell you anything. Then I heard about the sneaky messages he often sent, and I searched for any communications to make sure, but I guess he was smarter than the average nutcase." She sniggered. "You really need to tell your dad to lock your door when you're all out for the day. I thought you'd be done investigating after round two. I may have failed before, but they say the third time's a charm." She gritted her teeth. "Where's that awful Patty?" She waved the gun at me, then took careful aim.

My knees almost caved in, but I elevated my chin and stood my ground. If this was it, so be it. She raised the barrel, hatred pulsing through her arm as I stared into the black hole at the end of the gun. I closed my eyes. A gunshot rang out.

And I heard a scream.

FORTY-FIVE

I felt for pain. There was none. It wasn't me screaming. There were no holes, but the cacophony in the surrounding world filled my ears, and I peeled open one eye, then the other.

TnL whinnied and squealed. He pounded a frantic circle. Ann-Elizabeth's horse reared up, and she did all she could to hold on to the reins as my disobedient, rebellious, headstrong, insubordinate, handsome, wonderful, astonishing black Lab continued to bark, raising a ruckus and frightening her horse. Lightning split the sky with a roar, further terrifying her mount. Its front legs windmilled, pumping the air, and Ann-Elizabeth teetered. As she struggled to hang on, she lost her grip on the weapon. It hit the ground and fired again.

The horse went ballistic and threw her. Ann-Elizabeth fell off but rolled and scrambled toward the firearm. She stood up straight and swung the gun toward me but was confounded by TnL on one side, pawing the ground and whinnying, then rearing up, and Maverick barking, tail pointing at the ground, hackles raised, teeth bared on the other. She pointed the weapon at TnL and then at Maverick, at which time TnL moved in. One of his hooves connected with the metal and sent the gun flying.

We both clambered across the short stretch of yard. I reached it first, picked it up, and aimed it, but the end of the gun drooped, wavering under its weight compounded by the happenings of the day and my quivering noodle-like arms. Ann-Elizabeth steadily drew herself up, dusted herself off, and laughed. "You have to be willing to pull the trigger, and I don't see you able to do that." Her arrogant face twisted with something close to hatred or disgust. She took one step away from me and then another.

Maverick stopped barking and I could feel his eyes on me. He would do anything I asked. Maybe I couldn't pull the trigger. Maybe I could, but I bared my teeth. "Maverick, watch," I said, and he again bared his lethal mouthful and growled.

My concentration broke when headlights turned into the drive, and Ann-Elizabeth made a break for it, but Maverick, all claws and teeth, clamped down on her elbow, shaking his prize with ferocity. She screamed, "Get him off me. Let me go."

I slowly came back around with a tired, sweaty two-handed grip.

A car door thunked, but I couldn't take my eyes off Ann-Elizabeth and Maverick. I trusted Ann-Elizabeth had worked alone. I had to believe whoever had pulled in would be on my side.

A gentle hand reached around my shoulder and rested over mine. The other hand supported my back. Words wafted on warm, minty air, "I've got you."

The gun spun on the trigger guard over my finger and dropped into Amanda's hand as I melted into Pete's embrace. "I've got you," he whispered again.

My last ounce of strength swelled when I looked deep into those luscious eyes. "Patricia's in the horse barn. She's hurt."

I knew I said the words too loud, but it was the only way I could dispel the nightmare. Pete brushed a stray hair from my face, turned, and jogged to the barn. My legs gave out, and I slumped to the wet grass, tears mingling with the rain.

"Let go." Ann-Elizabeth cried hysterically over Maverick's ferocious snarl, but as tight as he gripped, he'd never break skin.

TnL, or rather, Foggy Bottom nudged my shoulder and blew warm soothing air onto my neck.

"What do you think? Should I call him off." I swiped at the rain and plastered a pseudo-smile on my face.

Amanda's eyebrows rose and her lips puckered before she sighed and said, "If you must."

FORTY-SIX

I'd just finished braiding my hair when I heard Dad answer the bell and laugh. "Look who the dog dragged in."

"Hi, Harry."

A smile stole across my face as I recognized the voice and skipped down the last two steps. Maverick stood on his hind legs and joined in as I wrapped her in a huge hug.

"What was that for?" Ellen said when she caught her breath again.

"You're my sister, or my half-sister, and I want you to know how happy that makes me. You are a real live connection to my mother—our mother. You're family." I grabbed Dad and hauled him close. "And I want you to know, although sometimes it doesn't seem like it, I do realize how very important family is."

Ellen thrust a flat gift-wrapped box into my hands. "This is for you."

I furrowed my brow. "But it's Mother's Day?"

"Open it." She nodded as if that could encourage me to peel away the wrapping faster.

I untied the silky brown ribbon, removed the textured tan paper, folded it in case I could reuse it, and shook the lid free. Nestled among rows of scrumptious-looking milk and dark chocolates in a variety of shapes and sizes lay a photo—the last photo taken of Ellen and our mother. I could see her in Ellen's smile and the tilt of her head. I could even see her in the firm set of my jaw and the intensity in our eyes.

"I don't know what to say."

Dad raised an eyebrow and said, "Say thank you."

"Thank you … for everything."

Fortunately, before I could become too maudlin, the doorbell rang again. Ransam and the Halloran gang stood on our top step. Supported by crutches and Kindra's arm wrapped tightly around her waist, Patricia stuck out her cast, already decorated with multi-colored signatures, shining like a beacon.

Debora said, her voice breaking, "How can we ever thank you?"

"Come in. Join us. We're having the best brunch in Columbia," Dad said, pulling the door as wide as possible.

Imagining what could have happened, tears threatened to spill down my cheeks until a very, merry Ida Clemashevski waltzed in toting fresh yeasty cinnamon rolls, dripping in white icing, singing, "Hail, hail, the gang's all here."

The salver tipped, and Dad relieved her of the heavy encumbrance. He set it on the counter. "I can help."

Ransam and Dad followed Ida out for who knew what other delicious foodstuffs. I seated the guests around our extended table, content to see Patricia and Kindra smiling.

Debora gestured to an unusually quiet Ellen to sit with them. No sooner had she sat, when the doorbell pealed again.

Pete and Lance entered, supporting a clean-shaven, well-dressed Ole Severson between them and helped him sink into one of Ida's overstuffed chairs. Debora gasped, and the Halloran girls nearly sucked the air out of the room. "Gramps."

Debora jumped to her feet and extended her hand, assisting him to her vacant chair. "You look so much like your dad. Mr. Severson—"

"It's Ole, please," the man said with gentleness. "I'm sorry I've acted the way I have. I hoped to drive you from the property, but I don't even know why I did that. Dad always said family was his biggest treasure."

"Ole, I'd love for you to meet my daughters."

He nodded shyly. "Pleased to officially meet both of you."

Patricia stuck out her hand. "I'm Patricia."

"The troublemaker," he said quietly shaking her hand.

Debora squinted.

"And I'm the smarter, older sister, Kindra," she said with gravitas, waiting for him to take her hand as well.

"The minder."

Ole's lopsided smiled elicited a wholehearted laugh from Debora. "He's got you two pegged. Ole, I do hope we can get better acquainted."

An engine roared outside, and a car door slammed. "Ida, are you expecting anyone?"

"No," she said gayly, "but whoever it is, they're invited anyway."

I opened the door. The boxy green Mercedes idled loudly at the curb. Mia looked like a filly ready to bolt, but Enzo held her hand tightly. He brought it to his lips and kissed her fingers and pulled her toward the stoop. "Go ahead," he said, giving her a hand.

On the top step, Mia lifted her head. "One of Debora Halloran's hands thought we'd find her here." She looked to the truck on the street with Halloran emblazoned across the side. "That's her truck, right?"

"Come in. We're having brunch."

"No. We couldn't," Mia said at the same time Enzo said, "We'd be delighted to come in, but we'll only stay a moment."

They stepped into the living room to complete silence, and Mia reddened. She mumbled, "I can't do this."

Enzo saw Debora and said, "Ms. Halloran. We have a pressing need to talk with you about."

She caught the eyes of her daughters. "We're all family here. Whatever you have to say to me you can say to everyone."

Mia cleared her throat. "Then you can expect a trailer to pick up the horses tomorrow. Please collect all their gear, and we'll get out of your way."

Patricia collapsed onto the couch next to Ole. He patted her hand as she stared out the window, barely breathing, not moving when Kindra sat carefully on her other side.

Debora knew this would shatter her daughters. "I'm sorry you feel you need to take the horses away."

I'll give Enzo credit. He was no dummy. In three long strides, he ended up in front of Patricia. She looked down at his shoes. He knelt on one knee. "Ms. Halloran, the horse shelter is ruined, and you can't expect them to thrive in the secondary barn. The doors have been wrenched free." He took a hand. "Therapy Thoroughbreds can use new strong blood, and I've heard they're looking for young volunteers."

Patricia's eyes moved first as she began to understand his

words and a grin took over her entire being. She and Kindra hugged and almost rocked each other off the sofa. Debora's eyes glistened with unspent tears. The horses would reside in Monongalia County after all.

With the happy chatter, I didn't hear another knock but noticed Maverick hop to attention and approach the door, so I did the same.

Carlee Bluestone. I rubbernecked both directions, looking for friends or family in tow. "Would you care to join us?"

"No, thank you. I have an exceptional day planned for my mother since I've missed the first sixteen, but I have something for you." She held out a package. "Open it later," she whispered and turned round, running into Amanda.

"Whoa."

"Sorry, Chief. Gotta go. See ya."

Amanda cocked her head, looking at the beautifully gold wrapped box in my hands. I shrugged.

"Join us," I said.

A dazzling smile graced her lips. "I'd like that." She hung her jacket on an empty hook by the door.

Pete draped his arms over my shoulders from the back. I leaned back into his strong chest. Amanda straightened the folds of fabric on her jacket, turned to us, and said, "Ronnie has temporarily withdrawn his request for a vote of confidence hearing."

"That's wonderful. It's over. Now life can get back to normal."

She shook her head. "It's not over, Katie. In fact, I think he's just begun."

IDA'S MINT JULEP

1 ¼ C super fine sugar
4 C cold water
Tea ball filled with dry mint leaves
1 ½ shots Bourbon
Fresh mint

Stir and dissolve sugar in water. Taste the sugar mix. It should be 'oily,' and if not, add sugar by the tablespoon. Suspend tea ball with mint leaves in the cold water. Cover tightly and refrigerate overnight. Strain through tea strainer from one vessel to another as needed to clear up simple syrup.

Pour Bourbon over ice into a glass. Add syrup to the top of the glass. Garnish with fresh mint sprig.

Pick a winning horse.

* * *

IDA'S MINT MOCKTAIL

2 C water
2 C granulated sugar
8 sprigs of mint leaves — plus garnish
4 C Ginger Ale

In a small saucepan bring the water, sugar and mint leaves to boil over medium high heat, stirring frequently. Dissolve the sugar completely. Let the simple syrup cool completely. Pour the simple syrup through a fine mesh strainer to remove the mint leaves. Fill cups with crushed ice and pour ½ cup of ginger ale into each cup, pour in ¼ cup of the mint simple syrup to each cup. Stir and top with additional mint sprigs if you'd like.

IDA'S FRUIT DIP

1 (8oz) cream cheese softened
1 (7oz) jar of marshmallow cream
Beat together until fluffy. Enjoy with all fruits.

COLUMBIA'S STAPLE—PISTACHIO SALAD

1 (3.25) box of pistachio pudding
1 tub Cool Whip (thawed)
1 (15 oz) can of pineapple tidbits (drain and reserve juice)
½ lb. miniature marshmallows

Stir together the pudding mix and pineapple juice. Fold in Cool Whip, pineapple tidbits, and marshmallow. Refrigerate.

Thank you for taking the time to read *Juleps, Jockeys & Justice*. If you enjoyed it please tell your friends, and I would be so grateful if you would consider posting a review. Word of mouth is an author's best friend, and very much appreciated.
Thank you,
Mary Seifert

What's next for Katie?

High school math teacher, Katie Wilk, is accompanying her state champion mock trial team to the national tournament in Atlanta, Georgia on a busy Memorial Day weekend. Mechanical issues and weather disrupt their travel plans and Katie sends the students on with the other chaperones. It's a good thing because when her flight is sabotaged, she lands in a world of trouble. What will it take to survive the wild and join her students in their quest to be the best?

Acknowledgments

I can't thank Stephanie Dewey, Lee Ellison, and their great team of beta readers (Marcia Koopmann, Susan Gross, Paula Webb, Isobel Tamney, Dawn Hasiotis, Gabi Hoffknecht) enough. They catch the lost connections and help polish the words to a high gloss. This wouldn't happen without them.

The Kentucky Derby has always occupied a special place in our family's traditions, right up there with Christmas, Thanksgiving, Fourth of July, and April Fool's Day, complete with hats, Mint Juleps, and choosing a winning horse. We've celebrated at home, at a bar, during a wedding reception, in a hospital room, and some have even visited Churchill Downs (so thanks for your insight, Luke Seifert, who directed me to Matthew Seifert as well).

Bouchercon connected me with Susan Elizabeth Tulis who lent her name to a character, and it would never have turned out the same. And thanks to Kim Sandry for the combination of names for Ole Severson. It fit right in.

I truly appreciate the feedback, edits, and comments about pacing and word choice from Brenna Gehlen. Who knew!

Colleen Okland and Dennis Okland hold a special place in my heart, encouraging, reading, questioning, and supporting my dream. They catch large and small infractions, and I am so grateful.

In checking facts and figures, if I can, I go to the source. Thanks to our local high school principal, Paul Schmitz, for trying to set me straight.

My SinC Guppy writing group always had a kind word,

a correct word, and an encouraging word. Thanks Kate, L.C. and Judy.

I am grateful to my friends who love horses and let me talk about wonderful animals. I learned much. Thank you, Lisa Piotrowski and Dr. Kathy Nelson Hund. And who better to explain wagering than horse racetrack teller, Barbara *Ann* Hall.

My friend, Kris Peterson, introduced me to the Granite Falls Lee-Mar Ranch Equine Center whose mission is *'to provide affordable, accessible, and effective equine-facilitated activities for individuals with disabilities and children at risk in a safe learning area. We are Healing Hearts with Hands & Hooves through our therapeutic riding programs!'* I appreciate Vicki Patterson allowing me to visit and watch what wonderful work is being done. Spending time with animals is beneficial. Their unconditional love is good for physical and mental well-being, improving strength, bettering balance, and building confidence. What comes to mind are usually dogs and cats, but horses are also valuable partners in individualized therapy programming. Equine-assisting professionals guide clients through activities with horses to give immeasurable benefits. Thanks to Melanie and Terry for your work at Lee-Mar.

And I couldn't do it without my family, especially my husband, John.

Get all the books in the Katie & Maverick Series!

Maverick, Movies, & Murder
Rescues, Rogues, & Renegade
Tinsel, Trials, & Traitors
Santa, Snowflakes, & Strychnine
Fishing, Festivities, & Fatalities
Diamonds, Diesel, & Doom
Creeps, Cache, & Corpses
Pranks, Payback, & Poison
Juleps, Jockeys & Justice

Get a free short story from Mary—Scan the QR code to find out how!

Visit Mary's website: MarySeifertAuthor.com/
Facebook: facebook.com/MarySeifertAuthor
Twitter: twitter.com/mary_seifert
Instagram: instagram.com/maryseifert/
Follow Mary on BookBub and Goodreads too!